PENGUIN BOOKS

HOW TO BE GOOD

'Brilliantly funny . . . undoubtedly Hornby's finest novel yet' *Heat*

'I loved this book' Julie Burchill, *Mail on Sunday*

'A bitingly clever novel of ideas, on a subject almost nobody else has written about – how would a totally good person get on in the modern world?' John Carey, *Sunday Times*

'Perhaps the most poised piece of writing Hornby has yet produced . . . only this writer has the wit and the stringency to take on this easy comedy and draw compelling, even universal pathos from it' Tim Adams, *Observer*

'Enormously readable and ultimately powerful, charming and affecting' Alex Clark, *Guardian*

'Hornby has raised his game. A good, dark espresso-strength comedy that nobody else could have written' *New Statesman*

'Hornby's is a lovely fictional voice: humane, amused, perceptive, free of vanity. He writes astonishingly well from a woman's perspective . . . entertains superbly' Libby Purves, *The Times*

'Hornby is without question a comic writer of great facility, warmth and lightness of touch. A very readable satire' *Literary Review*

Nick Hornby was born in 1957. He is the author of six novels: *High Fidelity, About a Boy, How to be Good, A Long Way Down* (shortlisted for the Whitbread Award), *Slam* and *Juliet, Naked*; three works of non-fiction: *Fever Pitch* (winner of the William Hill Sports Book of the Year Award), *31 Songs* (shortlisted for the National Book Critics Circle Award) and *The Complete Polysyllabic Spree*; and a Pocket Penguin book of short stories, *Otherwise Pandemonium*. He has written the screenplay for two films: *Fever Pitch* and *An Education*.

Nick Hornby lives and works in Highbury, north London.

How to be Good

NICK HORNBY

PENGUIN BOOKS

PENGUIN BOOKS

Published by the Penguin Group
Penguin Books Ltd, 80 Strand, London WC2R 0RL, England
Penguin Group (USA) Inc., 375 Hudson Street, New York, New York 10014, USA
Penguin Group (Canada), 90 Eglinton Avenue East, Suite 700, Toronto, Ontario, Canada M4P 2Y3
(a division of Pearson Penguin Canada Inc.)
Penguin Ireland, 25 St Stephen's Green, Dublin 2, Ireland (a division of Penguin Books Ltd)
Penguin Group (Australia), 250 Camberwell Road, Camberwell, Victoria 3124, Australia
(a division of Pearson Australia Group Pty Ltd)
Penguin Books India Pvt Ltd, 11 Community Centre, Panchsheel Park, New Delhi – 110 017, India
Penguin Group (NZ), 67 Apollo Drive, Rosedale, North Shore 0632, New Zealand
(a division of Pearson New Zealand Ltd)
Penguin Books (South Africa) (Pty) Ltd, 24 Sturdee Avenue, Rosebank, 2196, South Africa

Penguin Books Ltd, Registered Offices: 80 Strand, London WC2R 0RL, England

www.penguin.com

First published by Viking 2001
Published in Penguin Books 2001
Reissued in this edition 2010
This edition produced for The Book People Ltd,
Hall Wood Avenue, Haydock, St Helens, WA11 9UL

Printed in Great Britain by Clays Ltd, St Ives plc

ISBN: 978-0-241-95312-9

www.greenpenguin.co.uk

For Gill Hornby

Acknowledgements

Thanks to: Tony Lacey, Helen Fraser, Juliet Annan, Joanna Prior, Anya Waddington, Jeremy Ettinghausen, Martin Bryant, Wendy Carlton, Susan Petersen Kennedy, Amanda Posey, Ruth Hallgarten, Caroline Dawnay, Annabel Hardman, Mary Cranitch, Anna Wright and Gaby Chiappe.

I

I am in a car park in Leeds when I tell my husband I don't want to be married to him any more. David isn't even in the car park with me. He's at home, looking after the kids, and I have only called him to remind him that he should write a note for Molly's class teacher. The other bit just sort of . . . slips out. This is a mistake, obviously. Even though I am, apparently, and to my immense surprise, the kind of person who tells her husband that she doesn't want to be married to him any more, I really didn't think that I was the kind of person to say so in a car park, on a mobile phone. That particular self-assessment will now have to be revised, clearly. I can describe myself as the kind of person who doesn't forget names, for example, because I have remembered names thousands of times and forgotten them only once or twice. But for the majority of people, marriage-ending conversations happen only once, if at all. If you choose to conduct yours on a mobile phone, in a Leeds car park, then you cannot really claim that it is unrepresentative, in the same way that Lee Harvey Oswald couldn't really claim that shooting presidents wasn't like him at all. Sometimes we have to be judged by our one-offs.

Later, in the hotel room, when I can't sleep – and that is some sort of consolation, because even though I have turned into the woman who ends marriages in a car park, at least I have the decency to toss and turn afterwards – I retrace the conversation in my head, in as much detail as I can manage, trying to work out how we'd got from there (Molly's dental appointment) to here (imminent divorce) in three minutes. Ten, anyway. Which turns into an endless, three-in-the-morning brood about how we'd got from there (meeting at a college dance in 1976) to here (imminent divorce) in twenty-four years.

To tell you the truth, the second part of this self-reflection only takes so long because twenty-four years is a long time, and there are loads of bits that come unbidden into your head, little narrative details, that don't really have much to do with the story. If my thoughts about our marriage had been turned into a film, the critics would say that it was all padding, no plot, and that it could be summarized thus: two people meet, fall in love, have kids, start arguing, get fat and grumpy (him) and bored, desperate and grumpy (her) and split up. I wouldn't argue with the synopsis. We're nothing special.

The phone call, though . . . I keep missing the link, the point where it turned from a relatively harmonious and genuinely banal chat about minor domestic arrangements into this cataclysmic, end-of-the-world-as-we-know-it moment. I can remember the beginning of it, almost word-for-word:

Me: 'Hiya.'

Him: 'Hello. How's it going?'

Me: 'Yeah, fine. Kids all right?'

Him: 'Yeah. Molly's here watching TV, Tom's round at Jamie's.'

Me: 'I just phoned to say that you've got to write a note for Molly to take in to school tomorrow. About the dentist's.'

See? See? It can't be done, you'd think, not from here. But you'd be wrong, because we did it. I'm almost sure that the first leap was made here, at this point; the way I remember it now, there was a pause, an ominous silence, at the other end of the line. And then I said something like 'What?' and he said 'Nothing'. And I said 'What?' again and he said 'Nothing' again, except he clearly wasn't baffled or amused by my question, just tetchy, which means, does it not, that you have to plough on. So I ploughed on.

'Come on.'

'No.'

'Come on.'

'No. What you said.'

'What did I say?'

'About just phoning to remind me about Molly's note.'

2

'What's wrong with that?'

'It'd be nice if you just phoned for some other reason. You know, to say hello. To see how your husband and children are.'

'Oh, David.'

'What, "Oh David"?'

'That was the first thing I asked. "How are the kids?"'

'Yeah. OK. "How are the kids?" Not, you know, "How are you?"'

You don't get conversations like this when things are going well. It is not difficult to imagine that in other, better relationships, a phone call that began in this way would not and could not lead to talk of divorce. In better relationships you could sail right through the dentist part and move on to other topics – your day's work, or plans for the evening, or even, in a spectacularly functional marriage, something that has taken place in the world outside your home, a coughing fit on the *Today* programme, say – just as ordinary, just as forgettable, but topics that form the substance and perhaps even the sustenance of an ordinary, forgettable, loving relationship. David and I, however . . . this is not our situation, not any more. Phone calls like ours only happen when you've spent several years hurting and being hurt, until every word you utter or hear becomes coded and loaded, as complicated and full of subtext as a bleak and brilliant play. In fact, when I was lying awake in the hotel room trying to piece it all together, I was even struck by how clever we had been to invent our code: it takes years of miserable ingenuity to get to this place.

'I'm sorry.'

'Do you care how I am?'

'To be honest, David, I don't need to ask how you are. I can hear how you are. Healthy enough to look after two children while simultaneously sniping at me. And very, very aggrieved, for reasons that remain obscure to me at this point. Although I'm sure you'll enlighten me.'

'What makes you think I'm aggrieved?'

'Ha! You're the definition of aggrieved. Permanently.'

'Bollocks.'

'David, you make your living from being aggrieved.'

This is true, partly. David's only steady income derives from a newspaper column he contributes to our local paper. The column is illustrated by a photograph of him snarling at the camera, and is subtitled 'The Angriest Man in Holloway'. The last one I could bear to read was a diatribe against old people who travelled on buses: Why did they never have their money ready? Why wouldn't they use the seats set aside for them at the front of the bus? Why did they insist on standing up ten minutes before their stop, thus obliging them to fall over frequently in an alarming and undignified fashion? You get the picture, anyway.

'In case you hadn't noticed, possibly because you never bother to fucking read me . . .'

'Where's Molly?'

'Watching TV in the other room. Fuck fuck fuck. Shit.'

'Very mature.'

'. . . Possibly because you never bother to fucking read me, my column is ironic.'

I laughed ironically.

'Well, please excuse the inhabitants of 32 Webster Road if the irony is lost on us. We wake up with the angriest man in Holloway every day of our lives.'

'What's the point of all this?'

Maybe in the film of our marriage, written by a scriptwriter on the lookout for brief and elegant ways of turning dull, superficial arguments into something more meaningful, this would have been the moment: you know, 'That's a good question . . . Where are we going? . . . What are we doing? . . . Something something something . . . It's over.' OK, it needs a little work, but it would do the trick. As David and I are not Tom and Nicole, however, we are blind to these neat little metaphorical moments.

'I don't know what the point of all this is. You got cross about me not asking how you were.'

'Yeah.'

'How are you?'

'Fuck off.'

I sighed, right into the mouthpiece of the phone, so that he could hear what I was doing; I had to move the mobile away from my ear and towards my mouth, which robbed the moment of its spontaneity, but I know through experience that my mobile isn't good on non-verbal nuance.

'Jesus Christ! What was that?'

'It was a sigh.'

'Sounds like you're on top of a mountain.'

We said nothing for a while. He was in a North London kitchen saying nothing, and I was in a car park in Leeds saying nothing, and I was suddenly and sickeningly struck by how well I knew this silence, the shape and the feel of it, all of its spiky little corners. (And of course it's not really silence at all. You can hear the expletive-ridden chatter of your own anger, the blood that pounds in your ears, and on this occasion, the sound of a Fiat Uno reversing into a parking space next to yours.) The truth is, there was no link between domestic inquiry and the decision to divorce. That's why I can't find it. I think what happened was, I just launched in.

'I'm so tired of this, David.'

'Of what?'

'This. Rowing all the time. The silences. The bad atmosphere. All this . . . poison.'

'Oh. That.' Delivered as if the venom had somehow dripped into our marriage through a leaking roof, and he'd been meaning to fix it. 'Yeah, well. Too late now.'

I took a deep breath, for my benefit rather than his, so the phone stayed on my ear this time.

'Maybe not.'

'What does that mean?'

'Do you really want to live the rest of your life like this?'

'No, of course not. Are you suggesting an alternative?'

'Yes, I suppose I am.'

'Would you care to tell me what it is?'

'You know what it is.'

'Of course I do. But I want you to be the first one to mention it.'

And by this stage I really didn't care.

'Do you want a divorce?'

'I want it on record that it wasn't me who said it.'

'Fine.'

'You, not me.'

'Me, not you. Come on, David. I'm trying to talk about a sad, grown-up thing, and you still want to score points.'

'So I can tell everyone you asked for a divorce. Out of the blue.'

'Oh, it's completely out of the blue, isn't it? I mean, there's been no sign of this, has there, because we've been so blissfully happy. And is that what you're interested in doing? Telling everyone? Is that the point of it, for you?'

'I'm getting straight on the phone as soon as we've finished. I want to spin my version before you can spin your version.'

'OK, well, I'll just stay on the phone, then.'

And then, sick of myself and him and everything else that went with either of us, I did the opposite, and hung up. Which is how come I have ended up tossing and turning in a Leeds hotel room trying to retrace my conversational steps, occasionally swearing with the frustration of not being able to sleep, turning the light and the TV on and off, and generally making my lover's life a misery. Oh, I suppose he should go into the film synopsis somewhere. They got married, he got fat and grumpy, she got desperate and grumpy, she took a lover.

Listen: I'm not a bad person. I'm a doctor. One of the reasons I wanted to become a doctor was because I thought it would be a good – as in Good, rather than exciting or well-paid or glamorous – thing to do. I liked how it sounded: 'I want to be a doctor', 'I'm training to be a doctor', 'I'm a GP in a small North London practice'. I thought it made me seem just right – professional, kind of brainy, not too flashy, respectable, mature, caring. You think doctors don't care about how things look, because they're doctors? Of course we do. Anyway. I'm a good person, a doctor, and I'm lying in a hotel bed with a man I don't really know very well called Stephen, and I've just asked my husband for a divorce.

Stephen, not surprisingly, is awake.

'You all right?' he asks me.

I can't look at him. A couple of hours ago his hands were all over me, and I wanted them there, too, but now I don't want him in the bed, in the room, in Leeds.

'Bit restless.' I get out of bed and start to get dressed. 'I'm going out for a walk.'

It's my hotel room, so I take the keycard with me, but even as I'm putting it in my bag I realize I'm not coming back. I want to be at home, rowing and crying and feeling guilty about the mess we're about to make of our children's lives. The Health Authority is paying for the room. Stephen will have to take care of the minibar, though.

I drive for a couple of hours and then stop at a service station for a cup of tea and a doughnut. If this was a film, something would happen on the drive home, something that illustrated and illuminated the significance of the journey. I'd meet someone, or decide to become a different person, or get involved in a crime and maybe be abducted by the criminal, a nineteen-year-old with a drug habit and limited education who turns out to be both more intelligent and, indeed, more caring than me – ironically, seeing as I'm a doctor and he's an armed robber. And he'd learn something, although God knows what, from me, and I'd learn something from him, and then we'd continue alone on our journeys through life, subtly but profoundly modified by our brief time together. But this isn't a film, as I've said before, so I eat my doughnut, drink my tea and get back in the car. (Why do I keep going on about films? I've only been to the cinema twice in the last couple of years, and both of the films I saw starred animated insects. For all I know, most adult films currently on general release are about women who drive uneventfully from Leeds to North London, stopping for tea and doughnuts on the M1.) The journey only takes me three hours including doughnuts. I'm home by six, home to a sleeping house which, I now notice, is beginning to give off a sour smell of defeat.

No one wakes up until quarter to eight, so I doze on the sofa. I'm happy to be back in the house, despite mobile phone calls and lovers; I'm happy to feel the warmth of my oblivious children seeping down through the creaking floorboards. I don't want to go to the marital bed, not tonight, or this morning, or whatever it is now – not because of Stephen but because I have not yet decided whether I'll ever sleep with David again. What would be the point? But then, what is the point anyway, divorce or no divorce? It's so strange, all that – I've had countless conversations with or about people who are 'sleeping in separate bedrooms', as if sleeping in the same bed is all there is to staying married, but however bad things get, sharing a bed has never been problematic; it's the rest of life that horrifies. There have been times recently, since the beginning of our troubles, when the sight of David awake, active, conscious, walking and talking has made me want to retch, so acute is my loathing of him; at night, though, it's a different story. We still make love, in a half-hearted, functional way, but it's not the sex: it's more that we've worked out sleeping in the last twenty-odd years, and how to do it together. I've developed contours for his elbows and knees and bum, and nobody else quite fits into me in quite the same way, especially not Stephen, who despite being leaner and taller and all sorts of things that you think might recommend him to a woman looking for a bed partner, seems to have all sorts of body parts in all the wrong places; there were times last night when I began to wonder gloomily whether David is the only person in the world with whom I will ever be comfortable, whether the reason our marriage and maybe countless marriages have survived thus far is because there is some perfect weight/ height differential that no one has ever researched properly, and if one or other partner is a fraction of a millimetre wrong either way then the relationship will never take. And it's not just that, either. When David's asleep, I can turn him back into the person I still love: I can impose my idea of what David should be, used to be, on to his sleeping form, and the seven hours I spend with that David just about gets me through the next day with the other David.

So. I doze on the sofa, and then Tom comes down in his pyjamas, puts the TV on, gets a bowl of cereal together, sits down on an armchair and watches cartoons. He doesn't look at me, doesn't say anything.

'Good morning,' I say cheerily.

'Hi.'

'How are you?'

'All right.'

'How was school yesterday?'

But he's gone now; the curtains have been drawn over the two-minute window of conversational opportunity that my son offers in the morning. I get up off the sofa and put the kettle on. Molly's next down, already dressed in her school clothes. She stares at me.

'You said you were going away.'

'I came back. Missed you too much.'

'We didn't miss you. Did we, Tom?'

No answer from Tom. These, apparently, are my choices: naked aggression from my daughter, silent indifference from my son. Except, of course, this is pure self-pity, and they are neither aggressive nor indifferent, simply children, and they haven't suddenly developed an adult's intuition overnight, even over this particular night.

Last, but not least, comes David, in his customary T-shirt and boxer shorts. He goes to put the kettle on, looks momentarily confused when he realizes that it is on already and only then casts a bleary eye over the household to see if he can find any explanation for this unexpected kettle activity. He finds it sprawled on the sofa.

'What are you doing here?'

'I just came to check up on your parenting skills when I'm not around. I'm impressed. You're last up, the kids get their own breakfast, the telly's on . . .'

I'm being unfair, of course, because this is how life works whether I'm here or not, but there's no point in waiting for his assault: I'm a firm believer in pre-emptive retaliation.

'So,' he says. 'This two-day course finished a day early. What, you all talked crap at twice the normal speed?'

'I wasn't in the mood.'

'No, I can imagine. What sort of mood are you in?'

'Shall we talk later? When the kids have gone to school?'

'Oh, yeah, right. Later.' This last word is spat out, with profound but actually mystifying bitterness – as if I were famous for doing things 'later', as if every single problem we have is caused by my obsession with putting things off. I laugh at him, which does little to ease tensions.

'What?'

'What's wrong with suggesting that we talk about things later?'

'Pathetic,' he says, but offers no clue as to why. Of course it's tempting to do things his way and talk about my desire for a divorce in front of our two children, but one of us has to think like an adult, if only temporarily, so I shake my head and pick up my bag. I want to go upstairs and sleep.

'Have a good day, kids.'

David stares at me. 'Where are you going?'

'I'm whacked.'

'I thought that one of the problems with our division of labour is that you couldn't ever drop the kids off at school. I thought you were being denied a basic maternal right.'

I have to be at the surgery before the kids leave in the mornings, so I am spared the school run. And even though I am grateful for this, my gratitude has not prevented me from bemoaning my lot whenever we have arguments about who doesn't do what. And David, needless to say, knows that I have no genuine desire to take the kids to school, which is why he is taking such delight in reminding me of my previous complaints now. David, like me, is highly skilled in the art of marital warfare, and for a moment I can step outside myself and admire his vicious quick-wittedness. Well played, David.

'I've been up half the night.'

'Never mind. They'd love it.'

Bastard.

I've thought about divorce before, of course. Who hasn't? I had fantasies about being a divorcee, even before I was married. In my fantasy I was a good, great, single professional mother, who had fantastic relations with her ex – joint attendance at parents' evenings, wistful evenings going through old photograph albums, that sort of thing – and a series of flings with bohemian younger or older men (see Kris Kristofferson, *Alice Doesn't Live Here Anymore*, my favourite film when I was seventeen). I can recall having this fantasy the night before I married David, which I suppose should have told me something but didn't. I think I was troubled by the lack of quirks and kinks in my autobiography: I grew up in leafy suburbia (Richmond), my parents were and still are happily married, I was a prefect at school, I passed my exams, I went to college, I got a good job, I met a nice man, I got engaged to him. The only room I could see for the kind of sophisticated metropolitan variation I craved was post-marriage, so that was where I concentrated my mental energy.

I even had a fantasy about the moment of separation. David and I are looking through travel brochures; he wants to go to New York, I want to go on safari in Africa, and – this being the umpteenth hilarious you-say-tomayto-I-say-tomato conversation in a row – we look at each other and laugh affectionately, and hug, and agree to part. He goes upstairs, packs his bags and moves out, maybe to a flat next door. Later that same day, we have supper together with our new partners, whom we have somehow managed to meet during the afternoon, and everyone gets along famously and teases each other affectionately.

But I can see now just how fantastical this fantasy is; I am already beginning to suspect that the wistful evenings with the photograph albums might not work out. It is far more likely, in fact, that the photographs will be snipped down the middle – indeed, knowing David, they already have been, last night, just after our phone call. It's kind of obvious, when you think about it: if you hate each other so much that you can't bear to live in the same house, then it's unlikely you'll want to go on camping holidays together afterwards. The trouble with my fantasy was that it skipped straight from the happy wedding to the happy separation; but of course in between weddings and separations, unhappy things happen.

*

I get in the car, drop the kids off, go home. David's already in his office with the door closed. Today isn't a column day, so he's probably either writing a company brochure, for which he gets paid heaps, or writing his novel, for which he gets paid nothing. He spends more time on the novel than he does on the brochures, which is only a source of tension when things are bad between us; when we're getting on I want to support him, look after him, help him realize his full potential. When we're not I want to tear his stupid novel into pieces and force him to get a proper job. I read a bit of the book a while ago and hated it. It's called *The Green Keepers*, and it's a satire about Britain's post-Diana touchy-feely culture. The last part I read was all about how the staff of Green Keepers, this company that sells banana elbow cream and Brie foot lotion and lots of other amusingly useless cosmetics, all require bereavement counselling when the donkey they have adopted dies. OK, so I am not in any way qualified to be a literary critic, not least because I don't read books any more. I used to, back in the days when I was a different, happier, more engaged human being, but now I fall asleep every night holding a copy of *Captain Corelli's Mandolin*, the opening chapter of which I still haven't finished, after six months of trying. (This is not the author's fault, incidentally, and I am sure the book is every bit as good as my friend Becca told me it is when she lent it to me. It's the fault of my eyelids.) Even so, even though I no longer have any idea of what constitutes passable literature, I know that *The Green Keepers* is terrible: facetious, unkind, full of itself. Rather like David, or the David that has emerged over the last few years.

The day after I'd read this scene, I saw a woman whose baby was stillborn; she'd had to go through labour knowing that she would produce a dead child. Of course I recommended bereavement counselling, and of course I thought of David and his sneering book, and of course I took a bitter pleasure in telling him when I got home that the reason we could rely on our mortgage being paid every month was because I earned money by recommending the very thing that he finds contemptible. That was another good evening.

When David's office door is closed it means he cannot be disturbed, even if his wife has asked him for a divorce. (Or, at least, that's what I'm presuming – it's not that we have made provision for precisely that eventuality.) I make myself another cup of tea, pick up the *Guardian* from the kitchen table and go back to bed.

I can only find one story in the paper that I want to read: a married woman is in trouble for giving a man she didn't know a blow-job in the Club Class section of an aeroplane. The married man is in trouble, too, but it's the woman I'm interested in. Am I like that? Not outside in the world I'm not, but in my head I am. I've lost all my bearings somehow, and it scares me. I know Stephen, of course I know Stephen, but when you have been married for twenty years, any sexual contact with anyone else seems wanton, random, almost bestial. Meeting a man at a Community Health forum, going out for a drink with him, going out for another drink with him, going out for dinner with him, going out for another drink with him and kissing him afterwards, and, eventually, arranging to sleep with him in Leeds after a conference . . . That's my equivalent of stripping down to my bra and pants in front of a plane full of passengers and performing a sex act, as they say in the papers, on a complete stranger. I fall asleep surrounded by pieces of the *Guardian* and have dreams that are sexual but not erotic in any way whatsoever, dreams full of people doing things to other people, like some artist's vision of hell.

When I wake up David's in the kitchen making himself a sandwich.

'Hello,' he says, and gestures at the breadboard with the knife. 'Want one?' Something about the easy domesticity of the offer makes me want to cry. Divorce means never having a sandwich made for you – not by your ex-husband, anyway. (Is that really true, or just sentimental claptrap? Is it really impossible to imagine a situation where, some time in the future, David might offer to put a piece of cheese between two pieces of bread for me? I look at David and decide that, yes, it is impossible. If David and I divorce he will be angry for the rest of his life – not because he loves me but because that is who and how he is. It is just about possible to imagine a situation in which he would not run me over if I was crossing the street – Molly is tired, say, and I'm having to carry her – but hard to think of a situation where he might offer to perform a simple act of kindness.)

'No thanks.'

'Sure?'

'Sure.'

'Suit yourself.'

That's more like it. A slight note of pique has crept in from somewhere, as if his strenuous attempts to make love not war have been met with continued belligerence.

'Do you want to talk?'

He shrugs. 'Yeah. What about?'

'Well. About yesterday. What I said on the phone.'

'What did you say on the phone?'

'I said I wanted a divorce.'

'Did you? Gosh. That's not very friendly, is it? Not a very nice thing for a wife to say to her husband.'

'Please don't do this.'

'What do you want me to do?'

'Talk properly.'

'OK. You want a divorce. I don't. Which means that unless you can prove that I've been cruel or neglectful or what have you, or that I've been shagging someone else, you have to move out and then after five years of living somewhere else you can have one. I'd get going if I were you. Five years is a long time. You don't want to put it off.'

I hadn't thought about any of this, of course. Somehow I'd got it into my head that me saying the words would be enough, that the mere expression of the desire would be proof that my marriage wasn't working.

'What about if I . . . you know.'

'No, I don't know.'

I'm not ready for any of this. It just seems to be coming out of its own accord.

'Adultery.'

'You? Miss Goody Two Shoes?' He laughs. 'First off you've got to find someone who wants to adulter you. Then you've got to stop being Katie Carr GP, mother of two, and adulter him back. And even then it wouldn't matter 'cos I still wouldn't divorce you. So.'

I'm torn between relief – I've stepped back from the brink, the confession of no return – and outrage. He doesn't think I've got the guts to do what I did last night! Worse than that, he doesn't think anyone would want to do it with me anyway! The relief wins out, of course. My cowardice is more powerful than his insult.

'So you're just going to ignore what I said yesterday.'

'Yeah. Basically. Load of rubbish.'

'Are you happy?'

'Oh, Jesus Christ.'

There is a certain group of people who will respond to one of the most basic and pertinent of questions with a mild and impatient blasphemy; David is a devoted member of this group. 'What's that got to do with anything?'

'I said what I said yesterday because I wasn't happy. And I don't think you are either.'

'Course I'm not bloody happy. Idiotic question.'

'Why not?'

'For all the usual bloody reasons.'

'Which are?'

'My stupid wife just asked me for a divorce, for a start.'

'The purpose of my question was to help you towards an understanding of why your stupid wife asked you for a divorce.'

'What, you want a divorce because I'm not happy?'

'That's part of it.'

'How very magnanimous of you.'

'I'm not being magnanimous. I hate living with someone who's so unhappy.'

'Tough.'

'No. Not tough. I can do something about it. I cannot live with someone who's so unhappy. You're driving me up the wall.'

'Do what the fuck you like.'

And off he goes, with his sandwich, back to his satirical novel.

There are thirteen of us here in the surgery altogether, five GPs and then all the other staff that make the centre work – a manager, and nurses, and receptionists both full- and part-time. I get on well with just about everyone, but my special friend is Becca, one of the other GPs. Becca and I lunch together when we can, and once a month we go out for a drink and a pizza, and she knows more about me than anyone else in the place. We're very different, Becca and I. She's cheerfully cynical about our work and why we do it, and sees no difference between working in medicine and, say, advertising, and she thinks my moral self-satisfaction is hilarious. If we're not talking about work, though, then usually we talk about her. Oh, she always asks me about Tom and Molly and David, and I can usually provide some example of David's rudeness that amuses her, but there just seems to be more to say about her life, somehow. She sees things and does things, and her love life is sufficiently chaotic to provide narratives with time-consuming twists and turns in them. She's five years younger than me, and single since a drawn-out and painful break-up with her university sweetheart a couple of years back. Tonight she's agonizing about some guy she's seen three times in the last month: she doesn't think it's going anywhere, she's not sure whether they connect, although they connect in bed . . . Usually, I feel old but interested when she talks about this sort of thing – flattered to be confided in, thrilled vicariously by all the break-ups and comings-together and flirtations, even vaguely envious of the acute loneliness Becca endures at periodic intervals, when there's nothing going on. It all seems indicative of the crackle of life, electrical activity in chambers of the heart that I closed off a long time ago. But tonight, I feel bored. Who cares? See him or don't see him, it doesn't make any difference to me. What are the stakes, after all? Now I, on the other hand, a married woman with a lover . . .

'Well if you're not sure, why do you need to make a decision? Why don't you just rub along for a while?' I can hear the boredom in my voice, but she doesn't detect it. I don't get bored when I see Becca. That's not the arrangement.

'I don't know. I mean, if I'm with him, I can't be with anyone else. I do with-him things instead of single things. We're going to the Screen on the Green tomorrow night to see some Chinese film. I mean, that's fine if you're sure about someone. That's what you do, isn't it? But if you're not sure, then it's just dead time. I mean, who am I going to meet in the Screen on the Green? In the dark? When you can't talk?'

I suddenly have a very deep yearning to go and see a Chinese film at the Screen on the Green – the more Chinese it is, in fact, the better I would like it. That is another chamber of my heart that shows no electrical activity – the chamber that used to flicker into life when I saw a film that moved me, or read a book that inspired me, or listened to music that made me want to cry. I closed that chamber myself, for all the usual reasons. And now I seem to have made a pact with some philistine devil: if I don't attempt to re-open it, I will be allowed just enough energy and optimism to get through a working day without wanting to hang myself.

'Sorry. This must all sound so silly to you. It sounds silly to me. If I'd known that I'd be the sort of woman who was going to end up sitting with married friends and moaning about my single status I would have shot myself. Really. I'll stop. Right now. I'll never mention it again.' She takes a parodic deep breath, and then continues before she has exhaled.

'But he might be OK, mightn't he? I mean, how would I know? That's the trouble. I'm in such a tearing hurry that I haven't got the time to decide whether they're nice or not. It's like shopping on Christmas Eve.'

'I'm having an affair.'

Becca smiles distractedly and, after a brief pause, continues.

'You bung everything in a basket. And then after Christmas you . . .'

She doesn't finish the sentence, presumably because she has begun to see that her analogy isn't going anywhere, and that dating and men are nothing like Christmas shopping and baskets.

17

'Did you hear what I said?'

She smiles again. 'No. Not really.' I have become a ghost, the comically impotent, unthreatening sort that you find in children's books and old TV programmes. However much I shout Becca will never hear me.

'Your brother's single, isn't he?'

'My brother's a semi-employed depressive.'

'Is that a genetic thing? Or just circumstance? Because if it's genetic . . . It would be a risk. Not for a while, though. I mean, you don't get so many depressed kids, do you? It's a late-onset thing. And I'm so old already that I won't be around when they become depressed adults. So. Maybe it's worth thinking about. If he's game, I am.'

'I'll pass it on. I think he would like children, yes.'

'Good. Excellent.'

'You know the thing you didn't hear?'

'No.'

'When I said, "Did you hear what I said", and you said "No".'

'No.'

'Right.'

'He's my age, isn't he? More or less?'

And we talk about my brother and his depression and his lack of ambition until Becca has lost all interest in the idea of bearing his children.

2

Nothing happens for a couple of weeks. We don't have another conversation about anything; we keep to the social arrangements we have already made, which means dinners at weekends with other couples with children, couples who live within roughly the same income bracket and postal district as ours. Stephen leaves three messages on my mobile, and I don't reply to any of them. Nobody notices that I failed to attend the second day of my Family Health Workshop in Leeds. I have returned to the marital bed, and David and I have had sex, just because we're there and lying next to each other. (The difference between sex with David and sex with Stephen is like the difference between science and art. With Stephen it's all empathy and imagination and exploration and the shock of the new, and the outcome is . . . uncertain, if you know what I mean. I'm engaged by it, but I'm not necessarily sure what it's all about. David, on the other hand, presses this button, then that one, and bingo! Things happen. It's like operating a lift – just as romantic, but actually just as useful.)

We have a great belief, those of us who live in this income bracket and postal district, in the power of words: we read, we talk, we write, we have therapists and counsellors and even priests who are happy to listen to us and tell us what to do. So it comes as something of a shock to me that my words, big words, it seemed to me at the time, words that would change my life, might just as well have been bubbles: David swatted them away and they popped, and there is no evidence anywhere that they ever existed.

So now what? What happens when words fail us? If I lived a different sort of life in a different sort of world, a world where action counted for more than words and feelings, I would do something, go somewhere, hit someone, even. But David knows that I don't live in that world, and has called my bluff; he won't obey the rules. Once we took Tom to play this shoot-em-up game in a funfair; you had to put on this electronic backpack thing, and when you were hit, it made a noise and you were dead. You could, of course, just ignore the noise and carry on, if you wanted to be anarchic and wreck the game, because a beep is just a beep, after all. And that, as it turns out, was what I was doing when I asked for a divorce. I was making a beeping noise that David won't recognize.

This is what it feels like: you walk into a room and the door locks behind you and you spend a little while panicking, looking around for a key or a window or something, and then when you realize that there is no way out, you start to make the best of what you've got. You try out the chair, and you realize that it's actually not uncomfortable, and there's a TV, and a couple of books, and there's a fridge stocked with food. You know, how bad can it be? And me asking for a divorce was the panic, but very soon I get to this stage of looking around at what I've got. And what I've got turns out to be two lovely kids, a nice house, a good job, a husband who doesn't beat me and presses all the right buttons on the lift . . . I can do this, I think. I can live this life.

One Saturday night David and I go out for a meal with Giles and Christine, these friends of ours we've known since college, and David and I are OK with each other, and it's a nice restaurant, an old-fashioned Italian in Chalk Farm with breadsticks and wine-in-a-basket and really good veal (and if we take it as read that doctors cannot, unless they are Dr Death-type doctors who inject young children and pensioners with deadly serums, be Bad People, then I think I'm entitled to a little veal once in a while); and halfway through the evening, with David in the middle of one of his Angriest Man in Holloway rants (a savage assault, if you're interested, on the decision-making process at Madame Tussaud's), I notice that Giles and Christine are almost helpless with laughter. And they're not even laughing at David, but with him. And even though I'm sick of David's rants, his apparently inexhaustible and all-consuming anger, I suddenly see that he does have the power to entertain people, and I feel well-disposed, almost warm, towards him, and when we get home we indulge in a little more button pushing.

And the next morning we take Molly and Tom to the Archway Baths, and Molly gets knocked over by one of the puny waves generated by the wave machine and disappears under eighteen inches of water, and all four of us, even David, get the giggles, and the moment we calm down I can see what an awful malcontent I have become. I'm not being sentimental: I am aware that this happy family snapshot was just that, a snapshot, and an unedited video would have captured a sulk from Tom before we arrived at the pool (hates swimming with us, wanted to go round to Jamie's) and a rant from David after (I refuse the kids permission to buy crisps from the vending machine because we're going straight home for lunch, David is compelled to tell me that I am a living embodiment of the Nanny State). The point is not that my life is one long golden summer which I am simply too self-absorbed to appreciate (although it might be, of course, and I am simply too self-absorbed to appreciate it), but that happy moments are possible, and while happy moments are possible I have no right to demand anything more for myself, given the havoc that would be wrought.

That night I have a huge row with David, and the next day Stephen turns up at work, and all of a sudden I've spilled the half-full glass all over myself.

The row isn't worth talking about, really: it's just a row, between two people who actually don't like each other enough not to row. It begins with something about a plastic bag with a hole in it (I didn't know it had a hole in it, and I told David to use it to . . . Oh, forget it); it ends with me telling David that he's a talentless and evil bastard, and with him telling me that he can't hear my voice without wanting to throw up. The Stephen thing is altogether more serious. Monday morning is a drop-in surgery, and I've just finished seeing a chap who has suddenly become convinced that he has cancer of the rectum. (He doesn't. He has a boil – a result, I would imagine, of his somewhat cavalier approach to personal hygiene, although I will spare you any further details.) And I go out to the reception to pick up the next set of medical notes, and I see Stephen sitting in the waiting area with his arm in what is very clearly a home-made sling.

Eva, our receptionist, leans over the desk and starts to whisper.

'The guy in the sling. He says he's only just moved into the area and he has no proof of residence and no medical card and he only wants to see you. Says someone recommended you. Shall I send him packing?'

'No, it's OK. I'll see him now. What's his name?'

'Ummm . . .' She looks at the pad in front of her. 'Stephen Garner.'

This is his real name, although I wasn't to know that he'd use it. I look at him.

'Stephen Garner?'

He jumps to his feet. 'That's me.'

'Would you like to come through?'

As I walk down the corridor, I'm aware that several people in the waiting room are bearing down on Eva to complain about Mr Garner's queue jumping. I feel guilty and I want to get out of earshot, but progress to my surgery is slow, because Stephen, clearly enjoying himself greatly, has also developed a limp. I usher him in and he sits down, grinning broadly.

'What do you think you're doing?' I ask him.

'How else was I supposed to see you?'

'No, you see, that was the message I was trying to convey by not returning your calls. I don't want to see you. Enough. I made a mistake.'

I sound like me, cool and slightly stroppy, but I don't feel like me. I feel scared, and excited, and much younger than I am, and this emergent juvenile finds herself wondering whether Eva noticed how attractive Mr Garner is. ('Did you see that guy in the sling?' I want her to say at some point in the day. 'Phwooar.' And I'd only just restrain myself from saying something smug.)

'Can we go for a cup of coffee and talk about this?'

Stephen is a press officer for a pressure group which looks after political refugees. He worries about the Asylum Bill and Kosovo and East Timor, sometimes, he has confessed, to the extent that he cannot sleep at night. He, like me, is a good person. But turning up at a doctor's surgery feigning injury in order to harass one of the doctors . . . That's not Good. That's Bad. I'm confused.

'I've got a room full of patients out there. Unlike you, all of them, without exception, aren't feeling very well. I can't skip out for a coffee whenever I feel like it.'

'Do you like my sling?'

'Please go away.'

'When you've given me a time when we can meet. Why did you leave the hotel in the middle of the night?'

'I felt bad.'

'What about?'

'Sleeping with you when I've got a husband and two kids, presumably.'

'Oh. That.'

'Yes. That.'

'I'm not leaving until we have a date.'

The reason I don't have him thrown out is because I find all this curiously thrilling. A few weeks ago, before I met Stephen, I wasn't this person who makes men feign serious injury in order to grab a few precious seconds of time with me. I mean, I'm perfectly presentable looking, and I know that when I make an effort I can still extract grudging admiration from my husband, but until now I have been under no illusions about my ability to drive the opposite sex demented with desire. I was Molly's mum, David's wife, a local GP; I have been monogamous for two decades. And it's not like I've become asexual, because I have had sex, but it's sex with David, and attraction and all the rest of it no longer seems to apply: we have sex with each other because we have agreed not to have sex with anyone else, not because we can't keep our hands to ourselves.

And now, with Stephen begging in front of me, I do feel a little bit of vanity creeping in. Vanity! I catch a glimpse of myself in the mirror in my surgery, and for a moment, just a second, I can see why someone would go to all the trouble of putting his arm in a sling. I'm not being monstrously vain, after all: I'm not saying that I could see why someone would want to throw themselves off a cliff, or starve themselves to death, or sit at home listening to sad music and downing a bottle of whisky. The sling must have taken him all of twenty minutes to knock up, and that's presuming a certain degree of incompetence; throw in the drive from Kentish Town and we're talking about a maximum of forty-five minutes of inconvenience, very little expense and absolutely no pain. It's hardly *Fatal Attraction*, is it? No, I have a sense of proportion about this, and though it would be preposterous to presume that I'm worth much more than a fake sling, I do suddenly have the sense of being worth that much, and this is an entirely new and not altogether unwelcome feeling. If I were single, or had recently embarked on the latest in a long string of relationships, I would think that Stephen's behaviour was pathetic, or threatening, or annoying, at least; but I'm not single, I'm a married woman, and as a paradoxical consequence I tell him that I'll meet him for a drink after work.

'Really?' He sounds amazed, as if he knows he's overstepped the mark, and no woman in her right mind would agree to a date in these circumstances; for a moment, my new-found sexual confidence takes a knock.

'Really. Ring me on my mobile later. But please go, and let me see someone who has something wrong with them.'

'Shall I take the sling off? Make it look as though you've cured me?'

'Don't be stupid. But maybe you could lose the limp on the way out.'

'Too much?'

'Too much.'

'Right-o. See you later.'

And he strides cheerfully out of the room.

With a choreographer's sense of timing, Becca walks in seconds later – she must have pushed past Stephen on her way.

'I need to talk to you,' she says. 'I owe you an apology.'

'What for?'

'Do you ever do that thing where you lie in bed and you can't sleep so you end up writing out recent conversations you've had? So they look like a play?'

'No.' I love Becca, but it has begun to occur to me that she might be potty.

'Well, you should. It's fun. I keep them. Look through them, sometimes.'

'You should get the person you had the conversation with to come round and read their part out loud.'

She looks at me, and makes a face, as if I am the potty one.

'What would be the point of that? Anyway. You know the last time we went out for pizza?'

'Yes.'

'I was, you know, writing out the conversation. And I remembered all that stuff about your brother. But – don't laugh, OK – did you say something about having an affair?'

'Shhh! Shhh!' I push the door shut behind her.

'My God! You did, didn't you!'

'Yes.'

'And I just ignored you.'

'Yes.'

'Katie, I'm so sorry. I wonder why I did that?'

I make a face to show that I cannot help her.

'Are you OK?'

'Yes. Just about.'

'So what's going on?'

It's interesting, listening to the tones in her voice. And there are tones plural there. There's the girly-golly-gosh, I-want-to-hear-all-about-it tone, of course, but she knows David, she knows Tom and Molly, so there is caution there, too, and concern, and probably disapproval.

'Is it serious?'

'I don't want to talk about it, Becca.'

'You did.'

'Yes, I did. But now I don't know what to say about it.'

'Why are you doing it?'

'I don't know.'

'Are you in love with him?'

'No.'

25

'So what is it?'

'I don't know.'

But I do, I think. It's just that Becca wouldn't understand. And if she did, she would begin to feel more sorry for me than I could bear. I could tell her about the excitement of the last couple of weeks, and the dreamy otherworldliness of the lovemaking. But I couldn't tell her that Stephen's interest in me, his attraction to me, seems like the only sense of future I have. That's too pathetic. She wouldn't like that.

I'm nervous when I meet Stephen again after work, because it feels as though I'm entering Phase Two of something, and Phase Two seems potentially more serious than Phase One. I know, of course, that Phase One involved all sorts of serious things – infidelity and deceit, to name but two – but it stopped, and I was OK about it stopping; I thought the Stephen thing was something I could brush off, like a crumb, leaving no trace of anything behind. But if it was a crumb, and I'd brushed it off, it wouldn't have walked in to the surgery wearing a fake sling this morning. It's beginning to look less like a crumb and more like a red wine stain, a grease spot, a nasty and very visible patch of Indian takeaway sauce. Anyway. The point is I'm nervous, and I'm nervous because I'm not meeting Stephen with the intention of telling him I never want to see him again.

I don't want him to pick me up from work because people are nosy, so we arrange to meet in a residential street around the corner; to avoid missing each other we choose a house to meet outside. And while I'm walking there I try to think of the man with the boil because this is bad, bad, underhand, deceitful, and you have to be good to look at boils in the rectal area (unless you're very, very bad, I suppose, sick and corrupt and decadent), so when I spot Stephen's car I'm not really in the right place to focus on what I'm doing, or how I should be with him. I get in and we drive off, all the way to Clerkenwell, because Stephen knows a quiet bar in a smart new hotel, and I don't wonder until later why a man who works for a pressure group based in Camden knows anything about smart new hotels in Clerkenwell.

But it is the right place for us, discreet and soulless and full of Germans and Americans, and they bring you a bowl of nuts with your drink, and we sit there for a little while and it occurs to me for the first time, really, how little I know this man. What am I supposed to say now? I can have state-of-relationship conversations with David, because I know the way into them – Jesus, I should do by now – but this guy . . . I don't even know the name of his sister, so how can I talk to him about whether I should leave my husband and two children?

'What's your sister's name?'

'Sorry?'

'What's the name of your sister?'

'Jane. Why?'

'I don't know.'

It doesn't seem to have helped.

'What do you want?'

'Sorry?'

'From me. What do you want from me?'

'How do you mean?'

He's making me angry, although he'd be surprised that his hitherto minimal contribution to the conversation – a couple of 'Sorrys' and his sister's first name, provided on request – could have provoked this response. He just doesn't seem to get it, somehow. I am facing the imminent destruction of all that I hold dear, or used to hold dear, anyway, and he sits there sipping his designer beer, oblivious to anything but the comfort of his surroundings and his delight in my presence. I'm scared that any second he's going to lean back in his seat, sigh contentedly, and say, 'This is nice.' I want anguish, pain, confusion.

'I mean, do you want me to leave home? Come and live with you? Run away with you? What?'

'Blimey.'

'"Blimey"? Is that all you've got to say?'

'I hadn't really thought about all that, to be honest. I just wanted to see you.'

'Maybe you should think about it.'

'Right now?'

'You do know I'm married with kids, don't you?'

'Yes, but . . .' He sighs.

'But what?'

'But I don't want to think about it right now. I want to get to know you better first.'

'Lucky you.'

'Why lucky?'

'Not everyone has that sort of time.'

'What, you want to run off with me first and find out about me later?'

'So you just want an affair.'

'Is this the right time to tell you that I'm staying here tonight?'

'I beg your pardon?'

'I booked a room here. Just in case.'

I drain my drink and walk out.

('What was that all about?' he asks me the next time I see him – because there is a next time, and I knew there would be even as I was getting into the taxi that took me back to my husband and family. 'Why did you walk out on me at the hotel?' And I make some weak what-kind-of-girl-do-you-think-I-am joke, but of course there's nothing much to joke about, really. It's all too sad. It's sad that he doesn't know why I didn't respond to his seedy nightclub-owner gestures; it's sad that I end up convincing myself somehow that the man capable of making them is a significant and valuable figure in my life. We don't talk about sad things, though. We're having an affair. We're having too much fun.)

When I get home, David has put his back out again. I don't know that this will turn out to be a turning-point in our lives – why should I? David's back is always with us, and though I'd rather not see him as he is now – in pain, lying motionless on the floor with a couple of books under his head and the cordless telephone, its battery in need of recharging (hence, presumably, no message on the mobile), balanced on his stomach – I've seen him like this often enough not to worry about it.

He's even more angry than I was expecting him to be. He's angry with me for being late (but so angry, luckily, that he isn't really interested in where I've been or what I've been doing), angry with me for leaving him to cope with the kids when he's incapacitated, angry that he's getting older, and that his back troubles him more frequently.

'How come you're a doctor and you can't ever fucking do anything about this?'

I ignore him.

'Do you want me to help you up?'

'Of course I don't want you to help me up, you silly bloody woman. I want to stay here. I don't want to stay here and look after two bloody kids, though.'

'Have they had their tea?'

'Oh, yes. Course. They had some of those fish fingers that climb under the grill on their own and cook themselves.'

'I'm sorry if that was a stupid question. I wasn't sure when your back went.'

'Fucking ages ago.'

There is no careless use of the f-word in this house; it's all done very, very carefully. When David swears like this in front of the children – who are only pretending to watch television, seeing as how their two heads swivel round immediately when they hear a word they shouldn't – he is communicating to all of us that he is unhappy, that his life is terrible, that he hates me, that things are so bad he can no longer control his language. He can, of course, and does, most of the time, so I in turn hate him for his manipulation.

'Shut up, David.'

He sighs and mutters under his breath, filled with despair at my prissiness and my lack of sympathy.

'What do you want me to do?'

'Put their tea on and leave me alone. I'll be able to get up soon. If I'm allowed to rest it.' As if I were about to ask him to limbo dance, or put a few bookshelves up, or take me upstairs to make love.

'Do you want the paper?'

'Already read it.'

'I'll put the radio on.'

So we listen to the arts review thing on Radio 4, and we listen to *The Simpsons*, and we listen to the fish fingers spitting under the grill, and I try not to tread on my husband while I long for hotel rooms in Leeds and Clerkenwell – not what went on in them, but the rooms themselves: their quiet, their bedlinen, their intimations of a better, blanker life than this one.

David spends the night on the futon in the spare room; I have to help him to take his clothes off, so I'm bound to end up thinking about needs and wants and rights and duties and men with boils in their rectums, although I don't get anywhere. And then I go to bed and read the paper, and the Archbishop of Canterbury has written about divorce, and the grass-is-greener syndrome, and how he wouldn't wish to deny anyone the right to end a brutal and degrading marriage, but . . . (Why is every newspaper full of stuff about me me me? I want to read about train crashes I haven't been in, unsafe beef I won't eat, peace treaties in places I don't live; instead my eye is drawn to stories about oral sex and the breakdown of the contemporary family.) So I'm bound to end up thinking about brutal and degrading marriages, and whether I'm in one, and however hard I try to kid myself – *ah, but the meaning of these words 'brutal and degrading' it's different in our particular postal district, he calls me a silly bloody woman, he creates bad atmospheres when my family visit, he is consistently negative about things I hold dear, he thinks old people should stay in the seats specially designated for them on buses* – I know, really, that I'm not. I'm neither brutalized nor degraded by my relationship with David; it's just that I don't really like it very much, and that is a very different kind of complaint.

What is the point of an affair, when it comes down to it? Over the next three weeks I have sex twice with Stephen, and I don't come on either occasion (not that coming is everything, although it sort of would be in the long run); we spend time talking about childhood holidays, my kids, his previous live-in relationship with a woman who moved back to the States, our shared antipathy to people who don't ask questions . . . Where does any of it get me? And where do I want to get anyway? It's true that I haven't talked to David about childhood holidays recently, for obvious reasons, but is that what's really missing from my marriage – the opportunity to look into the middle distance and wax lyrical about the joys of Cornish rock pools? Maybe I should try it, just like one is supposed to try weekends away without kids and saucy underwear. Maybe I should go home and say, 'I know you've heard this before, but can I repeat the story of how I once found half-a-crown under a dead crab that my dad had told me not to touch?' But it was a dull story the first time, made palatable only by David's endless fascination for absolutely anything that had happened to me before I met him. Now I would be lucky to get away with a sigh and an inaudible obscenity.

You see, what I really want, and what I'm getting with Stephen, is the opportunity to rebuild myself from scratch. David's picture of me is complete now, and I'm pretty sure neither of us likes it much; I want to rip the page out and start again on a fresh sheet, just like I used to do when I was a kid and had messed a drawing up. It doesn't even matter who the fresh sheet is, really, so it's beside the point whether I like Stephen, or whether he knows what to do with me in bed, or anything like that. I just want his rapt attention when I tell him that my favourite book is *Middlemarch*, and I just want that feeling, the feeling I get with him, of having not gone wrong yet.

I decide to tell my brother about Stephen. My brother is younger than me, no kids, no relationship at the moment; I'm almost sure that he won't judge me, even though he loves Molly and Tom and has even been out for a drink and the odd meal with David when I haven't been around. We're close, Mark and I, and I vow to trust what he says, respect his instincts.

What he says is, 'You're off your fucking head.' We're in a Thai restaurant in Muswell Hill, around the corner from where he lives, and the starters haven't even arrived yet; I wish I'd saved the difficult part of the evening for later. (Except I didn't think it would be difficult. How come I got that wrong? Why did I think my brother would shrug all this off? I'd imagined this whispery, jokey, conspiratorial chat over a cold beer and some satay sticks, but now I can see that this was a bit off the mark, and that my brother would be no sort of brother at all if he smiled and shook his head fondly.)

I look at him and smile feebly. 'I know that's what it must look like,' I say. 'But you don't really understand.'

'OK. Explain.'

'I've been so depressed,' I say. He understands depression. He's what passes for a black sheep in the Carr family: a chequered employment history, unmarried, pills, therapy.

'So write yourself a prescription. Go and talk to someone. I don't see how an affair is going to help. And a divorce certainly won't.'

'You're not going to listen, are you?'

'Course I'll listen. Listening isn't the same as cheering you on, though, is it? You can get one of your girlfriends to do that.'

I think of Becca, and I snort.

'Who else have you told?'

'No one. Well, someone. But she didn't seem to hear.'

Mark shakes his head impatiently, as if I am speaking in feminine metaphors.

'What does that mean?'

I gesture helplessly. Mark has always envied my relationships with people like Becca; he would find it hard to believe that she simply smiled at me indulgently, as if I were a stroke victim babbling nonsense.

'Jesus, Kate. David's a friend of mine.'

'Is he?'

'Well, all right, not, like, my best friend. But he's, you know, he's family.'

'And that means he's got to stay family for ever. Because he's your brother-in-law and you went out for a curry a couple of times. No matter what he does to me.'

'What has he done to you?'

'It's not . . . what he's done. Nobody we know does things. He's just . . . He's always down on me.'

'Diddums.'

'Jesus, Mark. You sound like him.'

'Maybe you should divorce me, too, then. You can run away from everyone who doesn't thoroughly approve of you every second of the day.'

'He's breaking my spirit. He's grinding me down. Nothing's ever right, I don't make him happy . . .'

'Have you thought about counselling?'

I snort, and Mark realizes that this is David we are talking about, and makes a Homer Simpson 'Doh!'-type noise, and for a moment we are brother and sister again.

'OK, OK,' he says. 'Bad idea. Shall I talk to him?'

'No.'

'Why not?'

I don't say anything; I don't know why not. Except that I didn't want anything to leak out of this conversation into the real world. I just wanted my brother to come into this little weird bubble I'm in for an evening. I wanted empathy, not action.

'What would make a difference to you?'

I know the answer to this one. I've thought about it, and I'm word-perfect.

'I don't want David to be David any more.'

'Ah. Who do you want him to be, then?'

'Someone different. Someone who loves me properly, and makes me feel good, and appreciates me, and thinks I'm great.'

'He does think you're great.'

I start to laugh. It's not an ironic laugh, or a bitter laugh, although surely if there was ever a moment that justified bitter laughter it would be now; it's a belly laugh. This is one of the funniest things I have heard for months. I am not sure of many things at the moment, but I do know, with every atom of my being, that David does not think I am great.

'What? What have I said?'

It takes a while to compose myself. 'I'm sorry. Just the idea that David thinks I'm great.'

'I know he does.'

'How?'

'Just . . . You know.'

'No. I really don't. That's the whole point, Mark.'

It's true that I don't want David to be David any more. I want things to be structurally the same – I want him to have fathered my children, I want him to have been married to me for twenty years, I don't even mind the weight and the bad back. I just don't want that voice, that tone, that permanent scowl. I want him to like me, in fact. Is that really too much to ask of a husband?

3

I come home from work and David almost skips out of his office to greet me. 'Look,' he says, and then proceeds to bow at me vigorously, as if I were the Queen and he were some kind of lunatic royalist.

'What?'

'My back. I don't feel anything. Not a twinge.'

'Did you go to see Dan Silverman?' Dan Silverman is an osteopath that we recommend at the surgery, and I've been telling David to see him for months. Years, probably.

'No.'

'So what happened?'

'I saw someone else.'

'Who?'

'This guy.'

'Which guy?'

'This guy in Finsbury Park.'

'In Finsbury Park?' Dan Silverman has a practice in Harley Street. There is no Harley Street equivalent in Finsbury Park, as far as I know. 'How did you find him?'

'Newsagent's window.'

'A newsagent's window? What qualifications has he got?'

'None whatsoever.' Information delivered with a great deal of pride and aggression, inevitably. Medical qualifications belong on my side of the great marital divide, and are therefore to be despised.

'So you let someone completely unqualified mess around with your back. Smart decision, David. He's probably crippled you for life.'

David starts to bow again. 'Do I look like someone who's been crippled?'

'Not today, no. But nobody can cure a bad back in one session.'

'Yeah, well. GoodNews has.'

'What good news?'

'That's his name. GoodNews. Capital G, capital N, all one word. D. J. GoodNews, actually. To give him his full title.'

'DJ. Not Dr.'

'It's, you know, a clubby thing. I think he used to work in a disco or something.'

'Always useful when you're treating back complaints. Anyway. You went to see someone called GoodNews.'

'I didn't know he was called GoodNews when I went to see him.'

'Out of interest, what did his advert say?'

'Something like, I don't know. "Bad Back? I can cure you in one session." And then his telephone number.'

'And that impressed you?'

'Yeah. Of course. Why mess around?'

'I'm presuming this GoodNews person isn't some sort of alternative therapist.' It may not surprise you to learn that David has not, up until this point, been a big fan of alternative medicine of any kind; he has argued forcefully, both to me and to the readers of his newspaper column, that he's not interested in any kind of cure that isn't harmful to small children and pregnant women, and that anyone who suggests anything different is a moron. (David, incidentally, is rabidly conservative in everything but politics. There are people like that now, I've noticed, people who seem angry enough to call for the return of the death penalty or the repatriation of Afro-Caribbeans, but who won't, because, like just about everybody else in our particular postal district, they're liberals, so their anger has to come out through different holes. You can read them in the columns and the letters pages of our liberal newspapers every day, being angry about films they don't like or comedians they don't think are funny or women who wear headscarves. Sometimes I think life would be easier for David and me if he experienced a violent political conversion, and he could be angry about poofs and communists, instead of homeopaths and old people on buses and restaurant critics. It must be very unsatisfying to have such tiny outlets for his enormous torrent of rage.)

'I dunno what you'd call him.'

'Did he give you drugs?'

'Nope.'

'I thought that was your definition of alternative. Someone who doesn't give you drugs.'

'The point is, he's fixed me. Unlike the useless NHS.'

'And how many times did you try the useless NHS?'

'No point. They're useless.'

'So what did this guy do?'

'Just rubbed my back a bit with some Deep Heat and sent me on my way. Ten minutes.'

'How much?'

'Two hundred quid.'

I look at him. 'You're kidding.'

'No.'

He's proud of this ludicrous amount, I can see it in his face. In other times he would have laughed in, or possibly even punched, the face of some unqualified quack who wanted to charge him two hundred pounds for ten minutes' work, but now GoodNews (and if GoodNews is to become a regular conversational topic, I will have to find something else to call him) has become a useful weapon in the war between us. I think two hundred pounds is too much, therefore he gleefully pays the two hundred pounds. The perversity of the logic is actually alarming, when you think about it, because where will it end? Is it possible, for example, that he would sell the kids to a paedophile ring – for a piffling amount of money – just because it would really upset me? True, he loves his kids. But he really, really hates me, so it's a tough one to call.

'Two hundred pounds.'

'I can go back as many times as I want. For anything. For free.'

'But he fixes everything first time. So you don't need to.'

'That's why he's worth the money. That's why he charges so much.'

He bows again, up down up down, and grins at me; I shake my head and go to find my children.

*

37

Later, we watch TV together, as a family, and not for the first time recently I wonder how an evening can be so ordinarily domestic when life isn't that way. Even over the last few weeks, despite Stephen, and despite all the viciousness, we have developed a new Monday night routine, supper on laps during *Walking with Dinosaurs*; family ritual seems to be like some extraordinarily hardy desert flower, prepared to have a go at blooming in the most inhospitable terrain.

David still attempts to ruin our harmony – first by lying on the floor and attempting to do sit-ups (he is foiled by his girth and his general fitness level, rather than his back, but because it is not his back that has stopped him, he spends several minutes extolling the virtues of GoodNews, and he has to be hushed by the children), and then by poking fun at the commentary. 'Three weeks later, the male returns for another attempt at mating,' says Kenneth Branagh. 'Are you sure it wasn't a fortnight, Ken?' says David. 'Because it was a hundred million years ago, after all. You might find you're a few days out.'

'Shut up, David. They're enjoying it.'

'Bit of critical rigour won't kill them.'

'That's just what you need when you're a kid. Critical rigour.'

But we settle, in the end, and we watch the programme, bath the kids, put them to bed, eat an almost silent meal. And all the time I'm on the verge of saying something, doing something, except that I don't know what to say or do.

Next morning Tom spends his breakfast time staring at me and David, and after a little while I begin to find it disconcerting. He is a disconcerting child, Tom – he's quiet, quick on the uptake, direct to the point of being rude. He has the personality of a child prodigy, but no discernible talent.

'What's the matter with you?' I ask him.

'Nothing.'

'Why do you keep staring at us?'

'I want to see if you're getting divorced.'

If this were a film I'd be holding a coffee mug to my lips, and

Tom's words would provoke a huge joke splutter, and coffee would be coming out of my nose and running on to my blouse. But as it is I'm putting toast in the toaster, and I have my back to him.

'Why would we be getting a divorce?'

'Someone at school told me.'

He says this with no sense of grievance; if someone at work told me that I was getting a divorce and I'd had no prior awareness of any marital difficulties, I would be more upset about the source of the news than anything else. But of course childhood is a time when information flies at you from all directions, and to Tom it's all the same whether he hears this news from his mother and father or from little Billy in 2C.

'Who?' says David, with slightly too much aggression, thus revealing himself immediately as the source of the leak.

'Joe Salter.'

'Who the hell's Joe Salter?'

'This kid at school.'

'What's it got to do with him?'

Tom shrugs. He's not interested in Joe Salter. He's interested in whether David and I are splitting up. I can see his point.

'Of course we're not getting a divorce,' I say. David looks at me triumphantly.

'Why did Joe Salter say you were, then?' Tom asks.

'I don't know,' I say. 'But if we're not, it doesn't really matter what Joe Salter says, does it?' I had never heard Joe Salter's name until three minutes ago, and I'm sick of him already. I have a very strong mental image of a smug, malevolent little blond boy, angelic looking to everyone but his classmates and, now, David and me, all of whom have had a glimpse into his stinking, poisonous soul. 'I mean, we know more about it than he does. And we're staying married, aren't we, David?'

'If you say so.' He's really enjoying this, and I can't say I blame him.

'Will you ever get divorced?' asks Molly. Jesus. I can now see, for the first time, just how many worms a can holds, and why it's not a good idea to open one under any circumstances.

'We're not planning to,' I tell her.

'Who would we live with if you did?'

'Who would you want to live with?' asks David. This is not a question you will find recommended in even the most brutal childcare books.

'Daddy!' says Molly. And then, as an afterthought, 'But not Tom.'

'Tom can go and live with Mummy, then. That's fair.'

'Daddy's joking,' I say to Tom quickly, but I suspect the damage has already been done: David has alienated brother from sister, daughter from mother and son from father in the time it takes to eat a bowl of Golden Grahams. And I've just promised not to divorce him. 'Doh!' as my brother and my son and Homer Simpson would say.

At my insistence, David comes to the surgery at lunchtime and we go to a greasy spoon around the corner, to talk about what was said at breakfast. David is unrepentant. (Or should that be: David is Unrepentant. Like James Bond is 007.)

'If we're not getting divorced, what harm can it do? It's a purely hypothetical situation.'

'Come on, David. You can do better than that.'

'Than what? What was I doing?'

'Setting traps.'

'What, the "if we're not getting divorced . . ." bit, you mean? That's a trap?'

'You want me to say "Ah, but we might be . . ." And then you'd hammer me for being inconsistent, and telling you one thing and the kids another.'

For some time now I have looked on David's verbal landmines with some contempt, so clunkingly obvious are they (and it should come as no surprise that the author of *The Green Keepers* is as clunkingly obvious in conversation as he is in prose). But clearly I've been getting sloppy, because David seizes on my last remark with an alacrity that suggests he'd been hoping I'd say precisely that.

'Hold on, hold on. What did you tell me when you called me from Leeds?'

'I didn't . . . Well, I did, but I just wanted . . .'

'No. What did you say?'

'You know what I said.'

'Say it again.'

'You don't have to do this, David. You know what I said then, and you know what I said to the kids this morning.'

'And that's consistent, is it?'

'I can see that from your point of view it might appear inconsistent.'

'And what about from yours? Because, really, I'm interested. I want to know how asking for a divorce and then saying you don't want one appears anything but.'

'None of this is the point.' And I really mean that. I want to find out how he could ask our daughter to choose between one parent and another, and why he was so unthinkingly cruel to Tom, and why he's been telling the parents of small boys called Joe Salter, or friends of the parents of small boys called Joe Salter, or even small boys called Joe Salter, about our marital difficulties. It's fair enough that I should want to know these things, just as it is fair enough that he should want to know why I told him I wanted the marriage to end, apparently out of the blue; but we only have a lunchtime to talk. And suddenly it seems that a lifetime wouldn't be long enough, let alone a lunchtime, because if a breakfast conversation can be broken down into this many tiny pieces, none of which can be put back together, then how many tiny pieces could we extract from the last quarter of a century? He said and I said and he said and I said and he thought and I thought and he thought and I thought and he did this and I did that and . . . It shouldn't be like this. This isn't the way it's supposed to be. If it had been what *we* thought and what *we* did, there wouldn't be anything to argue about, because we had thought and done it together, but the only thing we have managed to do together is create an enormous mess, and I just can't see how . . .

'David, I just can't see how we're going to get out of this mess.'

'What are you talking about now?'

I try to get the words out – the words I have used once, and retracted only this morning – but luckily they won't come, and instead I burst into tears, and sob and sob and sob, while David leads me out of the café and into the street.

It could well be that I am going mad; or, on the other hand, that I am simply confused and unhappy; or, on the third hand, that I know exactly what I want but cannot bring myself to do it because of all the pain it would cause, and the tension between those two states of being makes me want to explode. But when David touches me in that way, with tenderness, with love and concern, it all dribbles away to nothing, and I just want to be with him and my kids for the rest of my life. I don't want to touch Stephen, I don't want to row about what David may or may not have said to other people, or what he certainly said to Molly and Tom. I just want to do my job during the day, watch dinosaurs in the evening, sleep with David at night. Nothing else matters. All I need to do is hold on to this feeling, and I'll be fine.

We go and sit in the car for a little while, and David lets me cry.

'I can't let this go on,' he says.

'It won't. This is the end of it.'

'Do you want to tell me what's been going on?'

Typical David. Typical man. Something has to have been 'going on' for someone to be in this kind of state . . . Except, of course, he's right, and something has been going on, something that has, without any shadow of a doubt, contributed to my recent unhappiness. Suddenly, what with the dinosaur decision, and David being nice to me, and this conviction I have that the tears mark the end of all this, it seems very clear to me what I should do and say.

'David . . . I've been seeing someone.'

I tell him because I know I'm not seeing someone any more, and because I know in my own head what I want, and because I know that this will communicate itself to David. It doesn't occur to me for a moment that for David my confession marks the beginning of something, not the end of something, and just because he has known me for twenty-five years it doesn't mean that he knows me

42

or understands me now. He's quiet for a moment, and then he says, 'Can you come straight home tonight?'

'Yes. Sure. Of course. We'll talk about it then.'

'There's nothing to talk about. But I want to do something about Molly's eczema, and I need you to look after Tom.'

I play a game with myself, just to see what it feels like. The game goes like this: I am not sitting in the kitchen of the marital home watching my son doing his homework, but in the kitchen of a small flat nearby. In the game, this is where I now live, after my separation. Molly is not here because at the moment she is refusing to talk to me; she blames me for what has happened (David must have given her a very skewed account of events), and every time I try to talk to her she turns her back. David's terrible joke about dividing the family down the middle has turned out to be a prosaic and obvious prediction.

In some ways, this game is instructive. Why, for example, have I chosen to imagine this kitchen as a different kitchen? Why, in other words, do I find it so difficult to imagine that I would be the one who stays put in the event of domestic meltdown? It's not just because I'm the guilty party (although there are mitigating circumstances, and I'm not as guilty as all that, and my marriage is brutal and degrading, sort of, although admittedly it's a gentle, middle-class version of brutality and degradation); it's because I am the breadwinner. David takes the kids to school; David makes their tea, and supervises their homework; David picks them up from the homes of their friends, friends I have never met. If David and I split up, then my departure would cause minimal disruption, whereas if he left, I don't know how we would manage. I'm the man. I'm the daddy. Not because I have a job, but because David doesn't, not really, and is therefore the primary carer. That is why it is so easy for me to imagine moving out – because fathers always move out. And that's why it's so easy to imagine Molly not talking to me – she would never choose me over David, and in any case, a daughter always refuses to speak to her father after she has discovered he's been having an affair. There's all that stuff that goes on, the whole

43

Freudian thing. Is it too much to suggest that Molly is actually sexually jealous of me?

'Tom?'

'Yo.'

'Do you think of me as your mum or your dad?'

'What?'

'Don't even think about it, just say the first thing that comes into your head.'

'Mum.'

'Are you sure? You didn't have to think for a couple of seconds because you were confused?'

'No. I think of you as my mum, and Dad as my dad.'

'Why?'

'Mum, I'm really busy, OK?' And he shakes his head sadly.

Molly has always suffered from eczema, ever since she was very little. She gets it everywhere – hands, arms, legs, stomach – and no amount of creams or diets or homeopathic remedies have managed to affect it. This morning, before she went to school, I applied a very powerful and probably harmful steroid cream to her hands, which were covered in painful-looking cracks. But when she comes home, she runs down the hall and thrusts her hands at me, and there's not a trace of it anywhere. I lift up her fleece, and it's the same story on her stomach; she shows me the backs of her legs, and there's nothing there either. And of course my stomach turns over when I hear Molly and David come in, and of course I'm terrified about what this evening might hold; but all any of us can talk about is what has happened to Molly's ugly red sores. (And if Molly's eczema is more important than my adultery, then what is the point of adultery in the first place?)

'That's amazing,' I say.

'He just touched it and it went away,' says Molly. 'I could see it go.'

'He didn't just touch it,' says David. 'He used a cream.'

'He didn't, Daddy. I was watching. He didn't do anything. He just touched it.'

44

'With the cream.'

'He just touched it, Mummy.'

'Who just touched it?'

'DJ GoodNews.'

'Ah. DJ GoodNews. I should have known. Is there nothing DJ GoodNews can't do?'

'He happened to mention that he was good with eczema,' says David. 'So I thought it was worth a try.'

'Backs and eczema. That's quite an unusual combination of specialisms.'

'He did Daddy's headache as well,' says Molly.

'What headache?' I ask David.

'Just a . . . just a normal headache. I just happened to mention that I had one, and he . . . massaged my temples. It was good.'

'So, head, eczema, back. He's a real wizard, isn't he? Another two hundred quid?'

'And you don't think this is worth it?'

I snort, although I don't know what the snort is intended to convey. I don't know why I'm being like this. I would have paid double that to make Molly better, but the opportunity to snipe is always irresistible, whatever the circumstances.

'You should go, Tom,' says Molly. 'It's great. You go all warm.'

'That's the cream,' says David. 'He did that with my back.'

'He didn't use any cream. Daddy, why do you keep saying he used cream when he didn't?'

'You couldn't see what he was doing.'

'I could. Anyway, I know what cream feels like. It feels creamy . . .'

'Der!' says Tom. (For the benefit of those unfamiliar with apparently meaningless pre-teen monosyllables 'Der!' is completely different from 'Doh!' As I understand it, the latter is an admission of stupidity on the part of the speaker, whereas the former implies strongly that someone else is stupid. The former, incidentally, is accompanied by a rather unattractive face – screwed-up eyes, protruding teeth – intended to illustrate said stupidity.) Molly ignores him. '. . . And his hands didn't feel creamy at all.'

Something weird is going on here, because David won't let this drop; it is clear that this conversation will continue until Molly has denied the evidence of her own senses.

'That is complete nonsense, Molly. Read my lips: He . . . Was . . . Using . . . Cream.'

'Does it matter?' I ask him mildly.

'Of course it matters!'

'Why?'

'She's fibbing. And we don't like fibbing, do we, Molly?'

'Yeah,' says Tom, unpleasantly. 'Fibber! Liar!'

Molly bursts into tears, shouts 'It's not fair! I hate you all!' and runs up to her bedroom; and thus the first GoodNews we have had in weeks is deftly turned into yet another source of upset and difficulty.

'Well done, David. Again.'

'She shouldn't tell fibs, should she, Dad?'

'He was using cream,' says David, to no one in particular. 'I saw him.'

David apologizes to Molly (not, I have to say, because he wants to, but because I suggest that it would be the mature and fatherly thing to do), and Tom apologizes to Molly, and Molly apologizes to us, and we settle down again. And this, at the moment, is what constitutes peace in our time: the two hours between the argument about the quack doctor and his creams and the discussion about my affair with another man and whether it constitutes the end of my marriage.

'Shall we talk now?' I say to David when the kids are in bed.

'What about?'

'About what I told you at lunchtime.'

'What do you want to say about it?'

'I'd have thought you'd want to say something.'

'No.'

'You just want to leave it at that?'

'I don't want to leave it at anything. I'm just presuming that you'll be moving out in the next couple of days.' There's something different about David, but I'm not sure what. I was certain that he'd do his David thing, which would involve a lot of ranting, some raving, several million caustic remarks and an awful lot of contempt directed towards Stephen. But there's nothing like that; it's almost as if he doesn't care any more.

'The affair's over. As of this second.'

'I don't know about that. But I do know that no one asks Elvis Presley to play for nothing.'

I feel sick and panicky, and now I don't understand his words or his tone.

'What does that mean?'

'It's what Colonel Tom Parker told the White House.'

'Please talk to me properly.'

'Nixon's people phoned up Colonel Tom Parker and asked him to play for the President at the White House. And Parker said, you know, "Fine, but how much will we be getting?" And Nixon's aide said, "Colonel Parker, nobody asks for money for a private performance for the President", and Parker said, "I don't know about that, but no one asks Elvis Presley to play for nothing."'

'I don't understand! Please stop this! It's important!'

'I know. It's just . . . you know, I was reminded of that story, so I thought I'd pass it on. It's my way of saying that what you do or what you want doesn't really count for anything. You're the president, I'm the King. I'm in charge, you're on your bike. Off you go. Thank you and goodbye.'

'You don't mean that.'

I say this even though I know that he almost certainly does. He's that sort of man. Maybe when it comes down to it, this is the only way in which men in our particular postal district are unreconstructed. They know about changing nappies and talking about feelings and women working and all the basics, but he would still rather close things off right now than admit any possibility of doubt or confusion or hurt, however much it costs him, however much he is eaten up by what I have done. And he told me once, and I'm sure it will come up . . .

'Why don't you think I mean it? Don't you remember? We talked about it?'

'I remember.'

'So.'

We were in bed, and we'd just made love – we had Tom but not Molly, and I wasn't pregnant, so this must have been some time in 1992 – and I asked David if the prospect of having sex with me and no one else but me for the rest of his life depressed him. And he was uncharacteristically reflective about it: he said that it did get him down sometimes, but the alternatives were too horrible to contemplate, and anyway he knew that he would never be able to tolerate anything other than monogamy in me, so he could hardly expect indulgence for himself. So of course we ended up playing the game that all lovers play at some time or another, and I asked him whether there were any circumstances in which he would forgive me an infidelity – a drunken one-night stand, say, followed the morning after by immediate and piercing remorse. He pointed out that I never got drunk, and I'd never had a one-night stand in my life, so it was hard to imagine this particular circumstance; he said that if I were unfaithful, it would be for other reasons, and those other reasons he felt would spell trouble – trouble he wouldn't want to think about. I very rarely credit David with any perspicacity, but I take my hat off to him now: I wasn't drunk. It wasn't a one-night stand. I have been sleeping with Stephen for all sorts of other reasons, every one of which spells trouble.

'Have you thought about where you're going to stay?' he asks – still apparently untroubled by any of this.

'No, of course not. Are you telling me I'm the one that has to go?'

David just looks at me, and it's a look that is so full of contempt I want to run away from everything – my husband, my home, my children – and never come back.

I'm a good person. In most ways. But I'm beginning to think that being a good person in most ways doesn't count for anything very much, if you're a bad person in one way. Because most people are good people, aren't they? Most people want to help others, and if their work doesn't allow them to help others then they do it however they can – by manning the phones at the Samaritans once a month, or going on sponsored walks, or filling in standing orders. It's no good me telling you that I'm a doctor, because I'm only a doctor during weekdays. I've been sleeping with someone other than my husband outside working hours – I'm not so bad that I'd do it inside working hours – and at the moment, being a doctor can't make up for that, however many rectal boils I look at.

4

David tells me he's going away for a couple of nights. He doesn't say where, and he won't leave a number – he takes my mobile with him in case of family emergencies – but I presume he's gone to stay with his friend Mike (divorcee, local, good job, nice flat, spare bedroom). Before he leaves, he tells me that I've got forty-eight hours to talk to the kids; the unspoken assumption is that when I have told them how naughty I've been, I will pack my bags and go. That first night I don't sleep at all, and I feel that I'll never be able to rest until I've answered every single one of the questions that thrash around in my head like fish in a trawler net. Most of these questions (will David let me come round to watch the dinosaur programme on Monday nights?) choke and die; a couple of them, the bigger, more tenacious ones, just refuse to let go. Here's one: what rights do I have? You see, I don't want a divorce. OK, I know I did, before, when I didn't know what it meant and I didn't know what I felt and I didn't know how awful the prospect would seem – but now I don't, and I'm (almost) positive I'd do (almost) anything to get my marriage back on track. And if that is the case, why should I be the one who tells the kids? If he won't contemplate any pacific alternative, why should I do his dirty work? What if I just don't go? What would he do then? I go round and round on this other loop, too: we're never going to get out of this mess, things have gone too far, it's always going to be awful whenever it happens, best get out now . . . And all the time I know, somewhere in me, that I will never be able to sit down and tell my children that I'm leaving them.

'Where's Dad?' Molly asks next morning. It's always Molly who asks that question, especially since David's Wisdom of Solomon judgement the other day; Tom no longer seems interested.

'He's away on business,' I say, as if David were another person altogether. It's an answer born out of a lack of sleep, because it could never apply to David's life and work. For the last few years the children have listened to him grumbling about having to go down to the newsagent's to use the photocopier; how, then, has he suddenly become the kind of man who stays in hotels in the major capitals of Europe eating power breakfasts?

'He hasn't got any business,' says Tom matter-of-factly.

'Yes he has,' says Molly, sweetly and loyally.

'What is it then?' Tom may prefer his mother to his father at the moment, but his inability to resist cruelty when the opportunity presents itself does not, I would argue, come from me.

'Why are you always horrible to Daddy?'

'Why is it horrible asking what business he does?'

'Because you know he doesn't do any and you're rubbing it in.'

Tom looks at me and shakes his head.

'You're rubbish at arguing, Molly.'

'Why?'

'Because you just said he doesn't do any. That's what I said, and you told me I was being horrible.'

Molly stops, thinks for a moment, tells Tom that she hates him and wanders off to get ready for school. Poor David! Even his staunchest defender cannot actually convince herself that he does anything resembling a proper Daddy job. If I were any kind of right-thinking parent I'd get involved, explain that fathers do all sorts of different things, but I hate David so much at the moment that I can't be bothered.

'So where is he really?' Tom asks me.

'He's gone to stay with a friend.'

'Because you're getting divorced?'

'We're not getting divorced.'

'So why has he gone to stay with a friend?'

'You've been to stay with friends. Doesn't mean you're getting divorced.'

'I'm not married. And when I go to stay with a friend I tell you I'm going and I say goodbye.'

'Is that what's bothering you? He didn't tell you he was going?'

'I don't care whether he says goodbye or not. But I know something's wrong.'

'Daddy and I had an argument.'

'See. You're getting a divorce.'

It would be so easy to say something now. Not easy as in comfortable, but easy as in logical, natural, appropriate, right, no jerky changing of gear: Tom knows that something is up, I may well have to say something at sometime anyway, David may well tell them himself as soon as he comes home . . .

'Tom! How many more times! And when are you going to get ready for school?'

He gives me a long stare and then turns violently on his heels to convey anger without disobedience. I want to go to the surgery and work and work. I want the day to be as unpleasant and as demanding as any working day has ever been, just so that at the end of it I will have regained something of myself. I want to look at blocked rectums and oozing warts and all sorts of things that would make the rest of the world sick to its collective stomach, and hope that by so doing I will feel like a good person again. A bad mother, maybe, and a terrible wife, undoubtedly, but a good person.

On the way to work I have a sudden panic that Stephen will call the mobile, so I call him as soon as I get in and he wants to know what's happening and I don't want to talk about it and he asks to see me and I end up arranging to meet him and booking a babysitter.

'Where are you going?' Tom asks when I'm getting ready to go out.

'To meet a friend for a drink.'

'What friend?'

'No one you know.'

'Your boyfriend?'

Molly thinks this is one of the funniest lines she has ever heard, but Tom isn't joking. He wants me to answer the question.

'What are you talking about, Tom?'

Tom is beginning to give me the creeps. I feel that any moment now he will be able to tell me Stephen's name and describe what he looks like.

'What's this friend's name, then?'

'Stephen.'

'What's his wife's name?'

'He hasn't got a . . .' Tricked by a ten-year-old. 'He hasn't got a wife. His girlfriend's name is Victoria.' His girlfriend's name is Victoria because there is a photograph of Victoria Adams and David Beckham on the front of a magazine lying on the kitchen table; if Tom had asked me this morning, when I wasn't feeling very sharp, I would have told him that Stephen's girlfriend's name was Posh.

'Is she going?'

'I hope so. She's nice.'

'Do you think he'll marry her?'

'I've no idea, Tom. I'll ask him tonight, if you want.'

'Yes please.'

'Fine.'

There is almost no point in talking about the rest of the evening, such is its dismal predictability. Stephen flatters me, I feel desired and stimulated, I see, as if for the first time, how unhappy my relationship with David makes me, and I go home wanting out. Oh and when I get home David is there waiting, and everything changes again.

I'm frightened when I see him sitting there, and initially the fear consoles me, because it surely means that my marriage is brutal, and that therefore the Archbishop of Canterbury will approve my divorce. But on further reflection I can see that brutality is a less likely explanation for my fear than other factors: the existence of Stephen, say, or my failure to talk to the kids about what has been going on, and I can feel the Archbishop's approval vanish as quickly as it appeared.

'Did you have a nice evening?' David asks me. He says it quietly, and I take the quiet as menace.

'Yes. Thank you. I went . . . I was out . . .' For some reason

I'm trying to remember the name of Stephen's girlfriend until I remember she was a whole other lie told to someone else for different reasons.

'It doesn't matter,' he says. 'Listen. I haven't loved you enough.'

I gape at him.

'I haven't loved you enough, and I'm really sorry. I do love you, and I haven't communicated that properly or positively.'

'No. Well. Thank you.'

'And I'm sorry that I said I wanted a divorce. I don't know what I was thinking of.'

'Right.'

'And will you come to the theatre with me tomorrow night? I've booked tickets for the Tom Stoppard. I know you wanted to go.'

The theatre has provided David with more rant material than probably anything else in his ranting career, with the possible exception of the Germans. He hates the theatre. He hates the playwrights, he hates the plays, he hates the actors, he hates the critics, he hates the audience, he hates the programmes, he hates the little tubs of ice-cream they sell in the intervals. He once tried to write a column explaining why he hated safety curtains, but he couldn't quite find the requisite 800 words.

'Oh. Thank you.'

'I'd like us to go to bed and sleep in separate rooms, and wake up in the morning and try to start again from scratch. Rebuild our lives.'

'Right-o.' He probably thinks I'm being sarcastic, but I'm not. A daft, cheerful phrase like 'Right-o' seems, at that precise moment, the only appropriate response to David's blithe, bland suggestion, ignoring as it does all the complication and bitterness of the last few years of our lives together.

'Good. I'm going to bed, then. Good night.' He comes over and kisses me on the cheek, hugs me, and starts to walk upstairs.

'Which bedroom are you sleeping in?' I ask him.

'Oh. Sorry. I don't mind. Which would you prefer?'

'Shall I sleep in the spare room?' I don't mind either, and anyway, it seems churlish to ask this polite, accommodating man, whoever he is, to move out of his own bed.

'Is that what you want?' But he says this solicitously – he's double-checking, rather than drawing attention to his hurt at my desertion of him.

I shrug. 'Yeah.'

'OK. If you're sure. Sleep well.'

When I wake up I'm almost sure that I will be greeted with a snarl and an insult, possibly followed by a request to vacate the house by the evening, but he makes me tea and toast, pours the kids their cereal, tells me to have a nice day. After work I go straight home, we eat an early supper, and go out to the theatre. He asks about the surgery, even laughs at a story I tell him about a guy with a chest infection who had no idea that smoking really was bad for one's health. (I can't make David laugh. Nobody can make David laugh, apart from the people he is prepared to concede are funnier than him, namely, Woody Allen, Jerry Seinfeld, Tony Hancock and Peter Cook, 1960s model. Making people laugh is his job.) We go by Tube to the theatre, and he continues in this vein: he's friendly, curious, he listens, he asks questions, he buys me one of the much-despised tubs of ice-cream. (True, he buys it for me out of my money – it transpires that he has forgotten his wallet – but the point is not that he is being generous, but that he is choosing to overlook one of London theatre's myriad crimes.) I'm starting to feel giddy; I'm also starting to get confused about who I'm with. This is what Stephen's like, this is why I was seduced into the idea of Stephen in the first place, and I'm worried that the contrast between my lover and my husband is becoming blurred. Maybe that's the point. Maybe this is the most vicious and manipulative thing David has done yet: pretending to be a nice person so that . . . what? So that I'll be nice back? So that I'll want to stay married to him? Is that really so vicious and manipulative, trying to make one's marriage function properly? In most cases one would argue not, but my mistrust of David runs very deep.

*

55

I love every second of the play. I drink it, like someone with dehydration might drink a glass of iced water. I love being made to think about something else other than my work and my marriage, and I love its wit and its seriousness, and I vow for the millionth time to nourish myself in this way on a more regular basis, while knowing that I will wake up in the morning with my unread novel on top of me. I spend almost as much time trying to snatch glimpses of David's profile as I do watching the stage, though. Something weird has happened, definitely, because the struggle to enjoy the evening is written on David's face: a war is taking place there, around the eyes and the lips and the forehead. The old David wants to frown and scowl and make faces to indicate his contempt for everything; the new one is clearly trying to learn how to enjoy himself in a place of entertainment, watching a new and brilliant piece of work from one of the world's leading playwrights. Sometimes this attempt at self-education takes the form of simple imitation – when he remembers, he allows himself to laugh when the audience laughs, although he never quite times it right, and as a consequence he reminds me of Tom and Molly attempting to join in on songs when they were little – and sometimes he makes an attempt to self-start, as if a nod of the head here and a gentle smile there will stimulate his withered capacity for benign, as opposed to malicious, pleasure. And sometimes he forgets himself, and the odd line provokes a fleeting expression of rage and bile. (Such is my intimate acquaintance with David's bile that I can tell what kind of line will do this to him: it's the kind that flatters the intellectual pretensions of the audience, makes them feel that unless they laugh they'll be demonstrating their own ignorance. I don't like it much either, but it doesn't make me want to get a gun and kill people.) Even then, however, it's as if an invisible pair of hands grabs his face and twists it back into shape, smooths it out, makes David resemble somebody who's paid a reasonable amount of money to have a good time and is therefore determined to do so. It's so unlike him that it gives me the creeps.

*

We walk out into the cold as if we were simply another pair of contented theatregoers, and I can't resist asking.

'Did you enjoy that?'

'I did. Very much.'

'Really? Very much?'

'Yes.'

'But you hate the theatre.'

'I think . . . I think I thought I hated the theatre. It was, it was a prejudice I hadn't examined properly.'

'You want to be careful.'

'Why?'

'If you start examining your prejudices carefully there'll soon be nothing left of you.'

He smiles pleasantly and we walk on. We're looking for a cab, which is what we always do after a night in the West End – Tube in, treat ourselves coming home – and I suddenly feel the need to see a yellow taxi light right this second, because I'm tired, and disoriented, and the thought of having to battle on escalators with a lot of drunks fills me with dread.

And then something odd happens, and it becomes clear that something odd has happened to David, that the change in him is a result of something other than introspection and self-will. What happens is this. We pass a homeless kid in a doorway huddled up in a sleeping bag and David feels in his pockets, presumably for some change. (Let me be fair to David: he always does this. He does not, miraculously, Have Views on the homeless.) He doesn't find anything, and he asks me for my purse, with many apologies, and another explanation as to why he thought he had his wallet with him when he didn't. I don't think about what I'm doing – why should I? – and give it to him, and he proceeds to give the kid everything that's in there – about eighty pounds in notes, because I went to the cashpoint today, and three or four pounds in change. As far as I know, we're left with nothing.

'What are you doing?'

I snatch the notes from the kid's hands. A passing couple holding a programme from the Stoppard play stop when they see me taking money from a homeless person, and I want to tell them I'm a doctor. David takes the money off me, gives it to the boy again and tries to hustle me along the street. I resist.

'David, what are you doing? We haven't even got the Tube fare home.'

'I kept a fiver back.'

'I wanted to get a taxi.' The couple is still watching me, and I don't like the whine in my voice.

'I'll bet this chap would love to get a taxi,' says David with a maddening sweetness in his voice. 'But he can't.'

'Well, where's he going to go in a bloody taxi?' I shout. 'He hasn't got anywhere to go. That's why he's sleeping here.' I don't understand why I'm like this, but then, I don't understand why David's like that.

'Oh, that's nice,' says the male half of the theatre couple.

'My husband's just given away everything we own,' I tell him.

'That is just not true,' says David. 'Our house? The money in our joint account? The money in our savings account? We won't even notice this tomorrow.'

Two or three other people have gathered to watch, and I realize that this is an argument I can't win – not here, not now – so we walk towards the Underground station.

'You can't go round giving eighty quid to homeless people!' I hiss.

'I am aware that I cannot go around giving eighty quid to every homeless person. I just wanted to do it that one time. See how it felt.'

'And how did it feel?'

'Good.'

I don't get any of this. 'When were you ever interested in being good?'

'I wasn't talking about being good. I was talking about feeling good.'

'Well . . . Get drunk. Get stoned. Have sex. Don't give all our bloody money away.'

'I'm tired of all those things. I was stuck. I need to do something different.'

'What's happened to you? What happened when you went away? Where did you go?'

'Nothing bloody happened to me.' The old David, back with a bang. 'Just because I wanted to see a play and gave a few quid to a street kid? Jesus.' He takes a deep breath. 'I'm sorry. I know my behaviour must seem confusing.'

'Will you tell me what's been going on?'

'I don't know if I can.'

We reach Leicester Square Tube station and try to put the five pound note into the ticket machine, but it's too crumpled, and the machine spits it out again. We take our place in the queue behind two hundred Scandinavian tourists and three hundred British drunks. And I still want to be in a taxi.

On the way back – no seats on the Tube, not until we get to King's Cross, anyway – David becomes absorbed in the theatre programme, almost certainly in an attempt to deflect further questions. We pay the babysitter by raiding the emergency fund in the kitchen jar, and then David says he's tired and wants to go straight to bed.

'Will you talk to me tomorrow?'

'If I can think of anything to say. Anything to say that will make sense to you, anyway.'

'What are our sleeping arrangements, anyway?'

'I'd like you to sleep with me. But no pressure.'

I'm not sure I do want to sleep with David, because of Stephen, and because of being in a mess, and all that stuff, but it's not just David I don't want to sleep with. There's this other man, too, the one who likes the theatre and gives money away and tries to be nice to people, and I'm not sure I want to sleep with him either, because I don't really know him, and he is beginning to give me the creeps. To dislike one husband may be regarded as unfortunate, but to dislike both looks like carelessness.

But be careful what you wish for . . . I didn't want David to be David any more. I wanted things to be structurally the same – I just didn't want that voice, that tone, that permanent scowl. I wanted him to like me, and now he does. I go upstairs to our bedroom.

You may not want to know about how lovemaking got underway in the old days – the pre-Stephen, post-kids old days, rather than the old-old days, when lovemaking meant something different – but I'm going to tell you anyway. We would both be reading in bed, and if I fancied sex, my hand would wander idly down towards his crotch, and if he fancied sex his hand would wander idly over towards one of my nipples (invariably the right nipple, because he sleeps on my left and it was clearly easier for him to reach across me than to go for the near side, which would involve an uncomfortable bend of the arm). And if the other party was in the mood, it would carry on from there, and books, magazines or newspapers would eventually be placed on the appropriate bedside tables. And OK, you wouldn't want to see characters re-enacting this routine in a porn video, unless you actively dislike porn videos, but it worked for us.

Tonight, however, is different. I reach for my book and David begins kissing the back of my neck tenderly; then he pulls me over and attempts to give me a big swoony kiss on the mouth, like a horizontal (and, let's face it, slightly overweight) Clark Gable. It's as if he has been reading an article in a woman's magazine of the 1950s about reintroducing romance into marriage, and I'm not at all sure that I want romance reintroduced into my marriage. I was happy enough with David's button-pushing routine, which at least had the virtue of efficiency; now he is looking at me as though this were our first time in bed together, and we were about to embark on the most memorable interior journey of our lives.

I push him away a little so that I can look at him.

'What are you doing?'

'I want to make love to you.'

'Yes, well, fine. Get on with it. There doesn't have to be all this fuss.' I can hear how I sound – like Joyce Grenfell in 9½ Weeks – and I hate it, because I'm not some sexless bluestocking lie-back-and-think-of-England type. But the truth is that we'd have been finished by now if this was the old David. I'd have come, he'd have come and the lights would be off.

'But I want to make love to you. Not just have sex.'

'And what does that involve?'

'Communication. Intensity. I don't know.'

My heart sinks. The advantages of turning forty for me include: not having to change nappies, not having to go to places where people dance, and not having to be intense with the person I live with.

'Please try it my way,' says David pitifully. So I do. I look into his eyes, I kiss him the way he wants to be kissed, we take a long time over everything and, at the end (no orgasm for me, incidentally), I lie on his chest while he strokes my hair. I get through it, just about, but I don't see the point of it.

The following morning, David spends most of breakfast humming, smiling, and trying to relate to his children, who seem as perplexed as I am, Tom especially.

'What have you got today, Tom?'

'School.'

'Yes, but what at school?'

Tom looks at me anxiously, as if I can somehow intercede, prevent his father from asking perfectly harmless conversational questions. I stare back at him and try to convey unfeasibly complicated messages with my eyes: 'It's not my fault, I don't know what's going on, just tell him your timetable and eat your cereal, he's undergone a complete character transformation . . .' That sort of look, the sort that would require several eyes, and eyebrows with the agility of a teenage Eastern European acrobat.

'I dunno,' says Tom. 'Maths, I expect. English. Ummmmm . . .' He glances at David to see whether he has provided sufficient detail, but David is still smiling at him expectantly. 'Games, maybe.'

'Anything you need any help with? I mean, your old man's not Brain of Britain, but he's not bad at English. Writing and all that.' And he chuckles, we know not why.

Tom no longer looks anxious; the anxiety has been replaced by something akin to terror. I almost find myself feeling sorry for David – it's sad, after all, that what certainly appears to be a genuine attempt to convey warmth and concern should be met with such naked mistrust – but ten years of ill-temper are not easily forgotten, and David has been grumpy for as long as Tom has been alive.

'Yeah,' says Tom, clearly unconvinced. 'I'm all right at writing, thanks. You can help me with games, if you want.'

It's Tom's little joke, and it's not a bad one – I laugh, anyway – but these are different times.

'Sure,' says David. 'Do you want to, I don't know, kick a ball around after school?'

'Yeah, right,' says Tom.

'Good,' says David.

David knows what 'yeah, right' means; he has heard the expression several times a day for the last couple of years, and it has never before prompted the word 'good'. The words 'sarcastic little bastard', 'ungrateful little sod' or simply 'shut up' yes; 'good', no. So why would he choose to ignore the tone and meaning that he knows Tom wishes to convey and plough on regardless? I am beginning to suspect that there is a sinister medical explanation for David's behaviour.

'I'll go out and buy a new pair of trainers today,' he adds, for good measure. Tom and I look at each other, and then attempt to prepare for the day ahead as if it were like any other.

Stephen leaves a message for me at work. I ignore it.

When I get back from work there are two children and an adult playing Cluedo on the kitchen table and a dozen messages on the answerphone. The phone rings again as I'm taking my coat off, but David makes no attempt to pick it up, and everyone listens to Nigel, David's editor at the paper, attempting to attract the attention of the Angriest Man in Holloway.

'I know you're there, David. Pick the fucking phone up.'

The children giggle. David shakes the dice.

'Why aren't you answering?'

'Daddy's given up work,' says Molly proudly.

'I haven't given up work. I've just given up that work.'

Nigel is still chuntering away in the background. 'Pick *up* . . . Pick *up*, you bastard.'

'You've given up the column? Why?'

'Because I'm not angry any more.'

'You're not angry any more?'

'No.'

'About anything?'

'No. It's all gone.'

'Where?'

'I don't know. But it's gone. You can tell, can't you?'

'Yes. I can tell.'

'So I can't write a column about being angry any more.'

I sigh, heavily.

'I thought you'd be pleased.'

I thought I would be pleased, too. If, a few weeks ago, someone had offered to grant me one wish, I think I would probably have chosen to wish for exactly this, because I would not have been able to think of anything else, not even money, that could have improved the quality of my life – our lives – so dramatically. Oh, I'd have mumbled something about cures for cancer or world peace, of course, but secretly I'd have been hoping that the genie wouldn't let me do the good person thing. Secretly I'd have wanted the genie to say, 'No, you're a doctor, you do enough for the world already, what with the boils and everything. Choose something for yourself.' And I would have said, after a great deal of thought, 'I would like David not to be angry any more. I would like him to recognize that his life is OK, that his children are wonderful, that he has a loyal and loving and – sod it – a not unattractive or unintelligent wife, and enough money for babysitters and meals out and the mortgage . . . I would like all his bile gone, every inch, or ounce, or millilitre of it.' (I imagine David's bile to be in that difficult state between liquid and solid, like almost-set concrete.) And the genie would have rubbed his stomach, and hey presto! David is a happy person.

And hey presto! David is a happy person, or at least, a calm person, here, now, in the real world, and all I do is sigh. The thing is, of course, I don't really want the hey presto! part. I am a rationalist, and I don't believe in genies, or sudden personality changes. I wanted David's anger to vanish only after years and years in therapy.

'I am pleased,' I say, unconvincingly. 'I just wish you'd had the courage to tell Nigel.'

'Nigel's an angry man,' David says sadly. 'He wouldn't understand.' This last observation at least is incontrovertible, given that Nigel has just ended his attempt to attract David's attention with a volley of abuse. He even used the C-word, although we all pretended we hadn't heard it.

'Why don't you play Cluedo with us, Mummy?'

And I do, until tea time. And after tea, we play Junior Scrabble. We are the ideal nuclear family. We eat together, we play improving board games instead of watching television, we smile a lot. I fear that at any moment I may kill somebody.

5

At lunchtime the next day, Becca and I walk up the road to get a sandwich, and I tell her about GoodNews, and the theatre, and the street kid, and even about the lovemaking. ('Ugh!' she says. 'Your own husband? How disgusting!') And then, suddenly, she grabs my arm.

'Katie! My God!'

'What?'

'Shit!'

'What? You're frightening me.'

'David's sick.'

'How do you know?'

'Change of personality. And did you say something about a headache?'

My stomach lurches. This is text-book stuff. This is the sinister medical explanation for his behaviour. David almost certainly has a brain tumour. How could I have been so oblivious? I run back to work and phone him.

'David. I don't want you to panic, but please listen carefully and do exactly what I say. You probably have a brain tumour. You have to go to hospital and have a CAT scan, urgently. We can get you the referral here, but . . .'

'Katie . . .'

'Please listen. We can get you the referral here, but . . .'

'Katie, there's nothing wrong with me.'

'Well, let's hope not. But these are classic symptoms.'

'Are you saying this because I've started to be nice to you?'

'Well, yes. And then there was the theatre.'

'You think that if I enjoyed a play I must have a brain tumour?'

'And the money. And the sex the other night.'

There's a long pause.

'Katie, I'm so sorry.'

'And that's the other thing. You keep apologizing all the time. David, I think you may be very ill.'

'It's so sad.'

'It might not be. But I do think . . .'

'No, no. Not that. It's so sad that the only explanation you can come up with for all this is that I'm about to die. I'm really not, I promise. We should talk.'

And he puts the phone down.

David won't discuss his tumour until we are alone, and even then I don't really grasp what he's saying.

'He didn't use cream,' is how he chooses to begin.

'I'm sorry?'

'DJ GoodNews. He didn't use cream.'

'Right. So . . .' I attempt to locate the import of this clearly important announcement, and fail.

'So . . . Molly was right? Is that it?'

'Oh. Yes. Sure. Absolutely. She was right all along. But don't you see? He just used his hands.'

'Right. No cream, then.'

'No.'

'OK. Thank you for telling me. I've . . . I've got a clearer picture of the whole thing now.'

'That's what all this is about. How it all started, anyway.'

'All what?'

David gestures outwards impatiently, at everything in the world.

'All . . . well, me. This. The money the other night. The . . . the problem with my column. All of it. The change of . . . I don't know, the change of atmosphere. You've presumably noticed the change in atmosphere? I mean, that's why you thought I was ill, right? Well. That's . . . That's where it all comes from.'

'It all comes from your friend GoodNews not using cream?'

'Yeah. Sort of. I mean, no cream was . . . That was the . . . Oh, I can't explain this. I thought I could and I can't.' I cannot recall David ever being like this – inarticulate, agitated, acutely embarrassed. 'I'm sorry.'

'That's OK. Take your time.'

'That's where I went. For my two days. I went to stay with GoodNews.'

'Oh. Right.' This is how we were taught to respond: listen carefully to what the patient says, don't interject, let him finish, even if that patient is your husband and he has gone completely mad.

'You don't think I've gone completely mad?'

'No. Of course not. I mean, if that's what you thought you wanted to do, and it helped . . .'

'He's changed my life.'

'Yes. Well. Good for you! And good for him!'

'You're patronizing me.'

'I'm sorry. I'm finding it difficult to . . . to grasp, all this.'

'I can understand that. It's . . . It's all a bit weird.'

'Can I ask a question?'

'Yes. Of course.'

'Will you explain about the cream?'

'He wasn't using any.'

'Sure, sure, I have understood that much. He wasn't using any cream. I'm just trying to make the link between . . . between him not using any cream and you giving eighty quid to that homeless kid. It's not immediately obvious.'

'Yes. Right. OK.' He takes a deep breath. 'I only went to see him in the first place because I thought it would annoy you.'

'I guessed.'

'Yes, well. I'm sorry. Anyway. He lives in this little flat above a minicab office behind Finsbury Park station, a real dump, and I was just going to go home. But I sort of felt sorry for him, so . . . I told him about my back, and where it hurt, and I asked him what he thought he could do for me. Because if he'd said he was going to manipulate me or, you know, do anything that would make it worse, I wouldn't have let him anywhere near me. But he just said that he'd touch it, nothing more, just put his hands there and the pain would go away. He said it would take him two seconds, and if nothing happened I wouldn't have to pay him. So I thought, what

the hell, and anyway he's only a skinny little guy and . . . Anyway.
I took my shirt off and lay down on his couch, face down – he
hasn't even got a treatment table or anything – and he touched me
and his hands got incredibly hot.'

'How do you know they weren't hot already?'

'They were cold when he . . . when he first put them on my
back, and they just started to warm up. And that's why I thought
he was using Deep Heat or something. But he didn't massage me,
or rub anything in. He just touched me, very gently, and . . . and
all the pain went. Straight away. Like magic.'

'So this guy's a healer. Like a faith healer.'

'Yeah.' He thinks for a moment, as if trying to think of something
that might make this easier for a couple of middle-class, university-
educated literalists to understand – by which I mean, I suppose,
that he would like to find something that makes it seem more
difficult – less straightforward, more complicated, cleverer. It's
not very hard to grasp that someone is a healer, after all: he
touches you, you feel better, you go home. What is there not to
understand? It's just that everything else you have ever believed
about life becomes compromised as a result. David gives up the
struggle to complexify with a shrug. 'Yeah. It's . . . amazing. He has
a gift.'

'So. Great. Hurrah for GoodNews. He's made your back better,
and he made Molly's eczema go away. We're lucky you found
him.' I try to say all this in a way that draws a line under this whole
conversation, but I'm guessing that this is not the end of the story.

'I didn't want him to be a healer.'

'What did you want him to be?'

'Just . . . I don't know. Alternative. That's why me and Molly
had that row about the cream. It freaked me out a bit, and I wanted
there to be this, I don't know, this magic cream from Tibet or
somewhere that conventional medics knew nothing about. I didn't
want it just to be his hands. Do you understand?'

'Yes. Sort of. You're happier with magic cream than with magic
hands. Is that it?'

'Cream's not magic, is it? It's just . . . medicine.'

This is typical of ignorant rationalists. For all they know, aspirin could be the most dramatic example of white witchcraft known to mankind, but because you can buy it in Boots it doesn't count.

'It'd be magic if it cured back pain and eczema.'

'Anyway. It freaked me out a bit. And then the thing with the headache . . .'

'I had forgotten about the headache.'

'Well that was when things started to go weird. Because . . . I don't even know why I told him I had a headache, but I did, and he looked at me, and he said, I can help you with a lot of things that are troubling you, and he touched me on the . . . here . . .'

'The temples.'

'Right, he touched me on the temples, and the headache went, but I started to feel . . . different.'

'What kind of different?'

'Just . . . Calmer.'

'That was when you told me you were going away and I had to tell the kids we were getting divorced.'

'I was calm. I didn't rant and rave. I didn't get sarcastic.'

I remember my feeling that there was something different about him then, and in remembering find a new way to become sad and regretful and self-pitying: my husband visits a healer, is thus magically rendered calmer, and the only benefit for me is that he expresses without viciousness his desire for a separation. Except, of course, things have moved on since then, and there are countless benefits for me, none of which I enjoy. I hear my brother's 'Diddums' ringing in my ear.

'And then you went to stay with him?'

'I didn't know I was going to stay with him. I just . . . I wanted to see if he could do the thing with the head again, and maybe try to find out what was going on when he did it. I was thinking of writing about him, about the eczema and everything, and . . . I just ended up staying and talking for a couple of days.'

'As one does.'

'Please, Katie. I don't know how to talk about this. Don't make it hard.'

Why not? I want to ask. Why shouldn't I make it hard? How often have you made things easy for me?

'Sorry,' I say. 'Go on.'

'He doesn't say very much. He just looks at you with these piercing eyes and listens. I'm not even sure whether he's very bright. So it was me who did all the talking. He just sort of sucked it all out of me.'

'He seems to have sucked everything out of you.'

'Yes, he did. Every bad thing. I could almost see it coming out of me, like a black mist. I didn't realize I was so full of all this stuff.'

'And what makes him so special? How come he can do it and no one else could?'

'I don't know. He just . . . He just has this aura about him. This'll sound stupid, but . . . He touched my temples again, when I was talking to him, and I just felt this, this amazing warmth flood right through me, and he said it was pure love. And that's what it felt like. Do you understand how panicky it made me feel?'

I do understand, and not just because David is an unlikely candidate for a love bath. Love baths are . . . not us. Love baths are for the gullible, the credulous, the simple-minded, people whose brains have been decayed like teeth by soft drugs, people who read Tolkien and Erich Von Daniken when they are old enough to drive cars . . . let's face it, people who don't have degrees in the arts or sciences. It is frightening enough just listening to David's story, but to undergo the experience must have been terrifying.

'So now what?'

'The first thing I thought afterwards was that I had to do everything differently. Everything. What I have been doing isn't enough. Not enough for you. Not enough for me. Not enough for the kids, or the world, or . . . or . . .'

He grinds to a halt again, presumably because even though the laws of rhetoric and rhythm require a third noun, the reference to the world has left him with nowhere to go, unless he starts babbling about the universe.

'I still don't understand what you talked about for two days.'

'Neither do I. I don't know where the time went. I was amazed when he told me it was Tuesday afternoon. I talked about . . . about you a lot, and how I wasn't good to you. And I talked about my work, my writing, and I found myself saying that I was ashamed of it, and I hated it for its, I don't know, its unkindness, its lack of charity. Now and again he made me . . . God, I'm embarrassed.' A sudden thought – it may or may not be a fear, I'll have to think about that another time – comes to me.

'There's nothing funny going on, is there?'

'What do you mean?'

'You're not sleeping with him, are you?'

'No,' he says, but blankly, with no sense of amusement or outrage or defensiveness. 'No, I'm not. It's not like that.'

'Sorry. So what did he make you do?'

'He made me kneel on the floor and hold his hand.'

'And then what?'

'He just asked me to meditate with him.'

'Right.'

David is not homophobic, although he has expressed occasional mystification at gay culture and practices (it's the Cher thing that particularly bewilders him), but he is certainly heterosexual, right down to his baggy Y-fronts and his preference for Wright's Coal Tar soap. There is no ambiguity there, if you know what I mean. And yet it is easier for me to imagine him going down on GoodNews than it is for me to picture him kneeling on the floor and meditating.

'And that was OK, was it? When he asked you to meditate? You didn't, you know, hit him or anything?'

'No. The old David would have, I know. And that would have been wrong.' He says this with such earnestness that I am temporarily tempted to abandon my own position on domestic violence. 'I must admit, it did make me feel a little uncomfortable at first, but there's so much to think about. Isn't there?'

I agree that yes, there is an enormous amount to think about.

'I mean, just thinking about one's own personal circumstances . . .' ('One's own personal circumstances'? Who is this man, who talks to his own wife in his own bed in phrases from 'Thought

71

for the Day'?) '. . . That could occupy you for hours. Days. And then there's everything else . . .'

'What, the world and all that? Suffering and so on?' It is impossible not to be facetious, I am beginning to find, with someone from whom all trace of facetiousness, every atom of self-irony, seems to have vanished.

'Yes, of course. I had no idea how much people suffered until I was given the time and space to think about it.'

'So now what?' I don't want to go through this process. I want to take a short cut and go right to the part where I find out what all this means for me me me.

'I don't know. All I know is I want to live a better life. I want us to live a better life.'

'And how do we do that?'

'I don't know.'

I cannot help but feel that all this sounds very ominous indeed.

Stephen leaves a message on my mobile. I don't return the call.

I come home the next night to the sound of trouble; even as I'm putting the key in the lock I can hear Tom shouting and Molly crying.

'What's going on?' David and the kids are sitting around the kitchen table, David at the head, Molly to his left, Tom to his right. The table has been cleared of its usual detritus – post, old newspapers, small plastic models found in cereal packets – apparently in an attempt to create the atmosphere of a conference.

'He's given my computer away,' says Tom. Tom doesn't often cry, but his eyes are glistening, either with fury or tears, it's hard to tell.

'And now I've got to share mine,' says Molly, whose ability to cry has never been in any doubt, and who now looks as though she has been mourning the deaths of her entire family in a car crash.

'We didn't need two,' says David. 'Two is . . . Not obscene, exactly. But certainly greedy. They're never on the things at the same time.'

'So you just gave one away. Without consulting them. Or me.'

'I felt that consultation would have been pointless.'

'You mean that they wouldn't have wanted you to do it?'

'They maybe wouldn't have understood why I wanted to.'

It was David, of course, who insisted on the kids having a computer each for Christmas last year. I had wanted them to share, not because I'm mean, but because I was beginning to worry about spoiling them, and the sight of these two enormous boxes beside the tree (they wouldn't fit under it) did nothing to ease my queasiness. This wasn't the kind of parent I wanted to be, I remember thinking, as Tom and Molly attacked the acres of wrapping paper with a violence that repelled me; David saw the look on my face and whispered to me that I was a typical joyless liberal, the sort of person who would deny their kids everything and themselves nothing. And here I am six months later, outraged that my son and daughter aren't allowed to keep what is theirs, and yet still, somehow, on the wrong side, an agent of the forces of darkness.

'Where did you take it?'

'The women's refuge in Kentish Town. I read about it in the local paper. They had nothing there for the kids at all.'

I don't know what to say. The frightened, unhappy children of frightened, unhappy women have nothing; we have two of everything. We give away some, a tiny fraction, of what we have too much of. What is there for me to be angry about?

'Why does it have to be us who gives them something? Why can't the Government?' asks Tom.

'The Government can't pay for everything,' says David. 'We've got to pay for some things ourselves.'

'We did,' says Tom. 'We paid for that computer ourselves.'

'I mean,' says David, 'that if we're worried about what's happening to poor people, we can't wait for the Government to do anything. We have to do what we think is right.'

'Well, I don't think this is right,' says Tom.

'Why not?'

'Because it's my computer.'

David merely flashes him a beatific smile.

'Why isn't it just their bad luck?' Molly asks him, and I laugh. 'Just your bad luck' was, until relatively recently, David's explanation for why our kids didn't own a Dreamcast, or a new Arsenal away shirt, or anything else that every other person at school owns.

'These children don't have much luck anyway,' David explains with the slow, over-confident patience of a recently created angel. 'Their dads have been hitting their mums, and they've had to run away from home and hide, and they haven't got their toys with them . . . You have lots of luck. Don't you want to help them?'

'A bit,' says Tom grudgingly. 'But not as much as a whole computer.'

'Let's go and see them,' says David. 'Then you can tell them that. You can say you want to help them a bit and then ask for your computer back.'

'David, this is outrageous.'

'Why?'

'You can't blackmail your own children like that.'

I'm beginning to feel better. I was struggling for a while back there, pinned back by the moral force of David's arguments, but now I can see that he's gone mad, that he wants to humiliate us all. How could I have forgotten that this is what always happens with zealots? They go too far, they lose all sense of appropriateness and logic, and ultimately they are interested in nobody but themselves, nothing but their own piousness.

David drums his fingers on the table and thinks furiously.

'No, I'm sorry, you're right. It is outrageous. I've overstepped the mark. Please forgive me.'

Shit.

It is a fractious family dinner. Somehow David has managed to recruit Molly to the cause – possibly because she has spotted an opportunity to taunt Tom, possibly because Molly has never been able to see her father as anything less than a perfect and perfectly reasonable man, possibly because the computer David gave away was in Tom's bedroom rather than hers, although the one we have left has now been placed in the neutral territory of the spare bedroom. Tom, however, is clinging stubbornly to his deeply held Western materialist beliefs.

'You're just being selfish, Tom. Isn't he, Dad?'

David refuses to be drawn.

'There are children there who don't have anything,' she continues. 'And you've got lots.'

'I haven't got anything now. He's given it all away.'

'What are all those things in the bedroom, then?' asks David gently.

'And you've got half a computer.'

'Can I get down?' Tom has hardly eaten anything, but he's clearly had his fill of the great steaming bowls of sanctimony being pushed at him from all directions, and I can't say I blame him.

'Finish your dinner,' says David. He opens his mouth to say something else – almost certainly something about how fortunate Tom is to have a plate of lukewarm spaghetti bolognese in front of him given the plight of blah blah blah – but he catches my eye and thinks better of it.

'Do you really not want anything else?' I ask Tom.

'I want to go on the computer before she gets it.'

'Go on, then.' Tom shoots off.

'You shouldn't have let him, Mummy. He'll think he never has to eat his dinner now.'

'Molly, shut up.'

'She's right.'

'Oh, you shut up, too.'

I need to think. I need guidance. I'm a good person, I'm a doctor, and here I am championing greed over selflessness, cheering on the haves against the have-nots. Except I'm not really championing anything, am I? I am not, after all, standing up to my unbearably smug husband and – now – my unbearably smug eight-year-old daughter and saying, 'Now look here, we worked jolly hard to pay for that computer, and if some women are daft enough to shack up with men who beat them, that's hardly our fault, is it?' That would be championing. All I'm doing is thinking unworthy thoughts that nobody can hear, and then sniping about unfinished spaghetti bolognese. If I had any real conviction, I'd be passing on some offensive piece of homespun wisdom about how the Good Samaritan could only afford to be the Good Samaritan because he held on to his old computers and . . . and . . . gave them to a charity shop when they were knackered. Something like that, anyway.

So what do I believe? Nothing much, apparently. I believe that there shouldn't be homelessness, and I'd definitely be prepared to argue with anyone who says otherwise. Ditto battered women. Ditto, I don't know, racism, poverty and sexism. I believe that the National Health Service is underfunded, and that Red-Nose Day is a sort of OK thing, although slightly annoying, I grant you, when young men dressed as Patsy and Edina from *Absolutely Fabulous* come up to you in Waitrose and wave buckets in your face. And, finally, I am of the reasonably firm conviction that Tom's Christmas presents are his, and shouldn't be given away. There you are. That is my manifesto. Vote for me.

Three days later the children seem to have forgotten that they ever needed two computers – Molly has lost the little interest she had in the first place, and Tom is spending most of his time on Pokémon – and we receive a letter from the women's refuge telling us that we have made an enormous difference to some very unhappy young lives. I still believe the other things, though, the things about poverty and Health Service underfunding. You won't shake me on those – unless, that is, you have any sort of persuasive evidence at all to the contrary.

David has abandoned his novel, now, as well as his column. 'No longer appropriate' – like just about everything else he ever thought or did or wanted to do. During the day, as far as I can tell, he sits in his office reading; late afternoons he cooks, he plays, he helps with homework, he wants to talk about the days that everyone has had . . . in short, he is a model husband and father. I described him as such to Becca the other day, and a picture of a model husband and father came unbidden into my head: this particular model, however, is made of plastic and has his features moulded into a permanent expression of concern and consideration. David has become a sort of happy-clappy right-on Christian version of Barbie's Ken, except without Ken's rugged good looks and contoured body.

And I don't think that David has become a Christian, although it is hard to fathom precisely what he has become. Asking him directly doesn't really clarify things. The evening after we get the letter from the women's refuge, Tom asks – mournfully but rather percipiently, I thought – whether we are all going to have to start going to church.

'Church?' says David – but gently, not with the explosion of anger and disdain that would have accompanied that word in any context just a few weeks ago. 'Of course not. Why? Do you want to go to church?'

'No.'

'So why did you ask?'

'Dunno,' Tom says. 'Just, I thought, that's what we'd have to do now.'

'Why now?'

'Because we give things away. That's what they do in church, isn't it?'

'Not as far as I know.'

And that's the end of it; Tom's fears are assuaged. Later, though, when David and I are on our own, I make my own enquiries.

'That was funny, wasn't it? Tom thinking we'd have to go to church now?'

'I didn't understand where all that came from. Just because we gave a computer to someone.'

'I don't think it's just that.'

'What else is there?'

'They both know about you giving the money away. And anyway, it's . . . You asked me if I'd noticed a change of atmosphere. Well, I think they have, too. And they sort of associate it with church, somehow.'

'Why?'

'I don't know. I suppose . . . You do give off the air of someone who has undergone a religious conversion.'

'Well, I haven't.'

'You haven't become a Christian?'

'No.'

'What are you, then?'

'What am I?'

'Yes, what are you? You know, Buddhist or, or . . .' I try to think of other world religions that might fit the bill, and fail. Moslem doesn't seem right, nor Hindu . . . Maybe a Hare Krishna offshoot, or something involving self-denial and some podgy guru driving around in an Alfa Romeo?

'I'm nothing. I've just seen sense.'

'But what does that mean?'

'We've all been living the wrong life, and I want to put that right.'

'I don't feel I've been living the wrong life.'

'I disagree.'

'Oh, is that right?'

'You live the right life during the working week, I suppose. But the rest of the time . . .'

'What?'

'There's your sexual conduct, for a start.'

My sexual conduct . . . For a moment I forget that for the last twenty years I have had a monogamous relationship with my husband, punctuated only recently by a brief and rather hapless affair (and what happened to him, by the way? A couple of unreturned phone calls seem to have dampened his ardour considerably). The phrase enables me to see myself as someone who may have to check herself into one of those sex addiction clinics that Hollywood stars have to go to, someone who, despite her best intentions, cannot keep her pants on. It's quite a thrilling picture, but its main purpose, I can see, is to convince me that David is being preposterous; the truth is that I am a married woman who was sleeping with someone else just a couple of weeks ago. David's language might be pompous, but there is, I suppose, a case to answer.

'You've never wanted to talk about that.'

'There isn't much to talk about, is there?'

I think about whether this is true and decide that it is. I could waffle on about context, but he knows about that already; the rest of it makes for a short and banal little story without much resonance.

'So what else do I do wrong?'

'It's not what you do wrong. It's what we all do wrong.'

'Which is?'

'We don't care enough. We look after ourselves and ignore the weak and the poor. We despise our politicians for doing nothing, and think that this is somehow enough to show we care, and meanwhile we live in centrally heated houses that are too big for us . . .'

'Hey, hold on . . .' Our dream – before DJ GoodNews came into our lives, was to move out of our poky terraced house and into something that gave us room to turn around in without knocking a child over in the process. Now, suddenly, we are rattling around in Holloway's equivalent of Graceland. But I am allowed to say none of this, because David has the bit between his teeth.

'We have a spare bedroom, and a study, and meanwhile people are sleeping outside on pavements. We scrape perfectly edible food into our compost maker, and meanwhile people at the end of our road are begging for the price of a cup of tea and a bag of chips. We have two televisions, we did have three computers until I gave one away – and even that was a crime, apparently, reducing the number of computers available to a family of four by one third. We think nothing of spending ten pounds each on a takeaway curry . . .'

I plead guilty to this. I thought David was going to say '. . . forty pounds a head on a meal in a smart restaurant', which we have done, on occasions – occasions which have, of course, prompted all sorts of doubts and qualms. But ten pounds on a takeaway? Yes, guilty, I admit it: I have frequently thought nothing of spending ten pounds on a takeaway, and it has never occurred to me that my thoughtlessness was negligent or culpable in any way. One has to respect David for this thoroughness, at least.

'We spend thirteen pounds on compact discs which we already own in a different format . . .'

'That's you, not me.'

'. . . We buy films for our children that they've already seen at the cinema and never watch again . . .' There ensues a long list of similar crimes, all of which sound petty and, in any other household, completely legal, but which suddenly seem, with David's spin on them, selfish and despicable. I drift off for a while.

'I'm a liberal's worst nightmare,' David says at the end of his litany, with a smile that could be described, were one feeling uncharitable or paranoid, as malicious.

'What does that mean?'

'I think everything you think. But I'm going to walk it like I talk it.'

On Sunday my mother and father visit for lunch. They don't come very often – usually we all have to go there – and when they do come I have somehow allowed myself to turn the day into An Occasion, thus inflicting on my children the misery that was inflicted on me during equivalent Occasions in my childhood: combed hair, the best clothes they possess, assistance in tidying up, attendance at table compulsory for the whole of the meal, even though my mother talks so much that the last mouthful of Viennese Whirl does not disappear down her throat for what seems like hours after the rest of us have finished. And, of course, a roast dinner, which my brother and I detested (very possibly because it was invariably detestable: gristly, dry lamb, overcooked cabbage, lumpy Bisto, greasy and disintegrating roast potatoes, the usual 1960s wartime fare), but which Tom and Molly love. Unlike either of my parents, David and I can cook; unlike either of my parents, we very rarely bother to waste this skill on our children.

Finally the clothes argument is over, the tidying has been done, my parents have arrived, and we are drinking our dry sherry and eating our mixed nuts in the living room. David has just gone into the kitchen to carve the beef and make the gravy. Moments later – much too soon to have achieved the tasks he disappeared to do – he comes back.

'Roast beef and roast potatoes? Or frozen lasagne?'

'Roast beef and roast potatoes,' the kids yell happily, and my mum and dad chuckle.

'I think so, too,' says David, and disappears again.

'He's a tease, your dad, isn't he?' says my mum to Tom and Molly – an appropriate response to what she has just seen and heard in just about any domestic situation but ours. David isn't a tease. He wasn't a tease before (he hated my parents' visits, and would never have been able to muster the kind of cheery goodwill necessary for joshing everyone along), and he certainly isn't a tease since his sense of humour disappeared into DJ GoodNews's fingertips along with his back pain. I excuse myself and go into the kitchen, where David is transferring everything we have spent the last couple of hours cooking into the largest Le Creuset casserole dish we own.

'What are you doing?' I ask calmly.

'I can't do this,' he says.

'What?'

'I can't sit here and eat this while there are people out there with nothing. Have we got any paper plates?'

'No, David.'

'We have. We had loads left over from the Christmas party.'

'I'm not talking about the plates. You can't do this.'

'I have to.'

'I . . . I understand if you can't eat it.' (I don't understand at all, of course, but I'm trying to talk him off the ledge.) 'You could refuse, and . . . and . . . tell us all why.' There is no point in worrying just yet about the excruciating lunch ahead of us, the embarrassment and bewilderment as my poor mother and father (Tories both, but neither of them actively evil, in the accepted non-David use of the word) receive a lecture about their wicked, wicked ways. In fact I vow to myself that if we get as far as the lunch, if this food is actually served on to actual plates and people (by which I mean people I know, God forgive me) actually sit down to eat it, I will not worry at all; I will listen to David's views with sympathy and interest. I watch while David crams the Delia-style roast potatoes into the dish. The painstakingly achieved crunchy golden shells start to crumble as he attempts to wedge them down the side of the joint.

'I have to give this away,' says David. 'I went to the freezer to get the stock out and I saw all that stuff in there and . . . I just realized that I can't sustain my position any more. The homeless . . .'

'FUCK YOUR POSITION! FUCK THE HOMELESS!' Fuck the homeless? Is this what has become of me? Has a *Guardian*-reading Labour voter ever shouted those words and meant them in the whole history of the liberal metropolitan universe?

'Katie! What's going on?' My parents and my children have gathered in the doorway to watch; my father, still every inch of him a headmaster despite the decade of retirement, is red-faced with anger.

'David's gone mad. He wants to give our lunch away.'

'To whom?'

'Tramps. Alkies. Drug addicts. People who have never done an honest day's work in their lives.' This is a desperate and blatant appeal to win my father over to my side, and I'm not proud of it, but I want my roast lunch. I WANT MY ROAST LUNCH.

'Can I come, Daddy?' says Molly, whom I am learning to despise.

'Of course,' says David.

'Please, David,' I say again. 'Please let us have a nice lunch.'

'We can have a nice lunch. Just, not this lunch.'

'Why can't they have the other lunch?'

'I want to give them the hot one.'

'We can make the other stuff hot. The lasagne. We'll microwave it and take it down this afternoon. Family outing.'

David pauses. We have, I feel, reached the moment in the movie when the armed but scared criminal pointing the gun at the unarmed policewoman begins to doubt the wisdom of what he is doing; the scene always ends with him throwing the gun on the ground and bursting into tears. In our version, David will take the lasagne out of the freezer tray and burst into tears. Who says that you can't make authentic British thrillers? What could be more thrilling than that?

David thinks. 'It's more convenient for them, lasagne, isn't it?'

'Absolutely.'

''Cos you don't have to carve it.'

'No. You could just take the ladle.'

'Yeah. Or even the, you know, the metal spatula.'

'If you want.'

He stares at the joint and the beaten-up roast potatoes for a moment longer.

'OK, then.'

My mum and dad and I breathe the sigh of the unarmed policewoman, and we sit down to eat in silence.

6

None of us feels like eating that night – not that there is much to eat anyway. I had planned to microwave the frozen lasagne, but there is none left. It has already been driven to Finsbury Park, where it was served up in paper plates to the winos who hang out on benches just inside the gates on Seven Sisters Road. (David dished it out on his own while the rest of us sat in the car. Molly wanted to go with him, but I wouldn't let her – not, if I am honest, because I thought she was in any danger, but because she is nauseating enough at the moment as it is. I was worried that if I had to watch her feeding the poor like an eight-year-old Dickensian charity lady I would begin to hate her too much to provide proper maternal care.)

When we get back home, I excuse myself and go and lie down in the bedroom with the Sunday papers, but I can't read them. The stories no longer refer to me me me, but to David, and the sorts of things he would Do Something About. After a little while I find that I am beginning to see news stories not in terms of information, but in terms of potential trouble for my family, and for the contents of my bank account and freezer. One article, about a group of Afghan refugees holed up in a church in Bethnal Green, I actually tear out and throw away, because it contains enough misery and hardship to starve us all.

I look at the gaping hole in the newspaper and suddenly feel very tired. We cannot live like this. Not true, of course, because we can, comfortably – less comfortably than before, maybe, but comfortably nonetheless – we will not starve, no matter how much lasagne is given away. OK, then. So. We can, but I don't want to. This is not the life I chose for myself. Except that is not true, either, because I did choose, I suppose, when I said that I would marry David for richer, for poorer, in sickness and in health, as long as we both shall live: this, obviously, is now more relevant than it has ever been, because he may well be sick, and poverty may well be approaching fast.

What did I think I was choosing, when I married David? What do any of us think we are choosing? If I try to recapture now the semi-formed fantasies I had then, I'd say they erred on the side of prosperity and health. I suppose I thought that we would be poor but happy to begin with – meaning that we would be living in a small cute flat, and spending a lot of time watching TV or drinking halves of beer in pubs, and making do with our parents' hand-me-down furniture. In other words, the difficulties I was prepared to tolerate in the early years of my marriage were essentially romantic in their nature, inspired by the clichés of young married life as depicted in TV comedies – or possibly, given that most TV comedies are more sophisticated and complex than my fantasies, by building society advertisements. Then later on, I thought, one set of difficulties (the difficulties posed by watching TV in a small flat, and by eating baked beans on toast) would be replaced by another: the difficulties that arose when you had two lovely, bright and healthy children. There would be muddy football boots and teenage daughters hogging the phone and husbands who had to be torn from the TV to do the washing-up . . . Golly gosh, there would be no end to those sorts of problems, and I was under no illusions: muddy football boots would be awfully trying! I was prepared, though. I wasn't green. I wasn't born yesterday. There was no way I was going to buy white rugs . . .

What you don't ever catch a glimpse of on your wedding day – because how could you? – is that some days you will hate your spouse, that you will look at him and regret ever exchanging a word with him, let alone a ring and bodily fluids. Nor is it possible to foresee the desperation and depression, the sense that your life is over, the occasional urge to hit your whining children, even though hitting them is something you knew for a fact you would never ever do. And of course you don't think about having affairs, and when you get to that stage in life when you do (and everyone gets there sooner or later), you don't think of the sick feeling you get in your stomach when you're conducting them, their inherent unhappiness. And nor do you think about your husband waking up in the morning and being someone you don't recognize. If anyone thought about any of these things, then no one would ever get married, of course they wouldn't; in fact, the impulse to marry would come from the same place as the impulse to drink a bottle of bleach, and those are the kinds of impulses we try to ignore, rather than celebrate. So we can't afford to think about these things because getting married – or finding a partner whom we will want to spend our lives with and have children by – is on our agenda. It's something we know we will do one day, and if you take that away from us then we are left with promotions at work and the possibility of a winning lottery ticket, and it's not enough, so we kid ourselves that it is possible to enter these partnerships and be faced only with the problems of mud removal, and then we become unhappy and take Prozac and then we get divorced and die alone.

Perhaps I am getting things out of proportion. Maybe all this contemplation of bleach-drinking and Prozac-munching and solitary deaths is an inappropriate response to the crime of giving lasagne away to starving drunks. On our wedding day, the vicar asked us, in that bit where he talks to the bride and groom privately, to respect one another's thoughts, ideas and suggestions. At the time, this seemed an unexceptionable request, easily granted: David for example suggests going to a restaurant, and I say, 'OK then.' Or he has an idea for my birthday present. That sort of thing. Now I realize that there are all sorts of suggestions a husband might make to a wife, and not all of them are worthy of respect. He might suggest that we eat something awful, like sheep's brains, or form a neo-Nazi party. The same must apply to thoughts and ideas, surely? I am in the middle of pointing all this out to the vicar twenty years after the event when the doorbell rings. I ignore it, but a couple of minutes later David shouts up the stairs to tell me I have a visitor.

It's Stephen. My legs almost buckle when I see him, my husband standing next to him, my children running past him, like a scene from a film that mesmerizes simply because it is so far outside the scope of one's own imagination.

I start to introduce my lover to my husband, but David stops me.

'I know who it is,' he says calmly. 'Stephen introduced himself.'

'Oh. Right.' I want to ask whether Stephen gave both his name and his position, as it were, but the atmosphere gives me all the answers I need.

'I'd like to talk to you,' says Stephen. I look anxiously at David. 'Both of you,' Stephen adds, although if this is meant to reassure me somehow, it fails. I don't want to talk. I want David and Stephen to go into a room, come out and tell me what to do. I'd do it, too – anything they came up with, as long as I didn't have to sit at the kitchen table with the two of them. David ushers Stephen past him, and we go and sit down at the kitchen table.

David offers Stephen a drink and I pray he doesn't want one. I get an awful vision of what life would be like while we were all waiting for the kettle to boil, or while David was rummaging through the freezer drawers trying to find the ice tray, and then bashing away at it for ten minutes.

'Can I just have a glass of tap water?'

'I'll get it.'

I jump up, grab a glass from the dishwasher, rinse it, fill it from the tap without letting the water run cool, and plonk it in front of him. No ice, no lemon, certainly no grace, but the hope that this might expedite things is dashed by David standing up.

'How about you, Katie? Cup of tea? Shall I make a pot of real coffee?'

'No!' I shriek.

'How about if I put the kettle on, just in . . .'

'Sit down, please.'

'Right.'

He sits down, and we stare at each other.

'Who wants to kick off, then?' David asks, relatively cheerily. I look at him. I'm not entirely sure that he is responding to the gravity of the moment. (Or am I being melodramatic, maybe even self-aggrandizing in some way? Maybe there is no gravity here. Maybe out in the world people do this all the time, hence David's breeziness. Am I taking it all too seriously, as usual?)

'Maybe I should,' Stephen says. 'Seeing as how I'm the one who's called the meeting, as it were.'

The two men smile, and I decide that my instinct just now was correct: I'm taking things way too seriously, and clearly this sort of thing does happen all the time, and my discomfort is indicative of a disastrous and embarrassing twentieth-century squareness. Maybe Stephen calls round to see the husbands of the women he has slept with on an almost weekly basis. Maybe . . . Maybe David does, which is why he seems to know what to do and say, and how to be.

'I just kind of wanted to see where we were at,' says Stephen pleasantly. 'I'm sorry not to call first or anything, but I left a couple of messages for Katie, and she didn't return them, and so I thought, why not take the bull by the horns sort of thing?'

'Horns being the operative word,' says David. 'Seeing as I'm wearing them.'

'Sorry?'

'The horns. Cuckold. Sorry. Stupid joke.'

Stephen laughs politely. 'Oh, I see. That's quite good.'

'Thank you.'

Maybe it's me. Maybe it's nothing to do with current North London sexual mores that I know nothing about, and maybe it's nothing to do with GoodNews and his effect on David; maybe it's just because I am simply not exciting enough for anyone to get worked up about. OK, I'm just about attractive enough for Stephen to want to sleep with me, but when it comes to jealous rages and dementedly possessive behaviour and lovelorn misery, I simply haven't got what it takes. I'm Katie Carr, not Helen of Troy, or Patti Boyd, or Elizabeth Taylor. Men don't fight over me. They saunter over on a Sunday evening and make weak puns.

'If I can interrupt for a second,' I say tetchily, 'I'd like to speed things up a bit. Stephen, what the hell are you doing here?'

'Ah,' Stephen says. 'The 64,000 dollar question. OK. Deep breath. David, I'm sorry if this comes as a shock, because you seem a decent sort of a guy. But, well . . . I've come to the conclusion that Katie doesn't want to be with you. She wants to be with me. I'm sorry, but those are the facts. I want to talk about what . . . you know, about what we're going to do about it. Man to man.'

And now, when I hear the 'facts' as presented by Stephen, my bleach-drinking view of marriage mysteriously evaporates. In fact, it has now transformed into a bleach-drinking view of Stephen, and I panic.

'That's nonsense,' I tell anyone who will listen to me. 'Stephen, you should stop now and go, before you make an idiot of yourself.'

'I knew she'd say that,' says Stephen with a sigh and a sad, I-know-you-so-well smile. 'David, perhaps you and I should talk privately.'

The outrageous cheek of this enrages me – 'Sure, yes, right, I'll leave the room, and you tell me who I should be with when you've sorted it out' – but the truth is that I am tempted to leave, of course I am. I don't want to live through the next few hideous minutes of this conversation. I remember feeling the same way when I was giving birth to Tom: at one point, bombed out of my head on gas and air and then an epidural, I somehow became convinced it was the maternity room, rather than the baby, that was responsible for the pain I was in, and that if I left it then I could cop out of the whole thing. Not true then, and not true now – the agony has to happen regardless of where I am.

My snapping at Stephen seems merely to have emboldened and relaxed him.

'David,' he says, 'this might hurt, but . . . I know from having talked to Katie over the last couple of months that . . . Well, there are a lot of things that aren't right.'

David gently interrupts before Stephen has a chance to enumerate all the problems he thinks we have. 'Katie and I have talked about that. We're working on it.'

I can't help but love David at this moment. He's calm when he has every right to be angry with everything and everyone, and as a result I feel, for the first time in a long time, that we are a unit, a couple, a marriage, and that marriage is, after all, something we should all aspire to. At this precise moment I'm happy to be in a marriage, to be two against one, to combine with my partner against this destructive and dangerous outsider with whom I happen to have had sex. The alternative is three-cornered anarchy, and I'm too scared and too tired for that.

'There are some things you can't sort out,' Stephen says. He won't make eye contact with any of us; he's staring into his glass of water.

'Like?'

'She doesn't love you.'

David looks at me, requiring some sort of reaction. I settle for a shake of the head and a roll of the eyes – a suitably ambiguous response, I hope, to what is, after all, a very complicated issue (two seconds ago I loved him, twenty minutes ago I hated him, earlier in the afternoon I wasn't bothered one way or the other, and so on and on, right back to the college disco, probably) – but neither the headshake nor the eye rolling seem to do the trick, because both of them are looking at me now.

'I never said that,' I throw in hopefully.

'You didn't have to,' says Stephen, and I can't deny that whenever I did speak about David, no one listening could have claimed that I was besotted with him. 'And then there's the sex . . .'

'I definitely never said anything about . . .'

'You did, actually, Katie. You said something about the difference between art and science, and that you preferred art.'

Oh. Oh dear. There was no way that was a lucky guess. I hadn't realized that I'd ever voiced my art versus science theory, but I must have done.

'I never said I preferred art.'

'You said you were a scientist by profession and you didn't need science in bed.'

Now he comes to mention it, I do remember saying something like that, but it was intended to make Stephen feel better about, you know, nothing happening from my side. Ironic, then, that it has come to be used as a weapon against David, who did make things happen from my side. (If you're interested, there is another layer of irony here, because David is a great anti-science man, and constantly bangs on about the superiority of the arts over science, and how all scientists are idiots and so on and so forth. So first of all, in this particular situation, he's swapped camps and become a scientist, his own worst enemy, without knowing it. And, then, having swapped camps and actually achieved more than the artist – although maybe that's just me speaking as a scientist – he's attacked for it.)

'I'm sorry,' says David mildly. 'You've lost me.'

Neither Stephen nor I have the heart to explain, so we just let his rather plaintive (and, let's face it, perfectly understandable) bafflement hang in the air. But I hate the feeling that Stephen and I are now, suddenly, the unit, and that David's incomprehension isolates him. I don't want to form any sort of alliance with this twit. Not any more.

'Stephen, I was trying to be nice to you when I told you that. It was an explanation for why I didn't come.' I glance at David, hoping that this brutally plain information will cheer him up, and that the cheer will register somewhere in his face, but he is still blank and quiet. I want to make him feel better than he must be feeling, but I can see now that referring to my sexual relationship with Stephen, even given its relative failure, is not the way to do it.

'That's what you're saying now,' Stephen says. There's a whine in his voice that I've never heard before, and I don't like it. 'That's not what you were saying when you were lying on top of me in Leeds.'

David looks away momentarily, a flinch as the needle finally pierces the skin. 'No, that's not what I said then,' I say, and there is a real heat in my voice. He's really beginning to upset me now. 'We know what I said then. I said the thing about arts and science then. That's what we're talking about. We're interpreting the words we know I used. Please try and keep up, Stephen.'

'Oh, terribly sorry if I'm not quick enough for you.' We glower at each other, and it is this that finally makes David get to his feet.

'I'm sorry if I'm speaking out of turn here,' he says, 'but you two really don't strike me as a couple who stand much chance of a happy and successful relationship together. You don't seem to get on very well. And you really should be able to, at this stage. Early on. First flush and all that.'

It's such an obvious and welcome observation that it makes me smile, even though the 'you two' and the 'couple' stick in my throat.

'I mean . . . to be honest, Stephen, Katie doesn't appear to like you very much. I'll let her speak for herself, but I don't think she's in a hurry to rush off with you. And, you know . . . there's surely got to be a degree of . . . of . . . unanimity about it. Otherwise it's not going to happen, is it?'

'No it bloody isn't,' I say.

'Katie . . .' Stephen reaches for my hand and I snatch it away. I can't believe he wants to argue the point.

'I'm not sixteen, Stephen. This isn't like trying to persuade someone to go to the pictures. I have a husband and two children. You think I'm going to suddenly see your point and leave them? "Oh, yeah, you're right, I do want to be with you. Silly me." I made a mistake. I've got to live with it, and so has David. Please go.'

And he does, and I never see him again. (Oh, but I think of him, of course I do. He's not really a part of this story any more, but in months and years to come I will find myself wondering whether he has a partner, whether he remembers me, whether I left some small but disfiguring scar . . . I haven't slept with enough men to forget any of them, particularly the most recent. So even though you will not hear much about him again, do not make the mistake of thinking that it is as if he never was.)

'Thank you,' I say to David when we hear the door slam. 'Thank you, thank you.'

'What for?'

'That must have been horrible for you.'

'It . . . It really was. I was so jealous. I hated him so much. What were you thinking of?'

'I don't know.' And I don't. Stephen now seems to be not a person at all, but the hallucinatory product of some sort of sickness.

'You were brilliant. And I'm sorry I put you in such a ridiculous situation.'

He shakes his head, and is quiet for a moment. 'I put myself in it, too, didn't I? Wouldn't have happened if I'd been making you happy. So I'm sorry, too.'

And now I do feel I owe him. Not because of what I promised a long time ago, but because of what he just did five minutes ago. And that's how it should work, isn't it? That night, I go to bed feeling I'd do anything for him.

'There's a favour I wanted to ask you, actually,' he says as we're about to put the light out, and I'm pleased. I'm in the mood for favours.

'Sure.'

'I spoke to GoodNews yesterday, and . . . Well, he's got nowhere to live. His landlord's given him notice. I was wondering if he could come here for a couple of nights.'

I don't want GoodNews here, of course I don't: the prospect fills me with a great deal of apprehension. But my husband has spent some of this evening listening courteously while my ex-lover outlines his shortcomings, and has now asked me if a friend can stay for a while: you don't have to have had a spiritual conversion to come to the right decision.

He's a funny little man, GoodNews. Thirtyish, small, astonishingly skinny; he would be unwise to pick a fight with Tom. He has huge, bright-blue, frightened-looking eyes, and lots of curly, dirty-blond hair, although I suspect that personal hygiene might not necessarily be a priority for him at the moment, and perhaps I should reserve judgement on the hair colour until he has been persuaded to shower. There has been an unwise and spectacularly unsuccessful attempt to grow a goatee, hence a fluffy little tuft of something or other, just underneath the centre of his lower lip, that any mother would want to rub off with a bit of spit. What you notice first of all, however, is that both his eyebrows have been pierced, and he is wearing what appear to be brooches over each eye. The children are particularly and perhaps forgivably fascinated by this.

'Are those tortoises?' Tom asks, even before he's said hello. I hadn't wanted to stare at the eyebrow jewellery before, but now I can see that Tom is right: this man is wearing representations of domestic pets on his face.

'Nah,' says GoodNews dismissively, as if Tom's error was ignorant in the extreme, and he's about to expand when Molly steps in.

'They're turtles,' she says. I am momentarily impressed by her authority until I remember that she has met GoodNews before.

'What's the difference?' asks Tom.

'Turtles can swim, can't they?' says David over-cheerfully, as if trying to enter into the spirit of a completely different occasion – an occasion where we're sitting around eating pizza and watching a nature programme, rather than an occasion where we're welcoming a spiritual healer with animals dangling from his eyebrows into our home. The cheerfulness comes, I can see, from embarrassment – he has, after all, spent an awful lot of time kneeling on the floor with this man, and so he has a lot to be embarrassed about.

'Why did you want turtles and not tortoises?' Tom asks. It's not the first question that came to my mind, but DJ GoodNews is such a curious creature that any information he cares to give us is endlessly fascinating.

'You won't laugh if I tell you?' I laugh even before he tells us. I can't help it. The idea that one would laugh at the explanation for the turtles, but not at the turtles themselves, is in itself funny.

GoodNews looks hurt.

'I'm sorry,' I say.

'That was quite rude,' says GoodNews. 'I'm surprised at you.'

'Do you know me?'

'I feel like I do. David's talked a lot about you. He loves you very much, but you've been going through some bad times, yeah?'

For a moment I think he's asking me for confirmation – 'That's me!' – but then I realize that the 'yeah' is just one of those annoying verbal tics that this generation pick up like headlice. I have never met anyone like GoodNews. He talks like a dodgy geezer vicar, all cockiness and glottal stops and suspect solicitude.

'Anyway,' he says. 'The turtles. It was really weird, yeah? 'Cos I had this dream about blue turtles, and then Sting, you know, the singer, well, I don't like him much, I used to like the Police when I was a kid but I think his solo stuff is bollocks pardon my French, anyway he brings out an album called *The Dream of the Blue Turtles*. So . . .'

He shrugs. The rest – the eyebrow-piercing and the brooches – is clearly meant to be self-explanatory, although I can't help feeling that he's missed out a couple of steps of the decision-making process.

'And I've always had this thing about turtles anyway. I've always thought they could see stuff that we can't, yeah?'

The children stare at their father, clearly baffled.

'What can they see?' asks Molly.

'Good question, Molly.' He points at her. 'You're good. You're sharp. I'm going to have to watch you.' Molly looks pleased, but there is no attempt to answer the question.

'He doesn't know,' says Tom with a snort.

'Oh, I know all right. But maybe now's not the time.'

'When's the time, then?'

'Do you want to show GoodNews his room?' says David to the children, clearly with the intention of bringing the subject of turtles and their psychic powers to a close; and as GoodNews doesn't want to expand on his theories anyway, he picks up his bags and goes upstairs.

David turns to me.

'I know what you're thinking.'

'What am I supposed to think?'

'I know he talks nonsense some of the time. Try not to get bogged down in the superficial stuff.'

'What else is there?'

'You don't pick up a vibe?'

'No.'

'Oh. Oh well.' In other words: some people – the intuitive, soulful and spiritual among us – can pick up a vibe, and others – the flat, dull, literalists, like me – can't. I resent this.

'What vibe should I be picking up, then, according to you?'

'It's not according to me. It's there. It's interesting that Molly and I can feel it and you and Tom can't.'

'How do you know Tom can't? How do you know Molly can?'

'Did you notice that Tom was rude to him? If you pick up the vibe, you wouldn't be rude. Molly isn't rude. She got it the first time she saw him.'

'And me? Was I rude?'

'Not rude. But sceptical.'

'And that's wrong?'

'You can almost see it, what he has. If you know how to look.'

'And you don't think I do?' I don't know why this bothers me so much, but it does. I want to know how to look; or at least, I want David to think of me as the sort of person who might know how to look.

'Calm down. It doesn't make you a bad person.'

'That's not true, though, is it? According to you. That's precisely why I'm a bad person. Because all I saw was the eyebrows, not the . . . the . . . aura.'

'We can't all be everything.' And he smiles that smile, and goes to join the others.

'There are a few things GoodNews has a problem with,' says David when they have all come down again.

'I'm sorry to hear that,' I say.

'I don't really agree with beds,' says GoodNews.

'Oh,' I say. 'Do you mind if we sleep in them?' I want to sound dry and light, like a nice white wine, but I fear that what comes out is a lot more vinegary than that.

'What other people do is their business,' says GoodNews. 'I just think they make you soft. Take you further away from how things really are.'

'And how are things?'

David shoots me a look. Not the old-style, I-hate-you-and-I-wish-you-were-dead look I would have got, once upon a time; this is the new-style, I'm-sooooo-disappointed look, and for a moment I am nostalgic for the days when hatred was our common currency. It was a currency that worked, at the time, just as pigs and bales of wheat must have worked. And though you can see why pigs were abandoned, they at least had the virtue of simplicity.

'That's a big question, Katie,' says GoodNews. 'And I don't know if you're ready for the big answer.'

'You are, aren't you, Mum?' says Tom, loyally.

'Anyway,' says David. 'GoodNews would like the bed taken out of the spare room. Because there isn't really room for him to sleep on the floor if it stays there.'

'Right. And where shall we put it?'

'I'll put it in my office,' says David.

'Can I take my bed out?' Molly asks. 'I don't like it.'

'What's wrong with your bed?' I address this to David rather than Molly, just so that he can see what a mess of the world his friend is making.

'I don't agree with it,' says Molly.

'What, precisely, don't you agree with?'

'I just don't. They're wrong.'

'When you have your own flat, you can sleep on nails for all I care. While you're here, you'll sleep in a bed.'

'I'm sorry,' says GoodNews. 'I'm causing trouble, aren't I? Please, forget it. It's cool.'

'Are you sure?' David says.

'No, really. I can cope on a bed.' There is a pause, and he looks at David, who has clearly become GoodNews's representative on Earth.

'The other thing that GoodNews was – well, we both were – worried about was where he's going to heal people.'

'He was intending to heal them here?'

'Yes. Where else?'

'I thought he was only here for a couple of nights.'

'Probably he will be. But he needs to work. And he has commitments to people. So, you know. If it does turn out to be a bit longer than a couple of days . . .'

'The spare bedroom's no good?'

David looks at him, and he shrugs.

'Not ideal,' says GoodNews. 'Because of the bed. But if there's nothing else . . .'

'Funnily enough, we've got an empty healing room that we never use.'

'I'm afraid sarcasm is one of Katie's indulgences,' David says.

'I've got loads of others, though. Millions of them.' And I suddenly remember that one of my most recent indulgences recently visited our home, and David was incredibly nice about it, and I feel bad. 'Sorry. Maybe your bedroom is the best place for now.'

'Fine. I can do good work there. It has a nice atmosphere, you know?'

'And the last thing is, GoodNews is a vegetarian.'

'Fine.'

'A vegan, actually.'

'Good. Very sensible. Much better for you. Is that it?'

'I think so. For the time being.'

'Enjoy your stay,' I tell GoodNews, who is sure that he will be very happy here. For my part, I am sure that he will never ever leave.

David cooks chicken pieces for us and vegetables for everyone while he and GoodNews talk in the kitchen, and then we have our first meal together. The main topic of conversation is GoodNews: GoodNews and the turtles (what they see, it transpires, is not really explicable in, like, words), GoodNews and how things really are ('Bad, man. But there's hope, you know? Once you know where to find it') GoodNews and his healing hands: Molly wants him to warm them up there and then, on the spot, but David tells her that it's not a party trick.

'Have you always been able to do it? Could you do it when you were my age?'

'No. I couldn't do it till I was, like, twenty-five?'

'How old are you now?'

'Thirty-two.'

'So how did you know you could do it, then?' This from Tom, who has remained oblivious to the GoodNews charm.

'My girlfriend at the time – she had a cricked neck and she asked me to give her a massage and . . . everything went all weird.'

'What sort of weird?'

'Weird weird. The lightbulbs got brighter, the room got hot. It was a real scene.'

'And how do you think your gift came about?' There is, I am pleased to note, less vinegar in my voice. I'm learning. I'm still not a very good white wine, but I'm drinkable – you could put me in a punch, anyway.

'I know, but I can't tell you in front of the kids. Bad form.'

I have no idea what this means, but if GoodNews thinks that the story of how he became a healer is unsuitable for minors, I am not prepared to argue with him, even if the minors are.

'Oh, go on,' Tom says.

'No,' says GoodNews. 'I mean it. Ask me another question.'

'What was your girlfriend's name?' Molly asks.

'That's a stupid question,' Tom snorts. 'Who wants to know that? Idiot.'

'Hey, Tom, man. If that information is important to someone, then who are we to judge?' says GoodNews. 'There might be all sorts of reasons why Molly wanted to know what my girlfriend's name was. Probably some pretty good reasons, if I know Molly. So let's not be calling people idiots, eh? She was called Andrea, Molly.'

Molly nods smugly, Tom's face becomes a picture of smouldering hate – the kind of picture that a newspaper could use to illustrate an article on ethnic division in the former Yugoslavia – and I know that DJ GoodNews has made himself an enemy.

For the rest of the meal, we manage to avoid flashpoints; Good-News asks politely about our jobs and our schools and our maths teachers, and we all answer politely (if, in some cases, tersely), and we pass the time in this way until the last mouthful has been eaten and it is time to clear away.

'I'll wash up,' says GoodNews.

'We have a dishwasher,' I tell him, and GoodNews looks anxiously at David. It is not difficult to anticipate what is coming, and so I do.

'You don't hold with dishwashers,' I say, with a weariness exaggerated to convey the idea that GoodNews's various antipathies might at some point become grating.

'No,' says GoodNews.

'You don't hold with a lot of things that a lot of people don't have a problem with,' I observe.

'No,' he agrees. 'But just because a lot of people don't have a problem with something, it doesn't mean they're right, does it? I mean, a lot of people used to think that . . . I don't know . . . slavery was OK, but, you know. They were wrong, weren't they? They were so wrong it was unreal. Because it wasn't OK, was it? It was really bad, man. Slaves. No way.'

'Do you think that slavery and dishwashers are the same thing, GoodNews? Or not quite the same, really?'

'Maybe to me they're the same thing.'

'Maybe to you all sorts of things are the same thing. Maybe paedophilia is the same thing as . . . as . . . soap. Maybe fascism is the same thing as toilets. But that doesn't mean I'm going to make my children pee in the garden, just because your peculiar moral code would prefer it.' *Maybe fascism is the same thing as toilets* . . . I really said that, just now. This is the world I suddenly inhabit, a world where this might pass for a coherent line of argument.

'You're being silly. And sarcastic,' David says.

Sarcasm – my terrible indulgence. 'Oh, so it's me being silly, is it? Not the man who won't sleep on a bed because it's not, like, real?' I feel bad. I should be able to handle the slavery versus dishwashers argument without recourse to childish insult.

'I try to survive without things that not everybody has,' says GoodNews. 'I'm not joining in until everyone's got everything. When, like, the last peasant in the Brazilian rainforest has a dishwasher, or a, you know, like, a cappuccino maker, or one of those TVs that's the size of a house, then count me in, yeah? But until then, I'm making a stand.'

'That's very noble of you,' I say. *Nutter,* I think, with an enormous sense of relief. There is, after all, nothing to learn from this person, no way he can make me feel small or wrong or ignoble or self-indulgent: he is simply a crank, and I can ignore him with impunity.

'Everybody in the world's got a dishwasher,' Molly says, clearly puzzled, and all the times I feel I have failed as a mother are as nothing compared to this one, humiliating moment.

'That's not true, Molly,' I say quickly and sharply. 'And you know it.'

'Who hasn't, then?' She's not being cheeky. She just can't think of anyone.

'Don't be silly,' I say, but I'm just buying myself time while I dredge up someone in her universe who does their own washing-up. 'What about Danny and Charlotte?' Danny and Charlotte go to Molly's school and live in a council flat down the road, and even as I speak I realize I am guilty of the most ludicrous form of class stereotyping.

'They've got everything,' says Molly.

'They've got DVD and OnDigital,' says Tom.

'OK, OK. What about the children Daddy gave Tom's computer to?'

'They don't count,' says Molly. 'They've got nothing. They haven't even got homes. And I don't know any of them. I wouldn't want to know them, thank you very much, because they sound a bit too rough for my liking. Even though I feel sorry for them and I'm happy they've got Tom's computer.'

This is my daughter?

The moral education of my children has always been important to me. I have talked to them about the Health Service, and about the importance of Nelson Mandela; we've discussed the homeless, of course, and racism, and sexism, and poverty, and money, and fairness. David and I have explained, as best we can, why anyone who votes Conservative will never be entirely welcome in our house, although we have to make special arrangements for Granny and Grandpa. And though I was sickened by Molly's unctuous performance during the computer and lasagne episodes, there was a part of me that thought, yes, she's coming along, she gets it, all those conversations and questions have not been in vain. Now I see that she's a stinking patrician Lady Bountiful who in twenty years' time will be sitting on the committee of some revolting charity ball in Warwickshire, moaning about refugees and giving her unwanted pashminas to her cleaning lady.

'You see,' says GoodNews. 'This is why I don't want to play the game. The possessions game. Because I think people become lazy and spoiled and uncaring.'

I look at my lazy and uncaring and spoiled daughter, and then I tell GoodNews that my children would love to help him with the dishes.

7

I have about twelve hundred patients. There are some patients that I see a lot, and some I hardly see at all, and there are some I can help, and some I can't, and the patients that distress me the most are the ones I see a lot who I can't help. We call them heartsink patients, for obvious reasons, and someone once reckoned that most partners in a practice have about fifty heartsinks on their books. They come in, and sit down, and they look at me, and both of us know it's hopeless, and I feel guilty and sad and fraudulent, and, if the truth be told, a little persecuted. These people don't see anyone else who can't help them, who fail them on such a regular basis. The TV repairman who can't fix your picture, the plumber who can't stop a leak, the electrician who can't get your lights back on . . . Your relationship with these people ceases, after a while, because they cannot do anything for you. But my relationship with my heartsinks will never cease. They will sit and stare accusingly at me for ever.

I know and, I hope, Mrs Cortenza knows that I cannot do anything for her. Her joints hurt, her back hurts, she cannot sleep with the pain, and the painkillers no longer seem to do anything for her, and she comes back again and again and we talk and talk and I think and think and come up with nothing that works (and in the process I spend and spend and spend, on drugs and X-rays and exploratory operations), and now I just wish that she would go to see another doctor and leave me alone, leave me to treat people I feel I have a chance with. Hopeful people, *younger* people, because Mrs Cortenza is old, older even than her seventy-three years, and it is her age and a lifetime spent cleaning other people's houses that have damaged her. (Let's face it: these houses belong to people like me, so there is a peculiar circularity in all this. Maybe if we all forgot about being good and saving the world, and stayed at home and cleaned our own houses, then people like Mrs Cortenza wouldn't need doctors. Maybe Mrs Cortenza, thus liberated from her pain and her domestic drudgery, could have got on with something socially useful. Maybe she would have spent her life teaching adult literacy, or working with teenage runaways, if I hadn't been so hellbent on curing her, and thus never having time to scrub my own floors.)

The morning after GoodNews's arrival Mrs Cortenza shuffles in, grey with age and effort, and slumps into the chair, and shakes her head, and my heart does what it is supposed to do. We are silent for a couple of minutes while she recovers her breath; during this silence she points at the picture of Molly and Tom that I have pinned to the noticeboard, and then points at me, and I smile and nod, and she smiles and makes a thumbs-up sign and a gesture with her hand to indicate how big they are. I am sure that the same thought then seizes both of us: they didn't use to be big when she first started coming to see me. The photo on the noticeboard probably depicted a couple of toddlers, and thus my children serve only to emphasize my uselessness.

'How are you, Mrs Cortenza?' I say, when the wheezing has subsided sufficiently to make conversation seem feasible. She shakes her head. She is not good.

I look at my notes. 'How were the pills I gave you last time?' She shakes her head again. They were not good.

'And are you sleeping?' She is not sleeping. Her sleep is not good. Nothing is good. I look at her for as long as I can without embarrassment, and then stare at my notes intently, as if there might be something in them that will solve not only Mrs Cortenza's problems, but the problems of all the world.

And suddenly I realize that at home I have something which has worked for somebody, and if I am any kind of a doctor then I am compelled to try it. I call David, and ask him to bring GoodNews down to the surgery.

'You have to pay him,' he says.

'Out of what? My mystical healing budget?'

'I don't care. But you're not to take advantage of him.'

'How about this: he treats Mrs Cortenza, and we don't charge him for board and lodging. Or for electricity. Or for general inconvenience.'

'You're not taking him down there every day.'

'I won't need to bring him down here every day. I am a perfectly competent doctor, you know. I have managed to prescribe the occasional effective antibiotic.' But even as I am saying this, I am making a list of my other recidivists. Just imagine: a working life without Mr Arthurs! Or Mrs McBride! Or Barmy Brian Beech, as we call him here, with no affection whatsoever!

GoodNews arrives within fifteen minutes, a quarter-hour which seems as long but no longer than my usual consultations with Mrs Cortenza, but which I am happy to curtail. I get some funny looks from reception, but no vocal objections from anyone.

Mrs Cortenza stares at GoodNews's eyebrow-brooches with naked hostility.

'Hello, love,' says GoodNews. 'You're a smasher, aren't you? What's your name?'

She continues to stare.

'This is Mrs Cortenza.'

'Not that name. Her proper name. Her first name.'

I don't have a clue, of course. How would I know? I've only been seeing her for five years. I scrabble through my notes.

'Maria.'

'Maria,' says GoodNews, and then he says it again, this time in an exaggerated, all-purpose European accent. 'Marrrrriaaaaa. What are we going to do about Maria, eh? You know that song? *West Side Story*?'

'That's *The Sound of Music*,' I tell him. 'The *West Side Story* one is different.' I wonder for a moment whether this will be my only demonstration of expertise throughout the entire consultation.

'So you've had two songs written about you?' says GoodNews. 'I'm not surprised. Lovely girl like you.'

Mrs Cortenza smiles shyly. I want to throttle her for being so gullible.

'So what needs doing here? How can we get Maria dancing again?'

'She's got chronic inflammation around most of her joints. Hips, knees. A lot of back pain.'

'Is she sad?'

'I should think so, with that lot.'

'No, I mean, like, mentally.'

'Is she mentally sad? You mean, sad in her mind as opposed to sad in her knees?'

'Yeah, all right, I'm not as good at talking as you, Dr Smartypants. But let's see which one of us can do something for her.'

'Why, does she have to be unhappy before you can treat her?'

'It helps if I can really key into that stuff, yeah.'

'Are you sad, Mrs Cortenza?' I ask her.

She looks at me. 'Sad? Sadness?' Neither her hearing nor her English is perfect, and so it is difficult to know which of these difficulties is responsible for the confusion.

'Yes. Sadness.'

'Oh, yes,' she says, with the relish only the old can bring to such a subject. 'Very, very sad.'

'Why?' says GoodNews.

'Too many things,' she says. She gestures at her clothes – she has worn black ever since I have known her – and her eyes fill with tears. 'My husband,' she says. 'My sister. My mother. My father. Too many things.' One doesn't want to feel unsympathetic, and it is certainly unhelpful to be prescriptive about grief, but one wonders whether Mrs Cortenza should maybe have come to terms with being an orphan by now. 'My son,' she continues.

'Your son's dead?'

'No, no, not dead. Very bad. He move to Archway. He never call me.'

'Is that enough sadness?' I ask GoodNews. I didn't know we had to key into sadness, and suddenly the idea of GoodNews seeing Barmy Brian is a little less attractive. I would imagine that there is a lot of sadness hidden away somewhere in Barmy Brian, and not all of it would be easy to listen to.

'That all makes sense,' says GoodNews. 'I can feel most of that.

Explain to her that I will need to touch her shoulders, neck and head.'

'I understand,' says Mrs Cortenza, somewhat affronted.

'Is that OK?' I ask her.

'OK. Yes.'

GoodNews sits opposite her and closes his eyes for a while; then he gets up, stands behind her and starts to massage her scalp. He whispers while he's doing it, but I can't make out anything he's saying.

'Very hot!' Mrs Cortenza says suddenly.

'That's good,' says GoodNews. 'The hotter the better. Things are happening.'

He's right. Things are happening. Maybe it's just the momentary intensity of the experience, maybe it's just the collective concentration, but it seems to me that the room has become warmer, much warmer, and for a moment it seems to become brighter, too. I don't want to feel this heat, and I don't want to notice how the wattage of the one bulb in the ceiling seems to have increased from its dim forty to a dazzling one hundred; feeling and seeing these things seems akin to feeling and seeing a whole lot of other, more complicated things, and I'd really rather not, if you don't mind. So I shall forget about them, as best I can.

What will prove more difficult to forget is this: after a few minutes of gentle massage and attendant ambient disturbance, Mrs Cortenza stands up, stretches herself gingerly and says to GoodNews, 'Thank you. Is much better now. Much much better.' And she nods to me – I may be paranoid, but the nod seems quite cool, a way of telling me how negligible her problems were, and how easy to fix if I had any kind of expertise – and walks out at about five times the speed she walked in.

'So,' I say. 'You can cure old age. Well done. Hurrah for you. There should be a few quid in that somewhere.'

'Nah, she's not cured,' says GoodNews. 'Of course she's not cured. Her body's fucked. But life will be much better for her.' I can see that he's pleased, genuinely pleased – not for himself, but for Mrs Cortenza, and I feel small and petty and hopeless.

*

'You can tell me now,' I say before he leaves. 'The children aren't here. What's the secret?'

'I don't know what the secret is. That wasn't what I couldn't tell you.'

'So tell me what you couldn't tell me.'

'Drugs.'

'What do you mean, drugs? Drugs what?'

'That's how it started. E. That's what I think, anyway. I was doing loads, and it was all that "I love you, you're my friend" stuff in clubs every Friday night, and . . . I'm like one of those American comic-book guys. Spiderman and all them. It changed my molecular make-up. Gave me superpowers.'

'Ecstasy gave you superpowers.'

'I reckon.' He shrugs. 'Weird, innit? I mean, there's you at university and all that finding out about, like, your thigh-bone's connected to your knee-bone or whatever you do there. And there's me down the clubs dropping a few. And we've come out at the same place. I mean, don't get me wrong, I still think there's a place for what you do.'

'Thank you. That's very generous of you.'

'No, no problem. I'll see you back at the ranch.'

Later, I sit watching Molly in the bath, looking for and failing to find any traces of her eczema.

'Molly. Do you remember when you went to see GoodNews?'

'Yes. Course.'

'Do you remember what he said to you? Did he ask you anything?'

'Like what?'

'I don't know. Did he ask you how you were feeling?'

'Ummmm. Oh, yes. He asked me if I was feeling sad.'

'And what did you say?'

'I said I felt a bit sad sometimes.'

'What about?'

'I'm sad about Grandma Parrot.' David's mother, who died last year, so-called because she had a stone parrot on her gatepost.

'Yes. That was sad.'

'And Poppy.' Family cat, killed shortly after Grandma Parrot. Molly's proximity to these deaths was much closer than we would have wanted, in an ideal world. Grandma Parrot collapsed when she was visiting us, and although she didn't actually die until later that night, in hospital, it was clear that she wasn't well when she was taken away; and – foolishly, in retrospect – we organized a search party for the missing Poppy. Molly and I found her up (and in, and all over) the road. I wish she had seen neither casualty.

'That was sad, too.'

'And your baby.'

'My baby?'

'The baby that died.'

'Oh. That baby.'

I had a miscarriage, eighteen months or so before I had Tom. A run-of-the-mill, ten-week, first-baby miscarriage, distressing at the time, almost completely forgotten about now; I cannot for the life of me recall telling Molly about it, but clearly I must have done, and she has remembered and mourned, in her own way.

'Did that make you sad?'

'Yes. Of course. That was my brother or sister.'

'Well, kind of.' I want to tell her that it's OK really without getting into some huge thing about souls and foetuses and all sorts of other areas that eight-year-olds should be spared for as long as possible. I change the subject. 'Anything else?'

'I think I was sad about you and Daddy, too.'

'Why were you sad about us?'

'Because you might get divorced. And you'll definitely die.'

'Oh, Molly.'

I know there are loads and loads of replies to this, but for a moment they seem fundamentally untruthful, and I can't bring myself to play the requisite parental consolation game. We might get divorced; we'll definitely die. This seems, in my suddenly world-weary and bleak frame of mind, a precise and accurate summation of the situation, and I don't feel like telling Molly anything different. Instead, I reach forward and touch her forehead, like GoodNews might do, in a doomed attempt to draw these thoughts out of her. It feels to me as though this is the only physical contact I can allow myself; anything more would result in an unstoppable torrent of grief and despair.

'I don't worry about any of that now,' says Molly brightly, as if it is her job to console me, rather than the other way around.

'Really?'

'Yes. Really. GoodNews made it all go away.'

After the kids have gone to bed, I don't want to join GoodNews and David downstairs, so I sit in the bedroom for a while, and I think. My conversation with Molly has made it impossible for me not to think, even though not-thinking is currently my favourite mode of being. And what I think, I suppose, is this: we live what an awful lot of people would regard as a normal life. There are some – rock singers, novelists, young columnists in the newspapers, those who affect to think of anything involving children and day-jobs and package holidays as a long and agonizing spiritual death – who would regard us as beneath contempt, such has been our wholehearted embrace of some sort of conservative lifestyle ideal. And there are others, and you know who they are, who would regard us as being impossibly lucky, blessed, spoiled by our upbringing and our skin colour and our education and our income. I have no quarrel with the second bunch at all – how could I have? I know what we've got, and what we haven't had to experience. But the other lot . . . I don't know. Because it seems to me that normal life, or the kind of 'normal' life that these people despise, already has plenty in it that prevents an agonizing spiritual death, and plenty in it that is simply agonizing, and who are these people to judge anyone?

What has happened to Molly in her first eight years? More or less nothing. We have protected her from the world as best we can. She has been brought up in a loving home, she has two parents, she has never been hungry, and she receives an education that will prepare her for the rest of her life; and yet she is sad, and that sadness is not, when you think about it, inappropriate. The state of the relationship between her parents makes her anxious; she has lost a loved one (and a cat); and she has realized that such losses are going to be an unavoidable part of her life in the future. It seems to me now that the plain state of being human is dramatic enough for anyone; you don't need to be a heroin addict or a performance poet to experience extremity. You just have to love someone.

And the other thing I think is that I have failed my daughter. Eight years old, and she's sad . . . I didn't want that. When she was born I was certain I could prevent it, and I have been unable to, and even though I see that the task I set myself was unrealistic and unachievable, it doesn't make any difference: I have still participated in the creation of yet another confused and fearful human being.

I have sat on my own in the dark long enough; it is time to rejoin my normal life. So I go downstairs, to eat with my husband and the live-in guru with the eyebrow-brooches, and to talk about how everyone who lives in our street should invite a homeless kid into their house for a year.

They're serious; I realize that straight away. Plans are already sufficiently advanced that they have drawn up a list of the houses in the street, with as much information about the inhabitants therein as David possesses. Neither of them take any notice of me as I walk into the kitchen, so I stand behind David and listen and read over his shoulder. The list looks like this:

1. Not known.
3. Not known.
5. Not known.
7. Old lady. (Old man also? No difference, if sharing bed)
9. Not known
11. Richard, Mary, Daniel, Chloe
13. Nice Asian family. (4?)
15. Not known
17. Not known
19. Wendy and Ed
21. Martina
23. Hugh

25. Simon and Richard
27. Not-nice Asian family (6? + Alsatian)
29. Ros and Max
31. Annie and Pete + 2
33. Roger and Mel + 3
35. For sale

And the same for the other side of the street. For a moment, I am distracted by the obvious pattern of our acquaintance – we know who lives next to us, and opposite us, but we know almost nothing of the people who live sixty or seventy yards away – until the sheer lunacy of the conversation draws me back into the room.

'By my reckoning there are at least forty spare bedrooms in this street,' David is saying. 'Isn't that incredible? Forty spare bedrooms, and thousands of people out there without a bed? I'd never even thought of it in that way before. I mean, when I see empty houses it pisses me off, but empty houses aren't really the issue, are they? If there are forty spare bedrooms in this street, then our postcode alone should be able to take care of most of the homeless kids out there.'

'We should be aiming at filling, say, ten of them,' says Good-News. 'I'd be happy with ten.'

'Really?' David looks a little disappointed, as if persuading only ten of his neighbours to house someone they didn't know was the sort of terrible compromise he wasn't prepared to make. This, then, is what we have come to: the spiritual healer who can't get along with dishwashers is now the hard-nosed realist in my house, and my husband is the wide-eyed optimist. 'Wouldn't ten mean, I don't know, that we'd lost the argument? 'Cos it's pretty unanswerable, surely, if we pitch it right.'

'Some people just won't get it,' says GoodNews.

'Some people might need the spare rooms for other things,' I say.

'Like what?' David asks, slightly aggressively. He used to use exactly these tones when he wanted to challenge me in the old days – about why I wanted to teach the kids about other forms of religion, say (he didn't want them to know about any), or why I wanted to go and hear Maya Angelou read ('What, you're a *black* feminist now?'). I had forgotten how wearing these tones were.

'You used to work in one of ours, for example.'

'OK, so five out of the forty are used as offices.'

'And what about if people have their parents to stay?'

'God, you're literal-minded.'

'What's literal-minded about saying that people have parents?'

'It's not that. It's the spirit. You have none.'

'Thank you.'

'None of these things are real problems. You're just being negative.'

'You have no idea about these people's lives. You don't even know their names.' I gesture at the paper in front of them. 'But you're happy to tell me what's a real problem for them and what isn't. What gives you the right?'

'What gives them the right to own half-empty houses when there are all these people out there in cardboard boxes?'

'What gives them the right? Their bloody mortgages, that's what gives them the right. These are their homes, David. And it's not like they're enormous homes, either. Why don't you pick on Bill Gates? Or Tom Cruise? How many spare bedrooms have they got?'

'If they lived around the corner, I would pick on them. But they don't. And we don't need them, because there's plenty of room for everyone right here. You're just frightened of the embarrassment.'

'That's not true.' But it is, of course, completely true. I am terrified of the embarrassment, of which there will be lorryloads. I can hear the diesel engines rumbling towards us even as we speak. 'How do you plan to go about this, anyway?'

'I don't know. Door-to-door.'

'What about a party?' says GoodNews brightly. 'We'll have a party here, and you can speak to everyone, and . . . and it'll be great.'

'Brilliant,' says David, with the air of someone who knows he's in the presence of genius.

'Brilliant,' I say, with the air of someone who wants to put her

113

head in the oven. But that sort of air doesn't interest them in the slightest.

OK: so they're wrong, clearly. And also completely mad. It's just that I can't quite work out why. What is the difference between offering spare bedrooms to evacuees in 1940 and offering spare bedrooms to the homeless in 2000? You might point out that the evacuees were in mortal danger; David and GoodNews would point out that the street kids have a lower life expectancy than the rest of us. You might argue that in 1940 the nation was united in its desire to look after its own; they would say that it is precisely this spirit we need now, for similar reasons. You could laugh at them, and say they were pious and sanctimonious, holy fools, moral blackmailers, zealots; they would tell you that they don't care what you think of them, that there is a greater good at stake. And do we have a moral right to keep a spare bedroom as a junk room, or a music room, or for overnight guests who never come, when it is February and freezing and wet and there are people on the pavements? Why isn't a standing order with Shelter enough? And what if my husband, or GoodNews, or both of them, turned out to be Jesus, or Gandhi, or Bob Geldof? What if the country had been crying out for this kind of energy, and they revolutionized the way we thought about private property, and homelessness was never again a problem in London, or Britain, or the Western World? What about my embarrassment then?

I no longer have the answers to any of these questions. All I know is that I don't want this party, and I don't want to put my neighbours through this, and I wish David and GoodNews were interested in starting up an Internet company so that they could make millions of pounds to spend on Page Three girls and swimming pools and cocaine and designer suits. People would understand that. That wouldn't upset the neighbours.

David and GoodNews tell the kids about the party the next morning at breakfast. Molly is curious; Tom sits at the table playing on his Gameboy and eating his cereal in between lives, apparently uninterested. I sit between the two of them while the men lean side-by-side with their backs to the work surface, answering questions. It is impossible not to notice how the dynamic in this household has changed, how my place now is with the children. And I don't mean that in the maternal sense, either; rather, I am reminded of going to large family parties when I was fourteen or fifteen, when there was always confusion as to whether I should sit with my younger cousins or with my aunts and uncles at mealtimes.

'Are we going to get a homeless person to stay, too?' Molly asks.

'Of course,' says David.

'Haven't we got ours already?' I say, with meaningful looks at all the relevant parties.

'So who else will get one?'

'Anyone who wants one,' says David, and his reply makes me snort with laughter. *Anyone who wants one . . .* It's Christmas, and this year everyone wants a homeless person, just as a couple of years ago everyone wanted a Buzz Lightyear. But at the homeless shop they never go out of stock.

'Would you like to tell us what's so funny, Katie?'

That's what he says, I swear. And he even sounds like a teacher: stern, vaguely distracted, following a script that was written a hundred years ago.

'That's not the line,' I say. I suddenly feel that, as I am the oldest child, it is incumbent on me to be the naughtiest. 'The line is, "Would you like to share the joke with the whole class?"'

'What are you talking about?'

'I get it,' says Tom. 'Don't you get it, Dad? You're the teacher and Mum's being naughty.'

'Don't be silly.'

'It's true,' says Tom. 'That's what you sound like.'

'Well, I'm very sorry. I don't mean to. Anyway. Is everybody happy about this?'

'I've got a question.' Sitting at the table with the kids, and being told off like a kid, has liberated me; my disenfranchisement has empowered me.

'Yes, Katie.'

115

'What happens if a homeless person moves into a neighbour's house and cleans them out?' It takes a child to say the unsayable.

'What do you mean?'

'I mean . . . well, that. What if we assist in moving a thief into our neighbour's house? Someone who's broke and desperate with a drug habit?'

'You're stereotyping the homeless, Katie. I'm really not sure that's the right way to go.'

'I appreciate what I'm doing, David. It's just, you know . . . The stereotype of a football fan is someone who gets drunk and breaks bottles over people's heads. And I know it's a stereotype, and I know lots of people who go to Arsenal who aren't like that. Just . . . There might actually be one or two who are. And I'm not sure I'd like to tell Ros and Max that they have to live with them.'

'I just don't think this conversation is very helpful.'

'Have you even thought about it?'

'Of course not.'

'Right. Are you going to think about it?'

'No.'

'Why not?'

'Because I want to change the way people think. And I can't change the way people think if I think like everybody else, can I? I want to believe the best of everybody. Otherwise what's the point?'

There are many, many answers to that last rhetorical question, but I can't bring myself to utter any of them. I shake my head, and get up from the table, and go to work, so that I can become an adult again.

Except, of course, work too has now been altered by my domestic circumstances, and when I get to the surgery, Dawn, the receptionist, is standing behind the desk with her mouth open and her brow furrowed, trying to make sense of a lot of very old European ladies waving their hands in the air and saying 'Hot! Very hot!', and miming sudden sprightliness (which, because they are not sprightly in any way, they have to effect with their eyes, mostly), and trying to look sad.

Dawn looks at me despairingly. 'What have you been doing?' she asks.

'Nothing,' I say, quickly enough for Dawn to deduce the opposite. 'Well, I got this guy in yesterday. A masseur. For Mrs Cortenza's back. Is that what they're on about?'

'Is he very tasty or something?'

'Oh, I don't think it's that. I think he uses –' and as I'm saying it I get a flash of déjà vu – 'I think he uses some cream or another, and . . . I think it might have some kind of effect on old ladies.'

'So what shall I tell them?'

'Oh, just . . . I don't know. Tell them to buy some liniment. It'll have the same effect. Write it down on a bit of paper and send them packing.' And I wander off down the corridor, in the vain hope that by walking away from the scene I might be able to put the whole unhappy episode behind me, but within an hour Becca has been in to see me.

'There's a rumour sweeping through the waiting room that somebody cured one of our patients,' she says accusingly. 'Somebody who's got something to do with you.'

'I'm sorry. It won't happen again.'

'I should hope not. Hey, all these old ladies are coming in to see me gabbling about somebody with hot hands who's a friend of yours. Is that the guy?'

'Which guy?'

'Affair guy?'

'No. It's . . . someone else.'

'Really someone else? Or pretend someone else, but actually, between you and me, and I promise I won't tell anyone, the same man?'

'Really someone else. Affair Guy has gone. This is Spiritual Healer Guy. The one who gave David the brain tumour. He's moved in with us.'

'And you're not sleeping with him?'

'No, I'm not sleeping with him. Jesus. I thought you might be more interested in his apparent ability to heal the sick by touching them than who he's sleeping with.'

'Not really. I only came in to ask what it's like to have sex with someone who has hot hands. But you say you don't know.'

'No, I don't know.'

'Will you tell me if you find out?'

'Becca, you seem to be labouring under the misapprehension that because of . . . recent events I will now always have a lover of some description. Infidelity's not a career, you know. I'm embarrassed about what happened before. Can you please stop joking about it?'

'Sorry.'

'What should I do about this guy?'

'Which guy? There seem to be so many.'

'Shut up.'

'Sorry, sorry.'

'Should I use him again?'

'God, no.'

'Why not?'

'We're GPs, Katie. We trained for seven years. I'm sure the world's full of people who can do a better job than we do, but we can't let the patients know that, or it's finished.'

She's right, of course. I don't want GoodNews here every day, even if he has the power to make my patients well. Especially if he has the power to make my patients well. That's my job, not his, and he's already taken too much as it is.

8

Tom doesn't own a Gameboy. I knew this, and so did David, and we watched him playing with it all through breakfast, and the impossibility of what we were seeing didn't register with either of us. And nor did I get to work and become suddenly distracted by a puzzling image, something slightly odd that I couldn't quite put my finger on. I would like to claim that a mother's intuition made me pick up the phone in order to put my mind at rest, but that is not the case: I only pick up the phone because it is ringing, and I only realize Tom doesn't own a Gameboy when David calls to tell me that we have been invited to the school, to talk to his head-teacher about our son's recent spate of thieving.

'What's he stolen?' I ask David. 'That Gameboy, for starters,' he says.

Only then does my maternal-detective instinct kick in.

When we get to the school at four, there is an array of stolen goods displayed on the headteacher's desk, like one of those memory games: there's the Gameboy, but also a couple of videotapes, an S Club 7 CD, a Tamagotchi, a whole load of Pokémon stuff, a Manchester United shirt, some half-eaten bags of sweets and, somewhat bizarrely, a paper wallet containing a classmate's holiday snaps.

'What did you want those for?' I ask Tom, but he doesn't know, predictably, and he just shrugs. He knows he has done wrong, and he's hunched up in the chair, hugging himself; but there is some part of him that is angry, too. One of the things that has always broken my heart about Tom is that when he is in trouble he stares very intently at you, and one day I realized that what he was looking for was softness, evidence that, despite your disapproval of his misdemeanour, you still loved him. Today, however, he's not interested. He won't make eye contact with anyone in the room.

'He's basically been pinching anything that wasn't nailed down,' says the head. 'He's not very popular with his schoolmates at the moment, as you can imagine.' She's a nice, intelligent, gentle woman, Jeanie Field, and she's always been very complimentary about our kids, partly, I suspect, because they demand so little of her. They come to school. They enjoy their lessons. They don't hit anyone. They go home. Now Tom has become just another drain on her time and her energy, and it is that as much as anything that is making me feel wretched.

'Have his home circumstances changed in any way?'

Where would one begin? With the Damascene conversion of his father? The discussion about which parent he would live with in the event of a divorce? The appearance of GoodNews? I look at David, to let him know that it is his unhappy task to explain the events of the last few months in a way that will embarrass nobody in the room, and he shifts uncomfortably in his seat.

'We have had some difficulties, yes.' I realize with horror that since he met GoodNews, David regards the avoidance of embarrassment as a bourgeois hang-up with which he will have no truck.

'Tom, will you wait outside, please?' I say quickly. Tom doesn't move, so I grab him by the hand, pull him to his feet, and march him outside. David starts to protest, but I just shake my head, and he shuts up.

'I'm sure Katie won't mind me saying that she had an affair,' David is saying as I come back into the room.

'I do mind you saying that, actually.' I want him to know, just for the record.

'Oh,' says David, baffled. 'It was my fault, though. I was an inattentive and ill-tempered husband. I didn't love her enough, or appreciate her properly.'

'That . . . Well, that sort of thing can happen,' says Jeanie, who clearly wishes that she were having a meeting with the knife-wielding, drug-dealing parents of an illiterate sexual deviant.

'But I . . . well, I . . . My shortcomings were revealed to me when

I met a spiritual healer, and I think I've changed. Wouldn't you say, Katie?'

'Oh, you've changed,' I say wearily.

'And the spiritual healer is currently staying with us, and we're . . . we're re-examining a lot of our lifestyle choices, and . . . Maybe, thinking about it, some of this has unsettled Tom.'

'I'd say that was a possibility, yes,' says Jeanie. I look at her, but there's no trace in her face of the dryness in her words. She knows how to do the white wine thing.

There is a knock on the door, and Tom comes back in.

'Have you finished?' he says. 'I mean, have you finished the stuff that I can't hear? About Mum's boyfriend and everything?'

We all stare at our feet.

'Sit down, Tom,' says Jeanie. He sits down in the corner of the room, in a chair that faces none of us, so we all have to turn to look at him. 'We've been talking about what might have made you do this. Whether there's anything you're not happy with at school or at home, or . . .'

'I haven't got anything,' says Tom suddenly and angrily.

'What do you mean?' Jeanie asks him.

'I haven't got anything. At home. He keeps giving it away.' He nods at his father.

'Oh, Tom,' says David, wounded. 'That's silly. You've got so much. That's why we decided together to lose some of it.'

'Hold on, hold on.' I'm missing something here. 'Tom, are you telling me there's something else apart from the computer?'

'Yeah. Loads of stuff.'

'It wasn't loads,' says David, but the impatience in his voice gives him away.

'When did this happen?'

'Last week. He made us go through our toys and get rid of half of them.'

'Why didn't you tell me?' I address the question to Tom rather than David, which is indicative of something.

'He told us not to.'

'Why do you listen to him? You know he's a lunatic.'

Jeanie stands up. 'I think these are things more profitably discussed at home,' she says gently. 'But there seems a fair bit to work on, I'd say.'

It turns out that most of what they gave away – to the women's refuge, again – was junk, or at least stuff they no longer played with. According to David, it was Molly who raised the stakes: she felt that the gifts would be meaningless unless they were really good toys, things they both enjoyed playing with. So there was an agreement (an agreement to which Tom seems to have been a somewhat reluctant signatory) to donate something from the current playlist. He gave away his radio-controlled car, and regretted it almost immediately. Here, then, is the complex psychological explanation for his life of crime: he gave some stuff away, and then wanted some other stuff to replace it.

We have a chat with Tom when we get home, and extract all the necessary guarantees about future conduct; we also agree on a fair and appropriate punishment (no TV of any kind for a week, no *Simpsons* for a month). But it is not my son I need to talk to.

'I'm getting lost,' I say to David when we are on our own. 'You have to explain things to me. Because I don't know what any of this is supposed to achieve.'

'Any of what?'

'You're turning our kids into weirdos.' Please don't say it's everyone else who's weird please don't say that please please. Because it's not true, is it? It can't be true, unless the word 'weird' means nothing at all. (But then, is it weird not to want to watch *Who Wants to be a Millionaire?* when everyone else does? Is it weird to find Big Macs inedible, when millions of people eat almost nothing else? Aha: no it isn't, because I can draw a circle within a circle – a circle around my particular postal district, as it happens – and place myself in a majority, not a minority. The only circle I can draw encompassing people who want to give their Sunday lunch and their kids' toys away, however, would be a circle around my house. That's my definition of weird. It is also fast becoming my definition of lonely, too.)

'Is it really so weird to worry about what's happening out there?'

'I don't mind you worrying. You can worry yourself sick. It's trying to do something about it that's causing all the problems.'

'Tell me what you think the problems are.'

'What I think the problems are? You don't see any?'

'I can see what might seem like problems to you. But they're not problems to me.'

'Your son becoming the Artful Dodger isn't a problem to you?'

'He'll stop taking things. And there are bigger issues at stake.'

'That's where I'm lost. I don't understand what the issues are.'

'I can't explain them. I keep trying, and I can't explain them. It's just . . . It's just about wanting to live a different life. A better life. We were living the wrong one.'

'We? We? You were the one writing the shitty novel. You were the one writing the newspaper column about how awful everyone was. I was trying to make sick people better.' I know how this sounds, but he makes me so angry. I'm a good person, I'm a doctor, I know I had an affair but that doesn't make me bad, that doesn't mean I have to give away everything I own or watch while my children give away everything they own . . .

'I know I'm asking a lot. Maybe too much. Maybe it's not fair, and maybe you'll decide that you can't put up with it. That's your business. But there's nothing I can do about it now. I just . . . The scales have fallen from my eyes, Katie. I was living a wasted life.'

'But where is this going to get you?'

'That's not the point.'

'What is the point? Please tell me, because I don't understand.'

'The point is . . . The point is how I feel. I don't care what gets done. I just don't want to die feeling that I never tried. I don't believe in Heaven, or anything. But I want to be the kind of person that qualifies for entry anyway. Do you understand?'

Of course I understand. I'm a doctor.

Later, half-asleep, I start to dream about all the people in the world who live bad lives – all the drug-dealers and arms manufacturers and corrupt politicians, all the cynical bastards everywhere – getting touched by GoodNews and changing like David has changed. The dream scares me. Because I need these people – they serve as my compass. Due south there are saints and nurses and teachers in inner-city schools; due north there are managing directors of tobacco companies and angry local newspaper columnists. Please don't take my due north away, because then I will be adrift, lost in a land where the things I have done and the things I haven't done really mean something.

The next day is Thursday, when I have an afternoon off, so, when Tom comes back from school, I take him out for a walk. He is deeply resistant to and utterly confused by the idea – 'What are we going to do on this walk? Where are we walking to?' – and if he were in any position to refuse then he would. But he is in trouble, and he knows it, and he is smart enough to realize that if a stroll round the nearest park helps him in any way, then it is a detour worth taking.

It hurts and worries me to say it, but I have become less fond of Tom and Molly. I have been aware of this for a while, and have always presumed that this was perfectly normal – how could I feel the same about this quiet, occasionally surly boy as I did about his smiling, miraculous two-year-old counterpart? But now I'm not so sure. Now I'm beginning to wonder whether he should not, in fact, be more lovable than he is, and whether the shortfall in lovability is due to something unattractive in him, or something unmaternal in me.

'It's not my fault, so don't say it is,' he says when we're ten yards from the house. No, there's no doubt about it: he should be nicer than this.

'Why isn't it your fault?'

''Cos it's Dad's fault. And GoodNews's.'

'They stole that stuff?'

'No. But they made me steal it.'

'They made you. How did they make you?'

'You know how they made me.'

'Tell me.'

'They've been depriving me.'

'And what does "depriving" mean?'

'Like those kids at school. You said they were deprived.'

He asked me once why a certain group of boys at his school were always in trouble, and I – perhaps, in retrospect, unwisely – introduced the concept of deprivation. I thought I was doing my duty as a right-thinking mother; it turned out that I was merely providing mitigation for my own son's criminality.

'That's different.'

'Why is it?'

'Because . . .'

'You said they didn't have very much at home, and that's why they got in trouble. And now I haven't got very much at home. And that's why I'm getting in trouble.'

'You don't think you've got very much at home.'

'Not any more I haven't.'

I'm becoming heartily sick of liberalism. It's complicated, and tiring, and open to misinterpretation and abuse by . . . by sneaky, spoiled children. And it breeds doubt, and I'm sick of doubt, too; I want certitude, like David has certitude, or like Margaret Thatcher had certitude. Who wants to be someone like me? People like us? Because we're almost always sure that we're wrong; we're almost always sure that we will go to hell, even though an inordinate amount of our waking thoughts are directed towards achieving the opposite effect. We know what's right but we don't do it because it's too hard, it asks too much, and even trying to cure Mrs Cortenza or Barmy Brian is no guarantee of anything, so I somehow end each day in debit rather than credit. Today I have learned that I don't really like my children and that I have somehow encouraged one of them to steal from his classmates; David, meanwhile, has been plotting to save the homeless. And yet somehow I still cling to the belief that I'm better than him.

'Tom, you're turning into a horrible, whining boy,' I tell him, without any explanation, and without any acknowledgement that he has been created by horrible, whining adults. We finish our walk in silence.

*

We haven't had a meal with friends since Before GoodNews, but on the Friday night we go to our friends Andrew and Cam for supper. GoodNews is babysitting: he offered, and the kids seemed OK about it, and as we'd actually failed to arrange an alternative, the offer was gratefully accepted. Andrew and Cam are People Like Us, alarmingly so: Andrew has a perilous toehold on the bottom rung of the media ladder, except it's not really perilous, because if he lost his footing he wouldn't actually fall very far, nor would he do himself or his family very much damage. He has a monthly books column in a men's fitness magazine, and is therefore probably the world's least-read literary critic. He is, of course, writing something else – a screenplay, rather than a novel, felicitously, so David can commiserate rather than feel threatened, and they can – could – both bitch happily about awful films they have seen or terrible novels they have read, and the bitching miraculously becomes mutually supportive and comradely, rather than merely unpleasant. Cam works in the Health Service as a manager, and she's nice enough, but we don't have an awful lot in common: she is Health Service-obsessed and has never wanted children, whereas I am happy never to talk about work if there is another conversational topic, including children, on offer. We are nice to each other because we both recognize the value of this relationship to our angry, frustrated menfolk.

Except now, suddenly, my man is neither angry nor frustrated. Andrew doesn't know this yet. He phoned, he invited, I accepted, I hung up, and there was no opportunity to mention the Finsbury Park Miracle. David seems unconcerned. In the car on the way over (we usually take a minicab, but David has shown no desire to drink more than the occasional glass of wine, so he is driving), I ask him gently whether he'll be telling Andrew about GoodNews.

'Why?'

'No reason.'

'Do you think I shouldn't?'

'No. I mean . . . You know, if you want to, you should.'

'I'll be perfectly honest with you, Katie. I've found it's quite hard to talk about. Without coming across as a weirdo.'

'Yes.'

'Why do you think that is?'

'I've no idea.'

'People are blinkered, don't you think?'

'That must be it. Maybe best to leave the subject alone, then.'

'I think you're right. Until I've . . . Until I've developed the language to talk about it properly.'

All sorts of muscles all over me relax, and I hadn't even realized I was tense, although I still get the feeling that this evening might be tricky. 'What do you think you'll talk about, then?'

'I'm sorry?'

'What do you think we'll talk about? How will the conversation go?'

'How should I know? What a peculiar question, Katie. You've been for dinner at people's houses before. You know how it works. Things come up and then we discuss them.'

'That's true in theory.'

'What does that mean?'

'Well, that's how it works in most cases. But when we see Andrew and Cam, we walk in, and then Andrew says that so-and-so's a wanker and his new book is awful, and you say that the new film by somebody else is unintentionally hilarious – even though nine times out of ten I know for a fact you haven't seen it – and Cam and I sit there smiling and sometimes laughing if you're being funny instead of just plain nasty, and then you get drunk and tell Andrew he's a genius, and he gets drunk and tells you you're a genius, and then we go home.'

David chuckles. 'Nonsense.'

'Suit yourself.'

'Really? That's your impression of our evenings with Andrew and Cam?'

'It's not an impression.'

'I'm sorry if that's what you think.'

'It's not what I think. It's what happens.'

'We'll see.'

We walk in, we're offered a drink, we sit down.

'How are you?' Cam asks.

'We're fine, I think,' I reply.

'Better than that fuckwit J—, then,' says Andrew gleefully. That's all it takes – 'We're fine', because us being fine gives him the opportunity to talk about someone who isn't fine: J— is a well-known writer who has had a famously bad time of late. His new novel has had unanimously stinking reviews and failed to reach the bestseller lists; meanwhile his wife has left him for one of his younger rivals. The old David would have drunk deep from this cup, but the new one simply looks discomforted.

'Yes,' says David mildly. 'He's been having a bad time, hasn't he?'

'Yes,' says Andrew. And then, presumably because David has, in his own way, responded to the bit about J— having a bad time, but not to the bit about J— being a fuckwit, he adds, hopefully, 'Fuckwit.'

'How are you two?' says David.

Andrew looks mystified: twice he has offered the hand of enmity, twice it has been refused. He tries one more time. 'We're better than that fuckwit J—, too,' he says, and laughs at his own joke.

'That's good,' says David. 'I'm glad.'

Andrew chuckles maliciously, as if David has somehow taken the bait. 'Did you read that review in the *Sunday Times*? Man, I'd have thrown my WP out of the window and emigrated.'

'I didn't read it.'

'I've got it somewhere. I was thinking of having it framed. Shall I dig it out?'

'No, it's fine.'

Usually by this point Cam and I have left them to it, and the four has folded neatly into two pairs along the gender crease, but now there is no 'it' to which we can leave them, so we sit there listening quietly.

'How come you missed it?'

'I . . . well, I've stopped reading reviews. I'm too busy.'

'Ooooh, get you. That's put me in my place.'

'No, no, I'm sorry. I didn't mean to imply that those who had the time to read reviews were, you know, were inferior in any way. I don't want to judge anyone.'

'You don't want to judge anyone?' Andrew laughs delightedly. David, the man who sits at the head of the top table in the High Court of all judgements, saying he doesn't want to judge anyone! This, you can see Andrew thinking, is irony taken to new, impossibly sophisticated levels.

'So. How come you're too busy to read reviews all of a sudden? What have you been up to?'

'Right now I'm . . . Well, I'm trying to sort out a neighbourhood adopt-a-street-kid campaign sort of thing.'

There is a pause, and both Andrew and Cam study David's face before the laughter starts again, this time from both of them. The laughter clearly stings David: his ears go red, as if the laughs had little brambles on them that prick him as they enter his head.

'When you say you're trying to sort it out,' says Andrew, 'do you mean you're trying to stop it?'

'No,' David says meekly. 'I'm trying to start it.'

The first traces of doubt are visible on Andrew's face now.

'How d'you mean?'

'Oh, it's a long story. I'll tell you another time.'

'Right.'

There is a long, long silence.

'Who wants to eat?' Cam says.

Here is a list of the people that Andrew and David have hitherto regarded as talentless, overrated, or simply wankers: Oasis, the Stones, Paul McCartney, John Lennon, Robbie Williams, Kingsley Amis, Martin Amis, Evelyn Waugh, Auberon Waugh, Salman Rushdie, Jeffrey Archer, Tony Blair, Gordon Brown, William Shakespeare (although to be fair they despise the comedies and some of the history plays only), Charles Dickens, E. M. Forster, Daniel Day-Lewis, the Monty Python team, Gore Vidal, John Updike, Thomas Harris, Gabriel García Márquez, Milan Kundera, Damien Hirst, Tracey Emin, Melvyn Bragg, Dennis Bergkamp, David Beckham, Ryan Giggs, Sam Mendes, Anthony Burgess, Virginia Woolf,

Michael Nyman, Philip Glass, Steven Spielberg, Leonardo DiCaprio, Ted Hughes, Mark Hughes, Sylvia Plath, Stevie Smith, Maggie Smith, the Smiths, Alan Ayckbourn, Harold Pinter, David Mamet, Tom Stoppard, of course, all other contemporary playwrights, Garrison Keillor, Sue Lawley, James Naughtie, Jeremy Paxman, Carole King, James Taylor, Kenneth Branagh, Van Morrison, Jim Morrison, Courtney Love, Courteney Cox and the entire cast of *Friends*, Ben Elton, Stephen Fry, Andre Agassi, Pete Sampras and all contemporary male tennis players, Monica Seles and all female tennis players throughout history, Pele, Maradona, Linford Christie, Maurice Greene ('How can a sprinter who's faster than anyone else be overrated?' I asked once, despairingly, but I received no satisfactory reply), T. S. Eliot and Ezra Pound, Gilbert and Sullivan, Gilbert and George, Ben and Jerry, Powell and Pressburger, Marks and Spencer, the Coen Brothers, Stevie Wonder, Nicole Farhi and anyone who designs fucking suits for a living, Naomi Campbell, Kate Moss, Johnny Depp, Stephen Sondheim, Bart Simpson (but not Homer Simpson), Homer, Virgil, Coleridge, Keats and all the Romantic poets, Jane Austen, all the Brontës, all the Kennedys, the people who made the film of *Trainspotting*, the people who made the film of *Lock, Stock and Two Smoking Barrels*, Madonna, the Pope, anyone they were at school or college with who is now making a name for themselves in the fields of journalism, broadcasting or the arts, and many, many others, so many others, too many to list here. It is easier, in fact, to write down the people in world history that they both like: Bob Dylan (although not recently), Graham Greene, Quentin Tarantino and Tony Hancock. I can't remember anyone else ever receiving the double thumbs-up from these two guardians of our culture.

I got sick of hearing why everybody was useless, and ghastly, and talentless, and awful, and how they didn't deserve anything good that had happened to them, and they completely deserved anything bad that had happened to them, but this evening I long for the old David – I miss him like one might miss a scar, or a wooden leg, something disfiguring but characteristic. You knew where you were with the old David. And I never felt any embarrassment, ever. Weary despair, sure, the occasional nasty taste in the mouth, certainly, flashes of irritation almost constantly, but never any embarrassment. I had become comfortable with his cynicism, and in any case, we're all cynical now, although it's only this evening that I recognize this properly. Cynicism is our shared common language, the Esperanto that actually caught on, and though I'm not fluent in it – I like too many things, and I am not envious of enough people – I know enough to get by. And in any case it is not possible to avoid cynicism and the sneer completely. Any conversation about, say, the London mayoral contest, or Demi Moore, or Posh and Becks and Brooklyn, and you are obliged to be sour, simply to prove that you are a fully functioning and reflective metropolitan person.

I no longer understand very much about the man I live with, but I understand enough to know that this evening is almost bound to throw up a decisive moment, a moment where David's new-found earnestness, his desire to love and understand even the most way-ward of God's creatures, will be met with blank incomprehension. As it turns out, the wayward creature turns out to be the outgoing President of the United States, and it is Cam, not Andrew, who is on the receiving end of David's terrifying sincerity. We're talking – as best we can, from a position of almost fathomless ignorance – about the US primaries, and Cam says that she doesn't really care about who the next president is as long as he keeps his thing in his trousers and doesn't monster young interns, and David shifts in his seat and eventually wonders, with a patent reluctance, who we are to judge, and Cam laughs at him.

'I mean it,' says David. 'I no longer want to condemn people whose lives I know nothing about.'

'But . . . that's the basis for all conversation!' says Andrew.

'I'm tired of it,' says David. 'We don't know anything about him.'

'We know more than we want to.'

'What do you know?' David asks him.

'We know he puts it about.'

'Do we? And even if he does, do we know why?'

131

'What?' says Cam. 'Society is to blame? Or Hillary? I don't believe this, David.'

'What don't you believe?'

'You're sticking up for Clinton.'

'I'm not sticking up for him. I'm just sick of all the poison. The drip drip drip of slagging off and cheap cracks and judgements of people we don't know and the endless nastiness of it all. It makes me want to have a bath.'

'Be our guest,' says Andrew. 'There's a clean towel up there.'

'But Bill Clinton!' says Cam. 'I mean, if you can't be rude about him, who can you be rude about?'

'I don't know the facts. You don't know the facts.'

'The facts? The most powerful man in the world – the most powerful married man in the world – gets a blow-job off a twenty-something-year-old and lies about it afterwards.'

'I think he must have been a very troubled and unhappy man,' says David.

'I don't believe this,' says Andrew. 'You used to e-mail me filthy Clinton and Lewinsky jokes all the time.'

'I wish I hadn't,' David says with a vehemence that causes visible bafflement on a couple of the faces round the table. We all concentrate very hard on our tricolore.

I venture an entirely positive opinion on our hosts' newly reno-vated kitchen, and we are happy for a while, but it clearly occurs to all of us simultaneously that there are very few subjects which offer that kind of harmony, and every now and again one of the three of us slips up, as if we are suffering from cultural Tourette's. I make a disparaging remark about Jeffrey Archer's literary ability (a passing observation – not even an observation, more a simile – buried in the middle of an otherwise unexceptionable exchange about a TV programme) and David tells me that I have no conception of how hard it is to write a book. Cam makes a joke about a politician who has recently been jailed for embezzlement, a man who has become a byword for untrustworthiness, and David makes a plea for forgiveness. Andrew has a little sneer about Ginger Spice's role with the UN and David says it is better to do something than nothing.

In other words, it is impossible: we cannot function properly, and the evening ends in confusion and awkwardness, and very early. There is a consensus in our particular postal district that people like Ginger Spice and Bill Clinton and Jeffrey Archer are beyond the pale, and if someone goes around sticking up for them then that consensus fails, and all is anarchy. Is it possible to want to divorce a man simply because he doesn't want to be rude about Ginger Spice? I rather fear it might be.

9

The party invitations have been sent out, and most evenings now David and GoodNews lock themselves away in David's study to finesse their plan of attack. I attempted to use that phrase humorously the other day, but the generals concerned just looked at me blankly – not just because they react to most attempts at humour in that way, but because they really do see this as a military campaign, a crusade in the original, eleventh-century sense. Our neighbours have become infidels, barbarians; GoodNews and David are going to batter their doors down with the heads of the homeless.

'Can't you just enjoy it as a party?' David says at breakfast, when I have complained once too often. 'You like parties. Ignore the other bit.'

'Ignore the bit where you harangue our friends and neighbours in my kitchen about the homeless?'

'First, it's our kitchen. Second, I'm not haranguing them – I'm talking to them, making suggestions about how we can create a better society in our street. And third, I'm going to do it in the living room, standing on a chair.'

'You've completely turned me around,' I say. 'What can I do to help?'

'We're making cheese straws,' says Molly. 'You could do the sandwiches.'

'I'm not making cheese straws,' says Tom.

'Why not?' Molly is genuinely amazed that anyone could be this truculent when there is so much fun to be had.

'Stupid.'

'What do you want to make, then?'

'I don't want to make anything. I don't want this party.'

'Dad, Tom says he doesn't want this party.' She adds a little incredulous chuckle to the end of her report.

'Not all of us feel the same way about things, Molly,' says David.

'You going to give anyone any more of my stuff?'

'This thing isn't about that,' says David, somehow managing to imply that there might be another thing, later on, which is.

GoodNews comes in just as we're all about to leave for work and school. He gets up at five-thirty but never comes downstairs until after half-past eight; I don't know what he does up there for three hours, but I suspect that it's something that even the most spiritual of us wouldn't do for more than a few minutes. Molly and David greet him warmly, I nod, Tom glowers at him.

'What's up? What's the word?'

'Yeah, good,' says David.

'I'm going to make cheese straws,' says Molly.

'That's great,' says GoodNews, to whom everything is good news. 'I've been thinking. What about some kind of medal? For those who volunteer on the spot?'

I don't want to hear about medals. I don't want to hear about parties or cheese straws, and I fantasize about spending the evening of the party in a cocktail bar with a girlfriend, drinking Slow Comfortable Screws or some other equally vulgar and anti-homeless concoction, hopefully at seven pounds a throw. I say goodbye to my children, but not to my husband or to GoodNews, and go to work.

As I'm walking down the path a woman I don't know – mid-forties, slightly stroppy-looking, too much lipstick, lines around her mouth that suggests she's spent the last couple of decades pursing her lips disapprovingly – stops me.

'Did you invite me to a party?'

'Not me. My husband.'

'I got an invitation.'

'Yes.'

'Why?' This is the question that most of our neighbours would want answered, but which only the unpleasant or mad ones would actually ask.

'What do you mean, why?'

'Why did your husband invite me to a party? He doesn't know me.'

'No. But he'd like to.'

'Why?'

I look at her, and I can just about make out an aura of unpleasantness hovering above her head; I'm presuming that this particular 'why' is rhetorical, and that no one has ever wanted or could ever want to know her.

'Because he has this mad vision that everyone in this street could love each other and get on with each other and Webster Road would be this lovely, happy place to live and we'd be in and out of each other's houses and maybe each other's beds and in any case we'd really look after each other. And he really wants you to . . . What's your name?'

'Nicola.'

'He really wants you, Nicola, to be a part of all this.'

'What night is it? Wednesday?'

'Wednesday.'

'I'm busy Wednesdays. I do women's self-defence.'

I raise my palms and make a sad face, and she walks on. But I have a lot to thank her for: I can see the fun in this. Who would have thought that a desire to make the world a better place could be so aggressive? Maybe David hasn't changed at all. Maybe all he ever wanted to do was upset people who need upsetting.

'Would you like to come to a party?'

Mr Chris James stares at me. We have just been arguing for ten minutes about my refusal to provide a note explaining his absence from work for the previous fortnight; it is my belief that he was not ill. (It is my belief, in fact, that he has been in Florida or somewhere on holiday, because when he was rummaging in his pockets for a biro he managed to spill a whole handful of American small change all over the floor, and got very defensive when I asked him where he got it from.)

'What sort of party?'

'The usual sort. Drink, food, conversation, dancing.' There will be no dancing, of course – it's more your standing-around-listening-to-a-man-standing-on-a-chair-and-lecturing-you party than a dancing party – but Mr James isn't to know that. (He isn't to know that there is unlikely to be very much conversation, either, given the nature of the evening, but if I tell the truth then it doesn't really sound like much of an invitation.)

'What are you asking me for?'

'I'm asking all my regulars.' This is not true either, obviously, although I certainly intend to ask the patients I don't like very much, which may well turn out to be the regulars, many of whom I have learned to dislike.

'I don't want to come to a party. I want a doctor's note.'

'You'll have to settle for a doctor's invitation.'

'Shove it.'

I raise my palms and make a sad face, and Mr James walks out of my surgery. This is great! I'm not exactly killing with kindness, but I'm certainly leaving the odd flesh wound. I am a convert.

Barmy Brian Beech, Heartsink Number One, has come in to ask whether he can help me with the operations.

'I wouldn't want to do the actual cutting bits. Not straight away. I'd have to have a look at what to take out and all that.'

'I'm a doctor,' I tell him. 'I don't do operations.'

'Who does, then?'

'Surgeons. In hospitals.'

'You're just saying that,' he says. 'You're just saying that because you don't want me to help.'

It is true that if I were a surgeon, Barmy Brian would not be my first choice as assistant, but as I am not, I don't have to have that particular conversation. I just have to have this one, which is in itself tortuous enough.

'Just give me a chance,' he says. 'Just one chance. And if I mess it up, I won't ask again.'

'Do you want to come to a party?' I ask him. He looks at me, all surgical ambitions suddenly abandoned, and I have achieved my immediate ambition, namely, to lead Brian away from a putative career in medicine. I have, however, invited him to a party at my house – not something I had thought of doing before. This party isn't mine, though. It's David's.

'How many people are at a party? More than seventeen?'

'There'll be more than seventeen at this one, probably. Why?'

'I can't go anywhere where there's more than seventeen people. That's why I couldn't work at the supermarket, you see. There are loads of people there, aren't there?'

I concede that the combined staff and customer numbers at the supermarket regularly exceed seventeen.

'Well, there you are,' he says. 'Could I come maybe the day after, when they've all gone?'

'Then it wouldn't be a party, though.'

'No.'

'We'll try and have one with sixteen. Another time.'

'Would you?'

'I'll see what I can do.'

For the first time ever, Brian leaves the surgery happy. And that makes me happy, until I realize that all this happiness comes as a direct result of David's lunacy, and that, far from sabotaging David's plans, I'm actually endorsing them. I have just been nice to exactly the kind of person David thinks I should be nice to, and as a consequence that person's life has been momentarily ameliorated. I don't like the implications of that.

It goes without saying that the old David hated parties. To be precise, he *hated* throwing parties. To be even more precise, to be as precise as that BMW engineer in the TV ads, he hated *the idea* of throwing parties, because we never went as far as actually throwing one, not once in twenty years together. Why did he want a load of people he didn't like putting cigarettes out on his carpet? Why did he want to stay up until three in the morning just because Becca or some other arsehole friend of mine was drunk and wouldn't go home? These were, as you may have guessed, rhetorical questions. I never actually attempted to argue all the reasons why he might have wanted cigarette burns on the carpet.

The way the rhetorical questions were phrased, I felt, indicated that I was highly unlikely to persuade him that parties could be FUN!, or that seeing all one's friends together in one place was GREAT! That wasn't how things used to work.

I start thinking about all sorts of things that didn't use to work in the way that they are working now, and I don't know how I feel about it. Here's something: David used to spend a lot of money on CDs and books, and sometimes, when he wasn't working properly, we used to argue about it, even though – or probably because – I am unhappy that I have become a culture-free organism. I know that he tried to hide new things from me, by burying the CDs on the shelves, playing new ones when I was out, scuffing paperbacks around a bit so that I wouldn't notice their newness. But now he has lost interest completely. He doesn't go out much, and the review sections of newspapers are thrown away untouched. And, if I am honest, I miss what he brought to the household. I may have become an unwitting convert to an extremist religion that regards all forms of entertainment as frivolity and self-indulgence, but I secretly enjoyed living with someone who knew what Liam Gallagher does for a living, and now that has gone.

And here's another thing: he doesn't make jokes, not proper ones, anyway. He tries to make the kids laugh, in a 1960s children's television kind of way – he puts things that aren't hats on his head, which is always a hoot, he uses pieces of fruit as ventriloquist's dummies ('Hello, Mr Banana' 'Hello, Mrs Strawberry', that sort of thing), he pretends to be a Spice Girl, etc., and so on. Molly laughs falsely, Tom looks at him as if he were attempting to defecate rather than amuse. But adults (in other words, me, because Good-News doesn't look like he spends a lot of time at his local comedy club) . . . forget it. His relentless quest for the gag in everything used to drive me potty, because he'd get this look on his face when you were talking to him, and it would fool you into thinking that he was listening to what you were saying, and then some elaborate and usually nasty witticism would come darting out of his mouth like Hannibal Lecter's tongue, and I would either laugh, or, more often, walk out of the room, slamming the door on the way. But every now and again – say, five per cent of the time – something would hit me right on the end of my funny bone, and however serious I felt, or angry, or distracted, he'd get the reaction he was looking for.

So now I very rarely walk out of the room and slam the door; on the other hand, I never laugh. And I would have to say that as a consequence I am slightly worse off. Part of the reason I married David in the first place was that he made me laugh, and now he doesn't, doesn't even want to, and part of me wants my money back. Am I entitled to it? What if a sense of humour is like hair – something a lot of men lose as they get older?

But here we are, in the real world, the world of now, and in the world of now David doesn't make jokes and we are having a party, a party for all the people in our street, many of whom David has been extremely rude about, on very thin evidence (coats, cars, faces, visitors, shopping bags). And before I know it, the doorbell is ringing, and the first of our guests is standing on the doorstep with a puzzled but not altogether unfriendly smile on his face and a bottle of Chardonnay in his hand.

The puzzled face belongs to Simon, one half of a gay couple who have just moved in to number 25. His partner, Richard, an actor whom Tom claims to have seen in *The Bill*, is coming along later.

'Am I the first?' asks Simon.

'Someone's got to be,' I say, and we both chuckle, and then stare at each other. David comes over to join us.

'Someone's got to be first,' says David, and all three of us chuckle. (This does not qualify as a joke, by the way. Yes, David said something that was designed to lighten the atmosphere, and yes, I registered audible amusement, but these are special, desperate circumstances.)

'How long have you been living in the street?' I ask Simon.

'Oh, how long is it now? Two months? Long enough for it to feel like home. Not long enough for us to have unpacked all our boxes.' You remember that bit in *Fawlty Towers* when Basil's car broke down, and he got out, and started beating it with the branch of a tree? You remember how when the first time you saw it you laughed until you were almost sick? That is more or less the effect that Simon's box witticism has on David and me. You had to be there, I suppose.

Molly comes over with a bowl of cheese straws and offers one to all of us. 'Tom says you were in *The Bill*,' she says to Simon.

'That wasn't me. I'm not an actor. That was Richard.'

'Who's Richard?'

'My boyfriend.'

You may have thought that this was the first straight line (if you'll excuse both puns) that Simon has delivered since he arrived, but you'd be wrong, because if something makes somebody laugh, then by definition it must be funny, and by referring to Richard as his boyfriend, Simon makes Molly laugh. A lot. Not immediately: first she blushes, and stares at her parents in awe; then she collapses into uncontrollable giggles and whoops.

'Your boyfriend!' she repeats, when she has enough breath to do any repeating. 'Your boyfriend!'

'That's not funny,' says David, but because he is looking at Simon sympathetically when he says it, Molly gets the wrong end of the stick, and thinks that Simon is being told off.

'He was only being silly, Daddy. Don't be cross with him.'

'Go away now, Molly,' I tell her. 'Other people would like some of those cheese straws.'

'There aren't any other people.'

'Just go.'

'I'm so sorry,' David and I say simultaneously, although neither of us offers any explanation as to why our daughter thinks that a man with a boyfriend is the best joke she has ever heard.

'Never mind,' says Simon. And then, just to break the silence, 'This was such a good idea.'

I am so convinced that he is being sarcastic that I snort.

The doorbell rings again, and this time it is Nicola, the unpleasant woman with the pursed-lip lines who wasn't going to be able to come because of her self-defence class. She hasn't brought a bottle.

'I cancelled my self-defence class.'

'Good for you.' I introduce her to Simon, and leave the two of them talking about whether the council should introduce a parking scheme in our neighbourhood.

The room fills up. Richard from *The Bill* arrives, and I forbid Molly to talk to him. The Asian family from next-door-but-one arrives, and GoodNews attempts to engage them in a debate about Eastern mysticism. I am chatted up by the seedy-looking builder from number 17 whose wife is in bed with flu. My brother Mark turns up, looking baffled. David must have invited him, because I didn't. I have no idea whether Mark is supposed to be a recipient or a donor of the expected largesse: he's right on the dividing line.

'What's going on?' he asks me.

'I don't know,' I say.

'Who are these people?'

'I don't know.'

He wanders off.

Remarkably, the party has started to resemble a party: people are laughing, talking, drinking, and the doorbell keeps ringing, and before long there is no more space in the living room, and people have spilled over into the kitchen. After a couple of glasses of wine, I even begin to feel a little sentimental. You know – here we all are, black, white, gay, straight, a microcosm of swinging, multicultural, multisexual London, eating cheese straws and talking about traffic schemes and mortgages, and getting on and isn't this great? And then David stands on a chair and bangs a saucepan with a wooden spoon, and I am woken from my little reverie.

'Good evening, everyone,' says David.

'Good evening,' shouts Mike, the seedy looking builder, who, as luck would have it, is A Character.

'When our invitation dropped through your letterbox, you probably thought to yourself, "What's the catch? Why is this guy who I don't know from Adam inviting us to a party?"'

'I'm only here for the beer,' shouts Mike.

'Well, it is Double Diamond,' shouts somebody else.

'No it isn't,' Mike shouts back. The two shouters are convulsed for what seems like several minutes.

'I'd love to tell you that there isn't a catch, but there is. A big catch. Because tonight I'm going to ask you to change people's lives, and maybe change your own life, too.'

'Backs to the wall!' shouts Mike. You don't have to be a psychoanalyst to worry about someone who thinks that changing one's own life probably has something to do with homosexuality.

'How many of you have got a spare bedroom?' David asks.

'Yes, thank you,' Mike shouts. 'It's where I sleep when the missus won't have me in with her.'

'So that's one,' says David. 'Any more?'

Most people choose to examine either their wine glasses or their feet.

'Don't be shy,' David says. 'I'm not going to ask you to do anything you don't want to do. All I know is that this street is full of three-storey houses, and there must be quite a few empty rooms somewhere, because you haven't all got two-point-four children.'

'What about if you live in a flat?' asks a young guy in a leather jacket.

'Is it a one-bedroom flat?'

'Yes.'

'Well, you haven't got a spare bedroom.'

'Can I go home, then?'

'You can go home any time you want. This is a party, not a detention centre.'

'Could have fooled me,' shouts Mike. His partner in comedy, the man who made the Double Diamond witticism, has come to stand by him, and offers him his hand for a high-five.

'I'm sorry to hear you're not enjoying yourself.' For a moment I think I catch a glimpse of the old David, visible like old paint through the new undercoat: there's a sarcasm in there that only I would be able to hear. The old taste for verbal confrontation is peeking out, too, because he doesn't say anything else: he's waiting for Mike's follow-up, his next crack, and Mike hasn't got one, because in the end he's merely a bit of a twit, someone who would shout out daft things at any sort of gathering with alcohol, be it a wedding or a christening or a save-the-world party such as this, and

143

he wants to push things so far but no further, and now David is calling his bluff.

'Aren't you having a very nice time?'

'No, you're all right,' says Mike, deflated.

'Because *Eastenders* probably starts in a minute.' And that gets a laugh – not a huge one, but bigger than anything Mike has managed so far.

'I don't watch *Eastenders*,' says Mike. 'I don't watch any soaps, actually.' This gets the biggest laugh so far, but they're laughing at him, at the banality of the riposte, and the laughter clearly stings him a little bit.

'So you're staying?'

'I'll finish my drink, anyway.'

'Glad to hear it.'

Another chuckle, and now they're on his side. David has put down a heckler, and I feel obscurely, perhaps nostalgically proud. Now I come to think of it, heckler downputting would have been the perfect job for the old David. He had just the right combination of belligerence and quickwittedness. He'd have made a terrible stand-up, because he mumbles quite a lot, and loses the thread, in an unamusing, bumbling way, and anyway the objects of his derision were always obscure and complicated (theatre curtains, small tubs of ice-cream, etc.). But maybe if he'd teamed up with a comedian, he could have been brought on at crucial moments, like an anaesthetist. Maybe that was his calling. (And is that the nicest thing I can find to say about his talent? That it is perfectly suited to quelling verbal insurrection at alcoholic gatherings? This is hardly the mark of a polymath. Hardly the mark of someone lovable, either.)

He pauses, to let the mood change.

'Now, where was I? Oh yeah. Spare bedrooms. See, I don't know about you, but I turn on the TV, or I pick up a paper, and something terrible's happening in Kosovo or Uganda or Ethiopia, and sometimes I call a number and I give a tenner, and it changes nothing. The terrible thing continues to happen. And I feel guilty and powerless, and I continue to feel guilty and powerless when I go out later, to the pictures or for a curry or to the pub . . .'

The pub! The pub! Which 'pub' would that be, David? The 'local'? The Patronizing Bastard?

'. . . And maybe I'm feeling guilty and powerless enough to keep it going, this feeling of wanting to do something, and there's this kid sitting by the cashpoint with a blanket and a dog, and I give him fifty pence, and that changes nothing either, because next time I go to the cashpoint he's still sitting there, and my fifty pence has done nothing. Well, of course it's done nothing, because it's fifty pence, and if I give him ten fifty pences, well, that'll do nothing either, because that's five quid. And I hate him sitting there. I think we all do. If you think about it for ten seconds, you can sort of guess just how horrible it would be, sleeping in the cold, begging for change, getting rained on, people coming up and abusing you . . .'

I look around. He's doing OK, apart from the pub bit. People are listening, and one or two are nodding, but you couldn't say that the light of conversion was shining in their eyes. He needs to pull something out of the bag, before he loses them.

Luckily, someone does it for him.

'I don't believe this,' says Mike. 'They're all arseholes, these people.'

'Which people?'

'These bloody homeless people. And they're loaded, half of them. Loads of money.'

'Ah,' says David. 'Loads of money. Which is why they sit on the pavement begging?'

'That's how they get it, isn't it? And then they blow it on drugs. I've been looking for bricklayers for six months, and have I heard from any of that lot? Course I haven't. They don't want to work.'

There are a couple of snorts, one or two tuts, a great deal of head-shaking and exchanged glances followed by raised eyebrows. Mike is surrounded by gay actors, Health Service professionals, teachers, psychoanalysts, people whose hearts bleed right through their Gap T-shirts, and even if, in the middle of the night, they catch themselves thinking that the homeless only have themselves to blame and they all take drugs and have bank balances bigger than ours, they would never ever say so out loud, during waking hours, and especially not at a party. Mike has misjudged his audience, and in doing so, he changes the dynamic in the room. Two minutes ago, David was talking to a lot of bemused faces; no one here wished him any ill, but neither were they willing to pledge a substantial part of their house to his cause. Now, it's different. Whose side are they on? Are they going to line up with the forces of right-wing darkness, i.e., Mike? Or are they on the side of the (slightly eccentric, possibly misguided, but angelic nonetheless) angels? Hurrah for angels! the psychoanalysts cry. Down with the right-wing forces of darkness! shout the gay actors. Not that there's any actual shouting, of course. They're too restrained for that. But Mike certainly has a little more floor space than he did. People have shuffled away from him, as if he were about to launch into some fancy dance routine.

'If that's how you feel, then you wouldn't be interested in what I've got to say.'

'No. I'm not. But I'm still finishing my drink.'

'You're welcome to finish your drink. But could I ask you to keep your views to yourself? I'm not sure whether anyone here is very interested in them.'

'That's 'cos they're a lot of stuck-up ponces.'

Mike's floor space expands a little further. He could do a break-dancing routine now without landing on anyone's head. Even the other half of his comedy duo has moved away from him. Mike has called David the thing that most people in this room fear being called; after all, we want to fit in, become part of the neighbourhood. We want Mike to be one of us, and we want Mike to want us to be his neighbours. It is true that he probably paid a few hundred pounds for his house back in the late sixties, when nobody like us wanted to live here, and some of us paid a quarter of a million pounds for our houses a couple of years ago. (Not David and I, though! We paid a hundred thousand for our house ten years ago!) But does that make us ponces? After all, Mike's house is worth a quarter of a million, too, now. But of course that's not the point.

The point is that we are the sort of people who can afford to pay a quarter of a million for a house (or rather, we are the sort of people to whom banks will lend a quarter of a million for a house); which makes us the sort of people who give money to beggars (and no wonder, if we are mad enough to pay a quarter of a million for a house); and then there's the pub at the end of the road, which once upon a time Mike might have drunk in, but which has now changed hands and clientele and serves Spanish sausages on a bed of something-or-other for ten pounds, and isn't really a pub at all, and let's face it, the ponces are responsible for that, as well as for other things, like the corner shop becoming an organic delicatessen . . . Golly, do we have a lot to answer for.

So Mike's exit (he bangs down his drink on the mantelpiece and storms out) is both a blessing and a defeat, because even though we all feel guilty about the homeless, we also feel guilty that we have failed to accommodate Mike, that he no longer feels a part of his own neighbourhood, and maybe this double guilt helps David, too, because there is now so much collective guilt in the room that the ponces are just dying to compensate somehow. They want to do something gritty and difficult just to prove that they are not ponces, that they are good, thoughtful people who are unafraid of difficulty. If David wanted people to give up their homes at this precise second, a couple of them might do so; a bedroom – pah! Nothing!

And David detects this mood, and storms through the rest of his speech, while GoodNews stands beside him with a self-satisfied beam on his face. Do these people want to be like Mike? Do they want to do something better than anything they have ever done in their lives? Because David doesn't care what we're doing now: however caring our job is, however much we give to charity, nothing is going to make as much difference to individuals as this. Six months without the use of a spare bedroom could literally save a life, because with a home and a permanent address and somewhere to shave and shower, then these kids can apply for jobs, and then they can earn, and with a wage comes self-respect, and the ability to build a life without this kind of intervention . . .

'I'm forty-one years old,' says David, 'and I have spent half my life regretting that I missed the sixties. I read about the energy, and I imagine what the music would have sounded like when you hadn't heard it a thousand times before, and when it actually meant something, and I've always been sad that the world is different now. I got a bit excited about Live Aid, but then you realize that these problems . . . They're too big now. They're never going to go away. We can't change the world, but we can change our street, and maybe if we can change our street, then other people will want to change theirs. We have hand-picked ten kids who are living rough and who need some help. They're good kids. They're not winos or junkies or thieves or lunatics; they're people whose lives have gone badly wrong through no fault of their own. Maybe their stepfather has thrown them out, maybe someone died on them and they couldn't cope . . . But we can vouch for them. If I can find ten spare bedrooms for these kids I'd feel that it was the greatest thing I'd ever done.'

'Are you having one?' someone asks.

'Of course,' says David. 'How could I ask you to do this if I wasn't prepared to?'

'Can I ask where we'll be putting him or her?' This from the lady at the back, who already supports two children, a spiritual guru and a husband who has lost the will to work.

'We'll sort it out when everyone's gone,' says David. 'Does anyone want to talk more about this?'

Four people put their hands up.

'Four's no good to me. I need more.'

One more hand, then nothing.

'OK. Half now, half later.'

Weirdly, the whole room breaks into a spontaneous round of applause, and I feel as though I might cry the sort of tears that come at the end of soppy films.

GoodNews and David take the Famous Five into his study (a study that, presumably, is about to be converted into a bedroom) while the rest of us watch. It's like that bit in a church wedding where the bride and groom and a few others shuffle off round the corner to sign the register, and the congregation beam at them, without knowing quite what else to do. (Is there singing at that point? Maybe. Maybe we should sing now – *You've Got a Friend*, or *You'll Never Walk Alone*, something where the secular just starts to rub against the spiritual.)

For the record, the five volunteers are:

1. Simon and Richard, the gay couple at number 25.

2. Jude and Robert, a couple in their late thirties, who some-one once told me were unable to have kids, and were trying to adopt, without much success. They're at number 6.

(So, for those of you who have a need to understand why anyone should wish to do what these people are doing, a theme begins to emerge . . .)

3. Ros and Max, diagonally opposite us at number 29. Don't know anything about them, because they've recently moved into the street, apart from 1) they have a daughter of Molly's age and 2) just before David turned, he said he'd seen Ros on the bus reading his column and laughing, so perhaps her willingness to offer up a bedroom is some kind of penance.

4. Wendy and Ed, an older couple at number 19. They've always stopped to talk when we've been out with the kids; I don't know much about them either, other than that they are both enormous and their children no longer live with them.

5. (Terrifying, this one) Martina, an old (properly old, seventy plus), frail Eastern European lady who lives on her own at number 21. Her grasp of English has always struck me as being remarkably weak for someone who has lived here for forty years, so heaven knows what she thinks she's volunteered for; we'll probably be given a large cake tomorrow, and she'll be baffled and horrified when some-one with dreadlocks knocks on her door in a week's time.

A woman I've never seen before in my life comes up to me. 'You must be very proud of him,' she says. I smile politely, and say nothing.

We don't get to bed until after midnight, but David's much too hyper to sleep.

'Is five any good, do you think?'

'It's amazing,' I tell him, and I mean it, because I had anticipated nobody, nothing, a dismal and humiliating failure and the end of the story.

'Really?'

'Did you honestly think you could get ten people to volunteer?'

'I didn't know. All I can say is that when I was going through it in my head, I couldn't think of any arguments against it.'

That's it. That's the whole David/GoodNews thing, right there: 'I couldn't think of any arguments against it.' My problem exactly. I want to destroy David's whole save-the-world-and-love-everyone campaign, but I want to do it using his logic and philosophy and language, not the language of some moaning, spoiled, smug, couldn't-care-less, survival-of-the-fittest tabloid newspaper columnist. And of course it's not possible, because David's fluent in his language, and I'm a beginner. It's as if I'm trying to argue with Plato in Greek.

'What arguments are there?' he says. 'I mean, these people are . . .'

'I know, I know. You don't have to argue with me. But that's not the point, is it?'

'Isn't it?'

'There are never any arguments against anything you want to do. People are hungry, give them food if you've got it. Kids have nothing to play with, give them toys if you've got too many. I can never think of anything to say to you. But that doesn't mean I agree with you.'

'But it has to.'

'That isn't how the world works.'

'Why not? OK, I know why not. Because people are selfish and scared and . . . and brainwashed into thinking that they have no alternatives. But they have. They have.'

And what am I supposed to say now? That people have a right to be selfish if they want to? That they don't have any alternatives? And what's the Greek for 'Please shut up and leave me alone'?

The next morning I sit eating cereal with Tom while GoodNews and Molly and David clear up around me. I'm not moving. I'm selfish, and I have a right to be. In the *Guardian* there's an article about a gang of youths who beat a man unconscious and left him under a hedge in Victoria Park, where he died of hypothermia. Unless he was dead already – the coroner doesn't know. Three of the youths were homeless. OK, I accept that I shouldn't have read the story out loud, given that our children are relatively young, and we have a homeless youth coming to live with us imminently (I presume that still to be the case – no one's mentioned anything to me) and they will have nightmares for weeks about the poor and almost certainly harmless kid who'll be sleeping underneath them. But I'm feeling bolshie, and the ammunition was just sitting there, at the top of page five, waiting to be fired.

'Oh, great,' says Tom. 'So now Dad's going to get us killed.'

'Why?' says Molly.

'Weren't you listening to what Mum was reading? A homeless person's going to come round here and rob us and then probably kill us.' He seems quite phlegmatic about it all; indeed, he seems to relish the prospect, possibly because being murdered would prove a point, and make his father sorry. I suspect that he's being naive, and his father would be regretful and sad, but not sorry. Not the kind of sorry that Tom needs.

'That's not fair,' David says to me angrily.

'No,' I say. 'One against five! He didn't stand a chance.'

He looks at me.

'What? It's here, in the paper. It's nothing to do with fairness. It's a news story. A fact.'

'There are so many other things you could have read out. I'll bet there's an article about, I don't know, changes in the benefit laws. I'll bet there's something about Third World Debt.'

'David, Third World Debt isn't coming to live in our house. Third World Debt hasn't killed . . .' I stop dead, knowing that I'm wrong, that I've lost, that Third World Debt has killed – has killed millions and millions, a zillion more than homeless youths have ever killed, I know that I know that I know that, but I'm going to hear all about it anyway, for hours and hours and hours.

10

The homeless kids all arrive on the same day, in a minibus that their hosts have hired for the morning. It's a sunny June Saturday, a little hazy because of the early heat and last night's rain, and a few people have gathered outside their houses, either to gawp or to welcome their new housemates, and suddenly I feel as though our street is, after all, special. No other street in London or Britain or the world is having a morning like this, and whatever happens hereonafter, David and GoodNews have, I can see now, achieved something.

The kids are loud and giggly as they get off the bus – 'Er, look at her, I'll bet she's yours' – but it's bravado, and a couple of them are clearly scared. We are all scared of each other. David talks to each one – three boys, three girls – as they stand on the pavement, and points them towards their new houses. He shakes hands with one of the boys and points at me, and a couple of minutes later I am making tea while an eighteen-year-old who wants me to call him Monkey rolls a cigarette at my kitchen table.

'What are you doing?' asks Molly.

'Rolling a cigarette.'

'Do you smoke?' says Molly.

'Duh,' says Tom, who promptly disappears to his bedroom. Molly, however, is awestruck. Her father Has Views on smoking, and her mother is a GP; she has heard that people smoke, but she has never seen anyone prepare to do it in front of her. For my part, I don't know whether I want Monkey smoking in my kitchen, in front of the children. Probably I don't. But asking Monkey to smoke outside in the back garden might get us off on the wrong foot: it might give him the feeling that he is not wanted, or that we do not respect his culture. Or it might serve to accentuate the differences between us – he might think that passive smoking is essentially a bourgeois fear, presupposing as it does the sort of long-term future he might feel he is currently denied, which is why he doesn't worry about smoking roll-ups. Or asking him to go outside might simply make him angry, and his anger will compel him to steal everything we own, or murder us in our beds. I don't know. And because I don't know, I say nothing, apart from, 'I'll find you an ashtray.' And then, 'You'll have to use this saucer.' And then, when I replay that last sentence in my head, and hear a) a note that could be perceived as tetchiness and b) what could be construed as implicit disapproval, the buried suggestion that there are no ashtrays in this house FOR A REASON, I add 'If you don't mind.' Monkey doesn't mind.

He is very tall and very thin – not like a monkey at all, more like a giraffe. He is wearing (from the bottom up) Dr Martens, combat trousers, a khaki jacket and a black turtle-neck sweater that is smeared with mud, or what I hope is mud. He has spots, but very little else: the rest of his wardrobe is contained in a plastic carrier bag.

'So,' I say. He looks at me expectantly, which is fair enough, considering that the word I have just used clearly induces expectation, but I'm temporarily stuck. I try to think of something to follow up with, something which won't patronize or offend, but which might indicate sympathy and curiosity. (I feel both sympathetic and curious, by the way, and so the question is not merely for show. I care. Really.)

'When was the last time you sat in someone's kitchen?'

That's not offensive, surely? Because if you've been sleeping rough, it's likely to have been a while, isn't it? And maybe the question will help to draw him out, get him talking, and I'll be able to understand a little more, learn something of what he's been doing, and where. The only danger, I suppose, is that it could sound smug – haven't we done well, we've got a kitchen, nah nah nah nah nah.

'Dunno. Ages ago. Last time I saw my mum, probably.'

'When was that?'

'A couple of years ago. Is Ali G really funny?'

'Who's Ali G?'

'That comedian on the telly.'

'I don't know. I've never seen him.'

'He isn't,' says Molly, who is drawing at the table.

'When have you seen him?' I ask her.

'I haven't. But I've seen a picture of him. He doesn't look very funny. He looks stupid. Why are you called Monkey?'

'I dunno. That's what they call me. Why are you called Molly?'

'Because Daddy didn't like Rebecca.'

'Oh. Have you got digital?'

'No.'

'Cable?'

'Yes.'

'Sky Sports?'

'No.'

'Oh.'

As it turns out, we are something of a disappointment to Monkey, and, if I am being honest, he is something of a disappointment to me. I cannot answer any of the questions he asks me, and nor do we have any of the things he seems to want most (apart from Sky Sports, we don't have Dreamcast, or a dog); meanwhile he will not help me to understand how it was he came to be sleeping on the streets, which means that I am unable to show him the side of me that I wanted him to see: Katie the therapist, the listener, the imaginative solver of insoluble problems. He goes for a bath; regrettably, we don't have a proper shower.

For a couple of days, all is quiet. We only see Monkey during the evenings; he doesn't talk about where he goes during the day, but it is clear that old habits are hard to break, and old friendships are as important to him as they are to everyone else. And, anyway, one night he comes back and attempts to give me housekeeping money out of a huge pile of coins that he dumps on the kitchen table, which gives us all an idea of his whereabouts during working hours. I am almost tempted to take the money: after all, he is the only person in the house other than me who is working. He is courteous, he keeps himself to himself, he reads, he watches TV, he plays with Tom at the computer, he enjoys every mouthful of food he is given, and he makes no dietary demands.

One night we leave our guests in charge of the children (imaginary conversation with my parents, or social services: 'Who's in charge of your children?' 'Oh, GoodNews and Monkey') and we go to the local cinema. We see a Julia Roberts film: she plays a struggling single mother who gets a job at a law firm and discovers that a water company is poisoning people, and she goes on a campaign to get compensation for them. Her relationship with a sexy bearded man suffers, and she becomes a bad, neglectful mother, but she is Fighting the Good Fight, and the water company is bad bad bad, and she only has two children and one boyfriend and there are hundreds of sick people, so it's OK. It's not a particularly good film, but I love it simply because it is a film, in colour, with a story that doesn't involve spacecraft or insects or noise, and I drink it down in one, like I drank the Stoppard play. David loves it because he thinks it is about him.

'Well?' he says afterwards.

'Well what?'

'Do you see?'

'Do I see what?'

'If you're going to do this stuff, it comes at a cost.'

'There was no cost. Not in the film. Everyone lived happily ever after. Apart from the sick people, perhaps.'

'Her boyfriend left her.'

'She made it up with him,' I point out.

'But weren't you on her side?'

And he used to have such a complicated, interesting mind. 'No. I was on the side of the water company. Of course I was on her side. I wasn't given much choice. Are you trying to say that you're Julia Roberts?'

'No, but . . .'

'Because you're not.'

We stop while he gives a kid fifty pence, and then continue in silence for a little while.

'Why not?'

'David, I'm not going to waste an awful lot of time on this.'

'Why not?'

'Why aren't I going to waste time explaining why you're not Julia Roberts?'

'Yes. This is important. Tell me the difference between what I'm doing and what she was doing.'

'What are you doing? Explain it to me.'

'You explain to me what she was doing first. And then we'll see what the differences are.'

'You're going to drive me mad.'

'OK, I'm sorry. The point is that she and I want to do something about things. A water company is poisoning people. Bad. She wants justice for the people affected. Kids are sleeping out on the street. Bad. I want to help them.'

'Why you?'

'Why her?'

'It was a film, David.'

'Based on a true story.'

'Let me ask you something: is this worth wrecking your family for?'

'I don't intend to wreck my family.'

'I know you don't intend to wreck your family. But two of us are very unhappy. And I don't know how much more I can take.'

'I'm sorry.'

'That's all you can say?'

'What else is there to say? You're threatening to leave me because I'm trying to do something for people who can't do much for themselves. And I . . .'

'That's not true, David. I'm threatening to leave you because you're becoming unbearable.'

'What can't you bear?'

'Any of it. The . . . the sanctimony. The smugness. The . . .'

'People are dying out there, Katie. I'm sorry if you think that I'm being smug.'

I cannot bring myself to say any more.

*

What with one thing and another – a broken leg one summer, post-college poverty the next – David and I did not go away on holiday together until the third year of our relationship. We were a proper couple by then, by which I mean that we had rows, that some days I didn't like him very much, that if he or I went away for a few days I didn't miss him, although I found myself jotting down inconsequential things to tell him, but that I never ever thought about whether I wanted to be with him or not, because I knew, somewhere in me, that I was in for the long haul. What I am saying, I suppose, is that this first holiday was not a honeymoon, and there was not very much chance of us spending the entire fortnight in bed, emerging only to feed each other spoonfuls of exotic fruits. It was more likely, in fact, that David would lapse into a two-week long sulk over a dispute about his loose interpretation of the rules of Scrabble, during the course of which I would call him a pathetic cheating baby. That was the stage we were at.

We found cheap flights to Egypt, with the intention of travelling around a bit, but on our second day in Cairo David became ill – sicker than he's ever been since, in fact. He became delirious, and he vomited every couple of hours, and at the height of it he lost control of his bowels, and we were in a cheap hotel and we didn't have our own toilet or shower, and I had to clean him up.

And there was a part of me that was pleased, because I'd set myself a test years before (probably when I first conceived of being a doctor, and realized that sometimes my private life would resemble my professional life): would I be able to see a man in that state and still respect him in the morning? I passed the test with flying colours. I had no qualms about cleaning David up, I could still bring myself to have sex with him afterwards (after the holiday, and after his restoration to health, I mean, rather than after his accident) . . . I was capable of a mature relationship after all. This was love, surely?

But now I can see I was wrong. That wasn't a test. What kind of woman would leave her boyfriend to rot in his soiled bedsheets in a strange hotel in a foreign country? This is a test. And Lord, am I failing it.

Wendy and Ed, the enormous couple who live at number 19, come to see us first thing the next morning. They took in a kid called Robbie, who they said they liked. Last night the three of them stayed in together and talked about Robbie's life, and how it had turned out in the way that it had, and Wendy and Ed went to bed feeling positive about the choice they had made to have him stay. But when they got up Robbie had vanished. Also vanished: a video camera, seventy pounds in cash, a bracelet that Wendy had left by the sink when she was doing the washing-up. GoodNews listens to the story with increasing agitation, which surprises me: I was presuming that he would be happy to write off the loss to experience, that he would argue – and as he is the owner of nothing very much, it is an easy argument to make – that these sorts of risks were worth running, that it was all for the greater good, and so on. It turns out, however, that it is not the theft that has agitated him, but our bourgeois logic.

'Oh, no, no, no, people,' he says. 'We're jumping to conclusions. We shouldn't be jumping. We should be sitting and thinking, not jumping.'

'How do you mean?' Ed is genuinely baffled. He, like me, is trying to see how any other interpretation of events is possible.

'Don't you see? We're putting two and two together and making the proverbial. I mean . . . OK, Robbie has gone. And OK, some stuff has gone. But it doesn't necessarily mean that they've gone to the same place.'

'I'm sure they haven't,' I say. 'I'm sure they've gone to different places. I'm sure the video camera has gone to the second-hand shop in Holloway Road and Robbie's gone to the off-licence.'

David gives me a look that lets me know I am being unhelpful, but I don't think that's true. Wendy and Ed are actually being pretty good about this. They could have come round here and thrown David from an upstairs window, or sat on him until he burst, but they just seem bewildered and hurt. And now they are being told that their powers of deduction are faulty.

'GoodNews is right,' says David, with a wearying predictability. 'We mustn't stereotype these kids. That's kind of how they got into this mess in the first place.'

Monkey comes into the kitchen, dressed in some of David's cast-offs and yawning.

'Do you know Robbie?' I ask him. 'The guy who was living with Ed and Wendy here?'

'Yeah,' says Monkey. 'He's a thieving little cunt. Pardon my language.'

'How do you know?' David asks.

'How do I know he's a thieving little cunt? 'Cos he steals everything.' Misjudging the mood somewhat, he laughs heartily at his own witticism.

'He's stolen some stuff from us and disappeared,' says Ed.

'Yeah, well, I could have told you that would happen. What's he taken?'

Ed tells him what is missing.

'Little fucker. Right.' And Monkey disappears too.

We make Ed and Wendy a cup of tea. David puts his head in his hands and stares mournfully at the floor. 'It was a high-risk strategy, I suppose. Thinking about it now.' That last phrase I would have found particularly difficult to swallow, if I were Ed and Wendy. They might have hoped that the thought had been done beforehand.

'You shouldn't worry too much about it,' GoodNews tells them cheerfully. 'You did the right thing. No matter how much you've lost. He could have taken everything you own, every last penny you've got, and you could go to sleep tonight knowing that your conscience is clear. More than clear. It's . . .' GoodNews struggles for a moment to find a word that means 'more than clear', and then gives up and settles for a beaming smile that doesn't seem to offer Ed and Wendy as much consolation as he might have anticipated.

*

Forty-five minutes later Monkey is back, with the camera, the bracelet, fifty of the seventy pounds, and Robbie, who is bleeding profusely from a cut above his right eye. David is angry, GoodNews anguished.

'How did he get that?' David asks.

Monkey laughs. 'He walked into a door.'

'Oh, man,' says GoodNews. 'This isn't what we're about.'

'I can't sanction violence,' David says.

'What does that mean?'

'It means I don't agree with it.'

'Yeah, well,' says Monkey. 'I asked him nicely but he wouldn't listen.'

'I was going to come back with the stuff,' wails Robbie. 'There wasn't any need for him to slap me around. I was only . . .' Robbie tries and fails to come up with a convincing explanation for why he would need purely temporary use of a video camera and a bracelet, and trails off.

'Is that true, Monkey?' David asks. 'Was he going to come back with the stuff?'

'I'll give you my honest opinion, David: No, it isn't true. He wasn't going to come back with the stuff. He was going to flog it.' Monkey delivers the line for laughs, and gets them – from Ed and me, anyway. David and GoodNews aren't laughing, though. They just look stricken.

I ask Monkey to take Robbie for a walk somewhere while we talk.

'So now what?' I ask. 'Do you want to get the police in, you two?'

'Ah, now, you really want to think hard about that,' says Good-News. 'Because the police, you know . . . That's quite heavy. If twenty pounds means so much to you, you know . . .'

Significantly, he trails off before completing the sentence in the way that sense and custom dictate. There will be no offers of recompense from this quarter, clearly.

'What?' I ask him.

'It's like, not much, is it, twenty quid? I mean, a young life has got to be worth more than that.'

'So you're saying that Ed and Wendy are mean. Callous.'

'I'm just saying that if it were me that lost the money, you know . . .'

'You're not involved,' I tell him. 'It's Ed and Wendy's decision.'

'If we get the police in,' David says, 'it'll make it very difficult for Robbie to carry on where he is. He might feel that Ed and Wendy don't want him.'

I don't think even I had quite realized, up until this point, just what a limp grasp on reality David now has.

'We don't bloody want him,' says Ed. 'Little shit.'

GoodNews is staggered. 'You don't want him? Because of this? Come on, guys. We knew it was going to be a hard road. I didn't think you two would fall at the first hurdle.'

'You told us you'd vetted everybody,' says Wendy.

'We did,' David says. 'We got recommendations from a local hostel. But, you know. It must have been very tempting for him. There's money lying around, and jewellery, and electronic goods, and . . .'

'So it's our fault?' says Ed. 'Is that what you're telling us?'

'Not your fault, exactly. But maybe we're not quite seeing the . . . the extent of the cultural gap here.'

Ed and Wendy look at each other and walk out.

'I'm very disappointed in them,' says David, almost to himself. 'I thought they were made of tougher stuff than that.'

I clean Robbie up and suggest to him that it might be politic to disappear. He's not entirely happy with the suggestion – like David and GoodNews, he seems to believe that I am indulging in some unhelpful stereotyping, and that he hasn't been given a chance. We have quite a lively debate about it all, as you can imagine, because my own feeling, a feeling that Robbie doesn't share, is that he has been given a chance, and he hasn't responded entirely positively to it.

He disagrees. 'That camera thing was cheap Korean crap,' he says. 'And like GoodNews says, it was only twenty quid.'

This, I try to point out, is beside the point – indeed, it is a non sequitur – but I don't make very much headway. After a much briefer conversation with Monkey he decides that Webster Road isn't for him after all. We never see him again.

News of the misfortune spreads up and down the street, and we receive several visits during the course of the day. All the other four hosts want to talk to David and GoodNews, of course, but Ed and Wendy's immediate neighbours – including Mike, whose ideological opposition to the project has predictably hardened overnight – are also unhappy. Mike pays us a visit.

'This isn't anything to do with you,' says David.

'What, when I've got a bloody tea-leaf living next door?'

'You don't know who you've got living next door,' says David. 'You're judging someone before you've got to know them.'

'You're jumping,' says GoodNews, pleased with his new verb. 'And we're not jumpers here.'

'What, so I've got to wait until half my fucking stuff has gone before I'm allowed to complain?'

'Why don't we call a street meeting?' says David.

'What good will that do?'

'I want to gauge the temperature. See how other people feel.'

'I don't give a fuck how other people feel.'

'That's not what living in a community is about, Mike.'

'I don't live in a fucking community. I live in my house. With my things. And I want to keep them.'

'OK. So maybe you should be given the opportunity to express that. Meet the kids and tell them you don't want them in your house.'

'Tell them! Tell them! If they have to be told not to break in, they shouldn't be here in the first place.'

'And where should they be?'

'In a hostel, back on the street, who cares?'

'I do, obviously. That's why I'm doing this.'

'Yeah, well, I don't.'

'What do you care about, Mike?' This is GoodNews's first contribution to the debate, but it is the most incendiary so far: Mike is now dangerously close to thumping somebody. I have conflicting loyalties. I don't like Mike very much, but on the other hand both David and GoodNews clearly need thumping, and it is difficult to see who else is going to do it.

'Listen,' says David. He has come back from the brink; I can hear the desire to pacify in his voice. 'I understand why you're worried. But I promise you you've got nothing to worry about. Please meet the other kids and listen to what they've got to say. And if anything else like this happens, well, I've got it all wrong and I'll have to think again. OK?'

It's enough, just; Mike calms down, and agrees to come round later on, although I suspect that David has some way to go before he manages to convert him to the cause. Meanwhile we prepare – some of us with heavier hearts than others – yet more cheese straws, for yet another community gathering in our house.

Rather sweetly, the kids all come with their hosts, rather than with each other, as if to demonstrate their new allegiances. They have to be nudged through the door, like much younger children attending a birthday party, and when they are in they stand there staring at the floor while the adults introduce them gently and, well, yes, proudly.

'This is Sas,' says Richard, the gay actor from *The Bill*. Sas is a chronically shy eighteen-year-old from Birmingham who arrived in London two years ago after being sexually assaulted by her step-father. She wants to be a nurse; she has recently been working as a prostitute. Some parts of her – her body language, the braids in her hair – make her look nine; her eyes make her look forty-five.

No one, not even Mike, could want anything else bad to happen to her.

Martina brings a girl called Tiz. Tiz is spotty and fat, and she and Martina, I notice, are holding hands when they come in. Ros and Max bring their own daughter Holly and her new best friend, Annie, who is older than the others, twenty-two or so, and is wearing what are clearly Ros's clothes – a long dress with a flowered print and a pair of sparkly sandals. Robert and Jude's Craig is wearing a suit, another cast-off, and his hair is wet from the shower and he looks like a sweet, scared little boy. That's what strikes you most about all of them: when they arrived they all looked as though they had seen too much, too young, and it's as if the comforts of Webster Road, the baths and the showers, have washed all that unimaginable filthy experience from their bodies and their faces. Now they all look as they should – and shouldn't, if the world were a different place. They look like terrified young people who are a long way from family and home and a life that any of us would want to live.

Mike doesn't stand a chance – he isn't even allowed to speak. Max points out that they have been burgled three times in the last two years, and it doesn't really matter if thieves are living next door to you or a couple of streets away. Martina tells Mike that she has lived alone for fifteen years, and enjoys Tiz's company so much that she would be devastated if she disappeared now. 'I would haf to go and find another Tiz,' she says.

Sas speaks last. She's not a good speaker – she's shy, and she looks at her shoes, and she stops and starts, and no one can really hear her anyway. But what is clear is that she is desperate for this chance – desperate to stay with Simon and Richard, desperate to go to college so that she can pass some exams, desperate not to return to how things were for her before. She wanted to kill Robbie, she said, because she knew what it meant, and what people would think of the rest of them, and she said if anything else got stolen while they were in the street she would personally pay the victims back out of her own pocket, even if it took her the rest of her life. When she has finished Richard comes up and hugs her, while everyone else claps. Mike goes home, looking as if he might burgle his own house and disappear.

Richard comes up to me afterwards to thank me for the evening – as if I have done anything apart from complain about yet more intrusion.

'I know Sas thinks we've done a lot for her,' he says. 'But I can't describe what she's done for us. I mean, look at me. A bad actor who's thrilled to bits if I survive more than one week in a hospital bed in *Casualty*. I've done nothing with my life. And now I'm on this permanent high. If Sas ever qualifies as a nurse I'll die a happy man. And I'd cry for a month. You must be very proud of David.'

'I am a doctor, you know,' I say. 'I've saved the odd life myself.' Richard stares at me until I run off and lock myself in the toilet.

This is not their story; it is mine, and David's. So I want to bring their story to an end, and tell you what has happened to them all. Craig and Monkey disappeared, after a few days in Monkey's case, and a few weeks in Craig's. Monkey took some money when he went, but it was money that David and I had put to one side to be stolen: when we began to suspect that Monkey was unhappy, and uncomfortable, and itching to move on to something else, I showed him the kitchen jar where we keep our emergency money, and then we put five twenty pound notes in it. We knew it would go, and it did. Craig was talking about going to find his mother, apparently, and we hope that's where he has gone. The girls are still here, in the street, and it is as if they never had a previous life at all. So. David wanted to rescue ten kids. He had to settle for six. Three of those six were beyond his reach. If the other three stay, and get jobs, and find homes of their own, and partners, maybe, then ... Oh, you can do the maths yourself. I don't mean the three-out-of-ten maths, of course. I mean the rest of it. Because I don't know the value of anything any more.

II

The only scenes I can stand in any of the *Star Wars* films are the quiet scenes in the second one, *The Empire Strikes Back*. Or rather, it used to be the second one, before the fourth one became the first one, thus making the second one the fifth one. A couple of years ago Tom used to watch his *Star Wars* videos over and over again, in sequence, and at first I preferred *The Empire Strikes Back* simply because it offered some respite from all the roaring and banging and whizzing. But later I came to appreciate its . . . I don't know what you'd call it. Message? Moral? Do *Star Wars* films have messages? Anyway, something in it began to chime somewhere in me, and I wanted to be Luke Skywalker, off somewhere on my own, learning to be a Jedi. I wanted a break from the war. I wanted someone wise to teach me how to do the things I needed to know to survive the rest of my life. And I know it's pathetic that it should have been a children's science-fiction film telling me this – it should have been George Eliot, or Wordsworth, or Virginia Woolf. But then, that's precisely the point, isn't it? There is no time or energy for Virginia Woolf, which means that I am forced to look for meaning and comfort in my son's *Star Wars* videos. I have to be Luke Skywalker because I don't know who else to be.

When Monkey and his pals moved into the street, I became acutely aware of the need to think; it seemed as though life were unsustainable without thought, in fact. I couldn't work out who was right and who was wrong, my house was full of people I didn't know . . . I was going mad, really. So I had to do this, didn't I? And of course it's selfish and indulgent and bad, but it seemed at the time as though I couldn't work out how to be good without being bad. Anyone would understand. God, the Archbishop of Canterbury, Miriam Stoppard, anyone. Wouldn't they? And it doesn't mean I love my children less, and it doesn't even mean I love my husband less (I don't think, although that's one of the things I need to think about) . . .

I've moved out. Sort of, anyway. Except that nobody knows. Well, David and GoodNews know, and a colleague called Janet, for reasons that will become clear, but Molly and Tom don't, not yet. I now live, or at least sleep, in a bedsit just around the corner, and I put the kids to bed at night, and I set the alarm for six-fifteen in the morning, get dressed, and walk straight out of the flat, no tea, no muesli, nightdress and dressing gown in a carrier bag, so that I am back in the familial house at six-thirty. The children usually need to be woken an hour later, but I'm there on the off-chance that either of them should get up earlier. (They rarely wake in the night now, and when they do, David has always been the one to deal with them, simply because I am the one with the proper job.) I then change back into my nightdress and dressing gown in order to remove any last doubts the children might have – although they would have to be very suspicious indeed to suspect that the mother who puts them to bed at night and is there at breakfast the next morning has moved out – and spend my extra hour reading the paper that I have brought with me. In theory, I get an hour's less sleep, but this is no hardship, because in practice it feels like I have slept for an hour longer, such is the revivifying effect of being on my own for the night.

I'm not paying for the room; it belongs to Janet Walder, the third person who knows about my new domestic arrangements. Janet works at the surgery and has gone back to New Zealand for a month to see her new niece. If it hadn't been for Janet's new niece, in fact, I would never have taken the decision to move out. Like those thieves who would never have dreamed of stealing a wallet if they hadn't seen it sticking out of somebody's pocket, the opportunity was all: she just happened to mention that she was leaving her room empty, and within seconds I had made my mind up. It was as if I were powerless to resist the temptation; my senses were overcome. I could hear the emptiness, and taste the silence, and smell the solitude, and I wanted it more than I have ever wanted anything before. (And what does that say about me? What kind of sensualist craves nothingness?) And then I invented my post-bedtime, pre-breakfast plan, on the spot, in seconds, because necessity is the mother of invention. And then I went home and told David what I was doing, and then I did it.

'Why?' David asked – not unreasonably, I suppose.

Because of everything, I told him. Because of GoodNews, and because of Monkey, and because I'm frightened of what you might do next. And because I'm disappearing, I wanted to tell him. Every day I wake up and there's a little bit less of me. But I couldn't say that, because I didn't know whether I was entitled to, and nor would I ever know, unless I got my Jedi training.

'I dunno, really,' I said. 'I just want some time out.'

'Time out of what?'

Time out of our marriage, I should have said. Because that, really, is what it comes down to. That's all there is left, when you take away working hours and family suppers and family breakfasts: the time I get on my own is the time I would have spent being a wife, rather than being a mother or a doctor. (And God, how frightening, that those are the only options available. The only times when I am not performing one of those three roles is when I am in the bathroom.) But of course I didn't say that either; I just waved a hand airily at what I hoped he would see was a decaying, wartorn planet that didn't have enough oxygen to support complex life forms.

'Please don't go,' he said, but I couldn't hear any conviction or desperation in his voice. Maybe I wasn't trying hard enough.

'Why don't you want me to go?' I asked him. 'What difference will it make to you?'

And there was a long, thoughtful, fatal pause before he said anything, a pause that allowed me first to ignore and then to forget what it was he eventually cobbled together.

Janet's bedsit is at the top of a large terraced house on Taymor Road, which runs parallel to Webster Road. The terrace is weird, because it's actually very beautiful, but was allowed to decay. Now the houses are being recovered, one by one, and I'm in the middle of a row of the last three tatty houses left.

There are three flats underneath me, and I now know and like the inhabitants of all of them. Gretchen, who works in PR and has promised me all sorts of free samples, lives in the garden flat, the biggest of the four; and above her is Marie, who teaches philosophy at the University of North London and goes home to Glasgow at weekends, and above Marie is Dick, a quiet, very nervous guy who works in a local record shop.

It's fun here. We make decisions together, decisions about how to live our lives, and where responsibilities lie, and what would be for the greatest possible good. Last week, for example, Gretchen hosted a house meeting, and we voted to get a bigger letter box: Marie orders a lot of books from Amazon and the postman can't put them through the door, so he has taken to leaving them out on the front step, where they get wet. Do you hear that, David? Letter box sizes! Those are the things we can change! (Probably – although we haven't yet got a quote, and we're not sure who instals letter boxes, or how to find out.) It was an entirely satisfactory discussion, short, logical, harmonious and just: Marie will pay two thirds of the installation costs, and I will pay nothing. And we drank wine, and listened to Air, who are French, and play mostly instrumentals that sound as if they are best heard in lifts. Air are my new favourite group, although Dick is a bit snooty about them, in his quiet, nervous way. He says there's much better ambient French pop than this, and he could do us a tape if we wanted.

But to me Air sound modern and childless and single, compared to, say, Dylan, who sounds old and married and burdened – who sounds like home. If Air are Conran, then Dylan is the greengrocers. Mushrooms, lettuce and tomato, home to cook bolognese and prepare a salad, and how does it feeeeel? To be on your oowwwn? Except I never am whenever Bob is singing. This, I can't help feeling, is what communal living should be about: cool music and white wine and letter boxes and a closed door when you need it. Next time we're going to talk about whether we need a table in the hall for post, and I'm looking forward to it. (My feeling is that we do, although I'm prepared to listen to those who disagree.)

Everyone is single here, and I like that, too. None of them want to be single, I suspect; even the other night there were lots of very forced, very self-deprecating and very well-rehearsed jokes about their romantic status, and I would surmise that if the subject came up during a house meeting about letter boxes – Gretchen wondered whether the size of the slot was responsible for the poor show on Valentine's Day, and we all laughed dutifully and mock-sorrowfully – it would come up in a discussion about anything at all. And though I'm sorry for them, if they are sorry for themselves, it suits my purposes that none of them should be in relationships, because it adds to that in-between, Empire-Strikes-Back atmosphere; it feels as though I have just started a fresh sheet on someone else's drawing pad. Mine got used up, every corner filled in, and I didn't like what I had done.

I don't think about how long I can live like this. Janet will be back in a few weeks, but already I have wondered whether Marie will be using her flat during the summer, and whether I could afford my own bedsit as well as the mortgage and two children and a husband and GoodNews and the homeless. And all this without considering whether this is a life worth living – whether these couple of hours every night, either on my own, or listening to Air with Dick and Marie and Gretchen and talking about letter box capacity, would do me for the next forty-odd years. At the moment it feels as though it would, but I'd probably be unwise to sign a forty-year lease on anything just yet.

But, bloody hell, I'm happy, for those precious two hours. I'm happier than I've been for years and years. I think. I watch Janet's tiny TV. I have even been reading the review pages of newspapers, and in the two weeks I've been here, I have got through seventy-nine pages of *Captain Corelli's Mandolin*. I pay for it during the night, I hasten to add. Those two hours cost me. On my first night here I woke up covered in sweat after a nightmare, and realized where I was, and where I wasn't. And I got dressed, and walked home and back, just so that I could hear the kids breathing. I have woken most nights since then at 2.25 a.m. precisely, feeling bereft and lonely and guilty and frantic with worry and fear, and it takes me ages to get back to sleep. And yet I still wake up in the morning feeling refreshed.

At the beginning of my third week in Janet's flat, I come home to find Tom watching TV with a new friend. The new friend is a little fat child with a boil near his nose and a boy-band fringe that only serves to accentuate, or perhaps even poke fun at, his almost startling unattractiveness. 'You know the kind of faces I'm usually found on?' the fringe seems to be saying. 'Well, have a look at this one!' Tom's friends don't look like this. They look handsome and cool. Cool is very important to Tom; fat and boils (and fluffy brown-and-white sweaters) are usually of even less interest to him than they are to anyone else.

'Hello,' I say brightly. 'Who's this?'

The new friend looks at me, and then looks around the room, head wobbling, to try to locate the stranger in our midst. Heartbreakingly, given his other disadvantages, he doesn't appear to be very bright; even after having ascertained that there is no one else with us, he declines to answer my question, presumably on the assumption that he would get it wrong.

'Christopher,' mumbles Tom.

'Hello, Christopher.'

'Hello.'

'Are you staying for tea?'

He stares at me again. Nope. He's not going to risk getting caught out on that one.

'She's asking you if you're staying for tea,' shouts Tom.

I am suddenly stricken with remorse and embarrassment. 'Is Christopher deaf?'

'No,' says Tom contemptuously. 'Just thick.'

Christopher turns his head to look at Tom, and then pushes him in the chest, feebly. Tom looks at me and shakes his head in what I can only interpret as disbelief.

'Where's your father?'

'In GoodNews's room.'

'Molly?'

'Upstairs. She's got a friend round, too.'

Molly is in her room with what appears to be the eight-year-old female equivalent of Christopher. Molly's new friend is tiny, grey-skinned, bespectacled and unambiguously malodorous – Molly's bedroom has never smelt like this before. The air in the room is a witch's brew of farts, body odour and socks.

'Hello. I'm Hope.' Hope. My God. The almost supernatural inappropriateness of Hope's name is an awful warning to all parents everywhere. 'I've come to play with Molly. We're playing cards. It's my turn.' She places a card carefully on a pile.

'The three of diamonds. It's your turn now, Molly.' Molly places a card on the pile. 'The five of clubs.' Hope is as loquacious as Christopher is silent. She describes everything that she does. And everything she sees. And she has an apparent fear of compound sentences. So she sounds like Janet, from 'Janet and John'.

'What are you playing?'

'Snap. This is our third game. Nobody's won yet.'

'No. Well, you see . . .' I begin to explain the fatal flaw in their approach and equipment, and then think better of it.

'Can I come round tomorrow?' Hope asks.

I look at Molly for signs of reluctance or active distaste, but her face is a mask of diplomacy.

'We'll see,' I say.

'I don't mind,' Molly says quickly. 'Really.'

It's a strange thing for a little girl to say about the prospect of a playdate with her new best friend, but I let it pass.

'Are you staying for tea, Hope?'

'I don't mind that, either,' Molly says. 'She can if she wants. Honestly. It would be good for me.'

This last phrase, cheerily and sincerely delivered, tells me everything I need to know about our guests.

As chance would have it, it is my turn to cook; David and GoodNews stay up in the bedroom, plotting. Christopher and Hope stay for tea, which is eaten in almost complete silence, apart from the occasional snatch of main-clause commentary from Hope – 'I love pizza!' 'My mum drinks tea!' 'I like this plate!' As Christopher seems only to be able to breathe through his mouth, his eating is a somewhat alarming cacophony of splutters, grunts and squelches which Tom regards with utter disdain. People talk about a face that only a mother could love, but Christopher's entire being would surely stretch maternal ties beyond the point of elasticity: I have never met a less lovable child, although admittedly Hope, whose peculiar personal aroma has not been dissipated by her proximity to food or other people, runs him close.

Christopher pushes his plate away from him. 'Finished.'

'Would you like some more? There's another slice.'

'No. Didn't like it.'

'I did,' says Tom, who has never once expressed approval for anything I have ever cooked, presumably because he has never hitherto been presented with an opportunity to make such approval sound aggressive. Christopher turns his head to look for the source of the remark, but once he has located it, cannot think of anything to say in reply.

'I like pizza,' says Hope, for the second time. Tom could normally be relied upon to leap upon that kind of repetition and rip the repeater to shreds, but he seems to have given up: he merely rolls his eyes.

'Your telly's too small,' says Christopher. 'And it dunt go very loud. When that thing blew up it sounded rubbish.'

'Why didn't you just ask for it to be turned up?' Tom says. Again, Christopher turns his head creakily, like some prototype robot, to study his friend; again, no response is forthcoming. In forty-five minutes Christopher has made me question my commitment to comprehensive education; suddenly I suspect that stupidity is contagious, and this boy should be thrown out of the house immediately.

'Where do you live, Christopher?' I ask him, in an attempt to find a conversational topic to which he might be able to make a contribution.

'Suffolk Rise,' he says, in exactly the same pugnaciously defensive rising tone – which other children use for the phrase 'No I never'.

'And do you like it there?' Molly asks. Another child might be suspected of satirizing the social situation, but Molly, I fear, is simply Trying Her Best.

'All right. Better than here. Here's a dump.'

It's Tom's timing that is so revealing. He counts to ten, maybe even twenty or thirty, and while he is counting he examines Christopher as if he were a chess problem, or a particularly complicated patient history. Then he stands up and punches Christopher squarely and calmly on the boil, which, on closer examination, turns out to have burst and spilled its dayglo yellow contents all over its former owner's cheek.

'I'm sorry, Mum,' he says sadly as he walks out, anticipating the first stage of his punishment before it has even been delivered. 'But you must understand a bit.'

'We're doing guilt,' David says after Christopher and Hope have gone home. (Christopher's mother, a large, pleasant and perhaps understandably disappointed woman, does not seem particularly surprised to learn that her son has been punched, and perhaps as a consequence does not seem particularly interested in my long and detailed outline of the sanctions we intend to take.)

'What does that mean?'

'We're all guilty, right?' GoodNews chips in enthusiastically.

'So you've always led me to understand.'

'Oh, no, I'm not talking about how we're all guilty because we're members of an unfeeling society. Even though we are, of course.'

'Of course. I wouldn't for a moment suggest otherwise.'

'No, I'm talking about individual guilt. We've all done something we feel guilty about. The lies we've told. The, you know, the affairs we've had. The hurts we've caused. So, David and I have been talking to the kids about it, trying to get a feel of where their own particular guilt lies, and then kind of encouraging them to reverse it.'

'Reverse it.'

'Yeah. Right. Reversal. That's what we're calling it. You take something you've done wrong, or some bad you've done to someone, and you reverse it. Do the opposite. If you stole something you give it back. If you were horrible, you have to be nice.'

'Because we're introducing the personal alongside the political.'

'Thanks, David. I forgot to say that bit. Right. The personal and the political. We've done the political thing, right? With the homeless kids and all that?'

'Oh, so that's finished now, is it? Homelessness cured? World a better place?'

'Please don't be facetious, Katie. When GoodNews says we've "done" it, he doesn't mean we've solved anything . . .'

'God, no way. There's still a lot to do out there. Phew.' And GoodNews fans himself with his hand, apparently to indicate the amount of sweat yet to be expended on the plight of the world's poor. 'But there's just as much to do in here, you know?' And he points at his own skull. 'Or in here, maybe.' His finger shifts towards his heart. 'So that's the work we're doing at the moment.'

'And that's why we had Christopher and Hope round for tea?'

'Exactly,' says David. 'We talked to Molly and Tom, asked them what they wanted to reverse, and we kind of pinpointed these two poor kids as particular sources of . . . regret. Molly always felt bad that she didn't ask Hope to her last birthday party, and . . . Well, you'll laugh, but Tom felt bad that he'd thumped Christopher at school.'

'Which is sort of ironic, isn't it? Seeing as he's just thumped him again.'

'I can see why you'd say that, yes.'

'And maybe what happened today was predictable?'

'Do you think?' David clearly hadn't anticipated the possibility of history repeating itself. 'Why?'

'Think about it.'

'I don't want my son bullying kids, Katie. And I don't want him disliking kids, either. I want him to find the good and the . . . the lovable in everybody.'

'And you think I don't?'

'I'm not sure. Do you want him to find what's lovable in Christopher?'

'Yes, well. Christopher may well prove to be a special case. A loophole in the law of universal love.'

'So you don't want him to love everybody.'

'Well, in an ideal world of course I do. But . . .'

'Don't you see?' GoodNews says excitedly. 'That's what we're doing! Building an ideal world in our own home!'

An ideal world in my own home . . . I'm not yet sure why the prospect appals me quite so much, but I do know somewhere in me that GoodNews is wrong, that a life without hatred is no life at all, that my children should be allowed to despise who they like. Now, there's a right worth fighting for.

'What about you?' David says after Tom and Molly are in bed and I'm about to leave.

'What about me?'

'What do you want to reverse?'

'Nothing. I take the view that anything we do, we do for a good reason. Like Tom thumping Christopher. This afternoon proved it. Tom thumped him twice because he can't not, so the best thing to do is keep them apart, not put them together.'

'So you don't believe that, like, warring tribes can ever live side-by-side in peace?' says GoodNews sadly. 'Belfast? Just give up? Palestine? That place with the, you know, the Tutsis and those other guys? Forget it?'

'I'm not sure that Tom and Christopher are warring tribes, are they? They're two small boys, more than warring tribes, surely?'

'You could argue that they are in a sense representative,' David says. 'You could argue that Christopher is a Kosovan Albanian, say. He's got nothing, he's despised by the majority . . .'

'Except unlike the average Kosovan Albanian, he could just stay at home and watch TV on his own, and nothing much would happen to him,' I point out. I point it out in my head on the way back to the bedsit; I closed the door on them somewhere during the second syllable in the word 'majority'.

But of course I find myself thinking about the whole reversal concept. How could one not? David knows I feel guilty about just about everything, which is why he launched the idea in my direction. Bastard. When I get back to Janet's place, I want to read, and I want to listen to the Air CD I borrowed from downstairs, but I end up making a mental list of the things I feel guilty about, and whether there is anything I can do about making any of it better. What alarms me is just how easy it is to remember things I've done wrong, as if they are floating on the surface of my consciousness all the time and I can simply skim them off with a spoon. I'm a doctor, I'm a good person, and yet there's all this stuff . . .

Number one, top of the pops: staying here. And it's because I feel bad about it that I've made it such hard work, what with the getting up at six-fifteen and all that. That's a sort of penance, I suppose, and maybe I can forgive myself for this one. (Except the real reason I get up at six-fifteen is because I don't have the courage to tell the children that I've moved out of their house, so in fact I should add the sin of cowardice to the sin of bedsit-dwelling. So in effect I'm doubly guilty, rather than completely absolved.)

Number two: Stephen. Or rather, David. Nothing much to say about that. I took marriage vows, I broke them, and I can't unbreak them. (Although there are mitigating circumstances, as I hope you are by now aware.) (Except there are never any mitigating circumstances when it comes to this sort of thing, are there? Whenever I have seen *Jerry Springer*, the guilty party always says to the devastated spouse 'I tried to tell you we wasn't happy, but you wouldn't listen.' And I always end up thinking that the crime of not listening does not automatically deserve the punishment of infidelity. In my case, however, I really do think that there is a case to be made. Obviously. How many of Jerry Springer's guests are doctors, for a start? How many of those transvestites and serial fathers ever wanted to do good works?) (Maybe all of them. Maybe I'm being a judgmental middle-class prig. Oh, God.)

Number three: my parents. I never call them. I never go to see them. (Or rather, I do, but not without a great deal of ill-will, procrastination, and so on.) (I really do think my parents are worse than anybody else's, though. They never complain, they never ask, they simply suffer in silence, in a way that is actually terribly aggressive, if you think about it. Or, even more provocatively, they affect to understand. 'Oh, don't worry about it. You've got so much on your plate, with work, and the kids. Just phone when you can . . .' Unforgivably manipulative stuff like that.) There is a paradox here, however, a paradox that provides some consolation: these feelings of guilt are harmful to one's mental health, yes, granted. But those who have no need to feel guilty are, in my experience, the most mentally unhealthy of all of us, because the only way to have a guilt-free relationship with one's parents is to talk to them and see them constantly, maybe even live with them. And that can't be good, can it? So if those are the choices – permanent guilt, or some kind of Freudian awfulness involving five phone calls a day – then I have made the sane and mature choice.

Number four: work. This seems particularly unfair. You'd think that my choice of profession would in itself be enough to absolve me from all worries on that score; you'd think that even a bad doctor on a bad day would feel better than a good drug dealer on a good day, but I suspect that this might not be true. I suspect that drug dealers have days when everything clicks, and it's all buzz buzz buzz, and they chalk off their jobs one by one, and they return home with a sense of accomplishment. Whereas I have days when I have been rude to people, and very little help, and I can see in my patients' eyes that they feel fobbed off, misunderstood, uncared-for (Hello, Mrs Cortenza! Hello, Barmy Brian!), and I never ever do my paperwork, and all the insurance claims are shoved straight to the bottom of my in-tray, and I promised at the last surgery meeting that I would write to our local MP about how refugees are being denied access to practices and I haven't done the first thing about it . . .

It's not enough just to be a doctor, you have to be a good doctor, you have to be nice to people, you have to be conscientious and dedicated and wise, and though I enter the surgery each morning with the determination to be exactly those things, it only takes a couple of my favourite patients – a Barmy Brian, say, or one of the sixty-a-day smokers who are aggressive about my failure to deal with their chest complaints – and I'm ill-tempered, sarcastic, bored.

Number five: Tom and Molly. All the obvious things, too dull to go into here, and much too familiar to anyone who has ever been a parent or a child. Plus, see number one above: I have moved out of their house (albeit temporarily, albeit because I was provoked, albeit to a small bedsit around the corner), and I haven't told them. I suspect that a number of mothers would find themselves wondering whether they had done the right thing in this particular circumstance.

These are, however, only the three-act dramas of conscience that are enacted daily in the Carr psyche. There are plenty of one-act dramas too, stuff that more properly belongs on the Fringe rather than in the West End, but provides some pretty compelling pre-sleep contemplation on occasions. There's my brother (see 'Parents' above), who I know is unhappy, and yet I haven't seen him since the day of the party; various other relatives, including mum's sister Joan, who is still waiting for a thank-you for a very generous . . . oh God, never mind that one. And there's an old school friend who once lent us her cottage in Devon and Tom broke one of her vases, but when she wanted to stay the night with us . . . Forget that one, too.

I don't wish to be melodramatic: I know I have not lived a bad life. But nor do I think that this crime-sheet amounts to nothing: believe me, it amounts to something. Look at it. Adultery. The casual exploitation of friends. Disrespect for parents who have done nothing apart from attempt to stay close to me. I mean, that's two of the ten commandments broken already, and given that – what, three, four? – of the ten are all about Sunday working hours and graven images, stuff that no longer really applies in early twenty-first-century Holloway, I'm looking at a thirty-three per cent strike rate, and that, to me, is too high. I can remember looking at the list when I was about seventeen and thinking that I wasn't going to have too much trouble, if you took out all the graven image restrictions and left in the ones that really mattered. In fact, I wouldn't have minded if you'd left all the finicky commandments in. God would understand the occasional emergency Sunday house-call, surely? And how many graven images am I ever likely to make? The score is nil to date – I haven't been tempted, and I'd be very surprised if I were ever to weaken. I haven't got the time, for a start.

When I look at my sins (and if I think they're sins, then they are sins), I can see the appeal of born-again Christianity. I suspect that it's not the Christianity that is so alluring; it's the rebirth. Because who wouldn't wish to start all over again?

12

When all the England football fans were rioting at some World Cup or another, I asked David why it was always the English and never the Scots, and he explained that the Scots' fans refusal to misbehave was a kind of weird form of aggression: they hate us so much that even though a few of them would probably like to fight, they won't, because they want to prove that they are better than us. Well, Molly has become a Scot. Ever since Tom hit the repulsive Christopher, she has insisted on being as nice as she possibly can to the repulsive Hope. Every day Hope comes round after school and smells the place out; and the more she smells, the keener Molly is for her to return the following evening, and the more Tom is made aware of his own unpleasantness to his Hope equivalent. I am seriously beginning to worry about Molly's mental health: how many eight-year-olds would want to spend day after day doing something so unappealing just to show that they are morally superior to a sibling?

And now we are approaching Molly's birthday, and she is insisting that she doesn't want a party; she wants to spend the day with us and her brother and her new best friend. To our immense discredit, two of the five people involved are not so keen.

'She never gets invited anywhere,' says Molly by way of explanation. They are very different, my son and my daughter, particularly at the moment. My son would make the same observation to justify the opposite course of action. Someone who was never invited anywhere would, *ipso facto*, be excluded from any party that Tom might contemplate throwing.

'But she smells,' Tom points out.

'Yes,' says Molly, almost affectionately. 'But she can't help it.'

'Yes, she can.'

'How?'

'She could have a bath. And use deodorant. And she doesn't have to fart all the time, does she?'

'I think she does, yes.'

I am struck suddenly both by the importance of this argument (it is, after all, about nothing less than how much we owe our fellow humans, and whether it is our duty to love everyone regardless of their personal attributes) and the form that it has taken – namely, a small child's flatulence. I stifle a laugh, because this is a serious business. The idea of driving to an amusement park in a small family car with Hope is not, ultimately, very funny.

'Why don't you just have a big birthday party and invite Hope to that?'

'She can do what she wants,' says David.

'Of course she can do what she wants. I just want to make sure that this is what she wants. I don't want to have to look at photos of Molly's ninth birthday party and try to remember who the hell she spent it with.'

'Why not? We don't know hardly anyone in our wedding photos any more.'

'Yes. And look what . . .' I stop myself just in time. Bitter contemplation of the wreck that is our marriage would be inappropriate right now. '. . . Look what was the cause of that.' In my anxiety to finish the sentence seamlessly I have begun to speak like an Eastern European exchange student.

However, if you wanted to look what was the cause of that, you couldn't have found a neater illustration of how our marriage became a wreck: over the next few years David taunted and teased and sneered at all the guests at our wedding, our friends and colleagues and relatives, for years and years until they dropped us.

'It's my birthday. I can do what I want.'

'It's not for a couple of weeks. Why don't you wait until you mention it to her, just to make sure?' It's not as if she'll be busy, after all.

'I don't want to.' And she goes to the telephone with more malicious glee, it seems to me, than is strictly appropriate for an act of such selfless generosity.

*

So. To recap: I wish to be forgiven for my trespasses (which include committing adultery, dishonouring my parents, being rude to the borderline mentally ill, e.g., Barmy Brian, and even lying to my own children about where I live), and yet I will not forgive those who trespass against me, even if they are eight-year-old girls whose only real trespass is smelling bad. And having grey skin. And not being terribly bright. Right. OK, then. Let me think about that, and I'll come back to you.

I don't even know I'm going to say the words until they come out of my mouth, and when they do I feel slightly faint. Perhaps I was feeling faint already – it is Sunday morning, and I have not yet eaten, despite having left the flat a couple of hours ago. Perhaps if I'd had a bowl of cereal as soon as I got home, I would never have said anything.

'I'm going to church. Does anyone want to come?'

David and the children look at me with some interest, for some time. It's as if, having said something eccentric, I might follow this up by doing something eccentric, like stripping naked or running amok with a kitchen knife. I am suddenly glad that it is not my job to convince people that going to church is a perfectly healthy leisure activity.

'I told you,' says Tom.

'What did you tell me? When?'

'Ages ago. When Dad was giving all our stuff away. I said we'd have to go to church in the end.'

I had forgotten that. So Tom was right, in a way he could never have predicted.

'This is nothing to do with your father,' I say. 'And no one has to go anywhere.'

'I'll come with you,' says Molly.

'What church?' says David.

Good question.

'The one round the corner.' There must be one round the corner. They're like betting shops, churches, aren't they? There's always one round the corner, and you never notice them if you don't use them.

'What corner?'

'We could go with Pauline,' says Molly. 'I know which church she goes to.' Pauline is a schoolfriend of Molly's. She's Afro-Caribbean. Oh, God.

'That wasn't . . . I was thinking of a different sort of church.'

'Pauline says it's fun, hers.'

'I'm not looking for a fun church.'

'What are you looking for?' David asks, relishing my discomfort.

'Just . . . I want to sit at the back and not join in. I expect Pauline's is a . . . well, a joining-in sort of church, isn't it?'

'What do you want to go for if you don't join in? What's the point of that?'

'I just want to listen.'

'I'm sure we can listen at Pauline's church.'

It's the lack of conviction I want, of course. I was hoping for a mild, doubtful liberal, possibly a youngish woman, who would give a sermon about, say, asylum seekers and economic migrants, or maybe the National Lottery and greed, and then apologize for bringing up the subject of God. And somehow in the process I would be forgiven my imperfections, permitted not to like Hope and Barmy Brian, made to understand that just because I wasn't good, it didn't mean I was bad. That sort of thing. And maybe that's exactly what Pauline's church is like – how would I know? I am, however, presuming that it isn't. I am presuming that at Pauline's church there is no doubt, simply joyful and committed worship, and I am presuming that because it is easier to stereotype racially than it is to find out the truth. So there we have it. I get up in the morning determined to do something approximating to the right thing, and within two hours find something else to feel guilty about.

'They go to a different sort of church, don't they, Mum?' says Tom.

'Who are "they"?' I ask sharply. If I'm going down, I'm going to take them with me.

'Pauline's family,' says Tom, puzzled.

'Oh. I thought you were being . . . Never mind.'

Because, of course, it wasn't him that was being anything. It was me. As usual.

Eventually I manage to convince Molly that we are Church of England, although this line of argument is not without its horrifying moments either, and the two of us cruise the neighbourhood in the car, looking for the right church putting on the right show at the right time. We strike it lucky almost immediately: Molly spots a few ancient parishioners hobbling into St Stephen's, a couple of streets away, and we park the car right outside. (If you are the kind of person whose choice of entertainment is governed by ease of parking, then I thoroughly recommend Anglican Sunday services. You can arrive at five to ten for a ten o'clock service, and you're away by two minutes past eleven. Anyone who's had to wait for an hour in the Wembley car park after a Spice Girls concert may find this attractive.)

It has everything I want. The vicar is indeed a kindly middle-aged lady who seems vaguely ashamed of her beliefs; the sparsity of the congregation, and its apparent lack of interest in anything or anyone, allows us to sit towards the back and pretend that we're nothing to do with anything or anybody. Molly is of course the youngest person in the pews on this side of the church, but I am probably the second youngest, by ten or fifteen years, although with a couple of them it's hard to tell: time has not, it is fair to say, been kind to some of these people. God knows what is cause and what is effect here.

We sing a hymn, 'Glorious Things of Thee are Spoken' – an easy one, easy-peasy, clearly remembered from school assemblies and assorted weddings, and both Molly and I join in with both energy and expertise, even if we do say so ourselves; and then there is a reading, and then there are notices. They're having a bring-and-buy sale. The reason there is no choir this week is that it has been invited to join forces with another choir to do something else somewhere else . . . I start to drift off. I have never been to an ordinary church service before. I have been to weddings, funerals, christenings, carol services and even harvest festivals, but I have never been to a bog-standard, nobody-there Sunday service.

It all feels a long way from God – no nearer than the bring-and-buy sale would be, and much further away than I imagine Molly's friend Pauline is at this precise moment. It feels sad, exhausted, defeated; this may have been God's house once, you want to tell the handful of people here, but He's clearly moved, shut up shop, gone to a place where there's more of a demand for that sort of thing. And then you look around and wonder whether the sadness isn't part of the point: those who are able to drag themselves here once a week are clearly not social church-goers, because there is nothing social happening here. This isn't a place to see and be seen, unless opera glasses are placed on the backs of the pews. You'd have to walk twenty yards to shake somebody's hand. No, these people are the hardcore, the last WASPs in Holloway, the beaten and the lonely and the bereaved, and if there is a place for them in the Kingdom of Heaven, they deserve it. I just hope that it's warmer there than here, and there is more hope, and youth, and there is no need for bring-and-buy sales, and the choir of angels isn't singing elsewhere that day, but you rather fear it might be; C of E heaven is in all probability a quarter-full of unhappy old ladies selling misshapen rock cakes and scratched Mantovani records. Every day of the week, for all eternity. And what about the nice lady reading the notices to us? Is she ever dispirited by her hobbling, careworn flock? I thought that I could detect a touch of weariness, maybe even despair, during the appeal for flower-arrangers, but maybe this is because flower-arranging is not her thing.

Sermons, however, clearly are her thing – electrifyingly, embarrassingly, hilariously so. She takes a deep breath, fixes us with a stare, and then shouts '1–2–3–4 GET WITH THE WICKED!', and we shrink back into our pews, afraid and confused – all of us apart from Molly, who recognizes the reference. '1–2–3–4 Get With the Wicked' is her favourite song in the charts at the moment – she bought it last Saturday afternoon with her pocket money, in Holloway Road, and she spent the afternoon dancing to it. The rest of the congregation, however, the varicose women and emphysemic men who constitute the nice lady's flock . . . I would wager that none of them have, as yet, bought the CD, so they do not know why the nice lady is shouting these things at them, and those who are physically capable of doing so stare hard at their shoes.

The nice lady pauses and smiles. 'Is that what Jesus wanted, for us to "get with the wicked"?' she asks. 'I think it is.' She points at us, suddenly and theatrically, as if she had a microphone in the other hand. 'Think about it.' Her invitation is welcome, because it means that we can continue to look at our shoes for a while longer as we struggle to tease out all the theological implications of the lyric. Who on earth does she think she is talking to? I can only presume she is literally looking at a different audience, that she has entered a parallel universe full of young, trendy Christians who wouldn't miss her sermons for the world and whoop with joy at each reference she makes to their culture. I want to run up to the pulpit and shake her.

'Think about it,' she says again. 'Mary Magdalene. Judas Iscariot. Zaccheus the tax collector. The woman at the well. One, two, three, four! That was Jesus getting with the wicked!' Suddenly, though, she switches her line of thought, and, with a grinding change of gears that would make even the most hopeless learner driver wince, she wonders whether God wants us to get with the good as much as He wants us to get with the wicked. She suspects not. She suspects that He wants us merely to be ourselves, and that if we spend all our time being falsely pious, then He won't be able to get to know us, which is what He wants to do.

Suddenly she starts singing 'Getting to Know You' from *The King and I*. I am blushing now. I can feel the blood pumping through every vein in my face and neck, and for the first time I wonder whether the nice lady is actually demented. It is only fair to point out, however, that not everyone is as agonized as I am by the performance. Some of us are waggling our heads and smiling, and it is clear that *The King and I* is closer to our collective heart than 'Get With the Wicked'.

'This is a good church, isn't it, Mum?' Molly whispers, and I nod with as much enthusiasm as I can access.

'Is this the one we'll be coming to every week?'

I shrug. Who knows? It is not easy to see how I might become a committed Christian through listening to a madwoman singing selections from musicals at me, but then again, I never really anticipated sharing my house with men called names like Good-News and Monkey.

'I know that song is from *The King and I*,' says the nice lady, 'but it could have been written about God. He wants to get to know you. And that's why He is not interested in you being artificially good, because that prevents Him from discovering you.'

Ha. This is more like it. 'Artificially good'. I like that phrase, and I will throw it in somebody's face at the first available opportunity. This is why I have moved out: because of the artificiality of David's behaviour, which prevents God from knowing him. In fact, David may well end up going to hell, paradoxically and ironically, because God will not have a clue who he really is. I am coming round to the Christian viewpoint. The nice lady is arguing that doing nothing – and anyway, I don't do nothing, because I am a doctor, a good person, but my goodness is organic and natural, rather than artificial – is better, more holy, than doing something. I decide, on the spot, to let God into my heart, in the hope that my new-found faith can somehow be used as a vicious weapon in the marital war. It is true that not everyone discovers the Lord in this way; some would argue that it is distinctly unChristian, in fact, to become a convert in the hope that it might really upset somebody. But God, famously, moves in mysterious ways.

The sermon is followed by a reading that I find so pertinent that it is all I can do to stop myself leaping out of my pew and punching the air. The reading is given by one of the very few men in the congregation with the puff to get up the steps to the pulpit; when he has recovered from his exertions, he launches in to one of St Paul's Letters to the Corinthians. It's famous, this reading, and I've heard it many times before (how? where?), and because I think I know it, I drift off. The word 'charity' reels me back in. ' "Charity vaunteth not itself, is not puffed up",' the man with puff says. Hurrah for St Paul! Right on! Vaunting and puffing! Puffing and vaunting! You want any of that, you should come round to Webster

Road, which has become a Puffers and Vaunters Social Club! Why have I never heard this stuff properly before?

I attempt to think about all this, and how it can best be used for maximum damage, by gazing across the church and into what I hope is a holy space, but I end up simply staring at someone I hadn't noticed before: a man of around my age, with my nose and my complexion, wearing my husband's old leather jacket. I am looking at my brother. My brother!

My first reaction – and this says something about the state of contemporary Anglicanism, and also why I suspect my new-found enthusiasm for the Church is likely to be short-lived – is to feel terribly sad for him; I really hadn't known things were this desperate. I watch him for a while, and manage to convince myself that the desperation is etched on his face. He clearly isn't listening to a word that the nice lady is saying, and at one stage he emits a sigh and props his head up on his fist. I nudge Molly and point, and after she has spent an abortive couple of minutes failing to attract his attention, she crosses the church and joins him. He does a double-take, kisses her, then looks round and locates me, and we exchange baffled smiles.

The nice mad lady is giving communion now, and the congregation gets shakily to its collective feet and begins to shuffle forward. The commotion, or what passes for a commotion here, allows me to scoop up the members of my family scattered around the church and lead them out.

'Hello.' When we get outside I kiss Mark on the cheek and look at him quizzically.

'It's like bumping into someone in a brothel, isn't it?' he says.

'Is it?'

'Yeah. I mean, I'm mortified that you've caught me. But then, you shouldn't really be here either, should you?'

'I've got a child.'

'That's an excuse for going to *Toy Story 2*, not church.'

'We're going every week,' says Molly. 'It was great, wasn't it?'

'Well, Uncle Mark can take you next week. Do you want to come back for coffee?'

'Yeah. Thanks.'

Mark and I walk to the car – thirty seconds, it takes us! – in silence, listening to Molly rapping '1–2–3–4 Get With the Wicked' and skipping along to the rhythm in her head. Neither Mark nor I are amused or delighted by her display, even though she is being relatively amusing and delightful, if you like that sort of thing; and I remember that when I was pregnant with Tom, I used to watch other parents reacting with either blankness or irritation to their children's childishness and wondering whether I would ever be able to take it for granted like that. I couldn't imagine it. The heady preparation of hope and hormones that courses through you during pregnancy had kidded me into believing I would always, always want to cry whenever my unborn child did anything joyful. But it just gets beaten out of you – not by the kids, but by life. You want to cry, but you're too busy trying not to cry about something else, and this morning I'm trying not to cry about the state of my brother.

Mark looks old, much older than I remember him looking: sadness has gouged some extra lines around his eyes and mouth, and there is some grey in his Sunday-morning stubble. He's usually clean-shaven, so allowing the grey to poke out like that seems significant somehow – not so much as if he's accepted the ageing process with dignity, but more that he has given up, that there's no point in reaching for the shaving foam because shaving is the first move of a game he's lost too many times already. Maybe I'm being silly and melodramatic, and maybe if I'd caught him coming out of a nightclub (or a brothel) looking like this the stubble and the weariness would prompt an entirely different interpretation, but I haven't caught him coming out of a nightclub. I've caught him coming out of a church, and I know him well enough to presume that this is not a good sign.

'So?'

'So what?'

'Was that a one-off?'

'A two-off.'

'Twice in a row? Or twice ever?'

'In a row.'

'And how's it going?'

'You were there. I mean, she's, you know . . . She's one wafer short of a communion, isn't she?'

'So why go back? Why not go to a different one?'

'I'm afraid that if I go to a good one I'll get sucked in. No chance of that there.'

'That's the logic of a depressive.'

'Well. Yeah. It would be, wouldn't it?'

I park outside the house and we go inside. GoodNews and David are at the kitchen table hunched over a piece of paper.

'This is my brother Mark. I bumped into him in church. Mark, this is DJ GoodNews.'

They shake hands, and GoodNews gives Mark a long, quizzical stare that clearly unnerves him.

'Can you both shove off now?' I say. 'Mark and I want to talk privately.' David shoots me a loving, wounded look, but they gather their stuff together and go.

'Can I listen?' says Molly.

'No. Bye.'

'That bloke was at the party,' Mark says. 'Who is he?'

'GoodNews? My husband's spiritual healer. He lives with us now. With them, anyway. I live in a bedsit round the corner. Not that the kids know.'

'Oh. Right. So. Anything else happening?'

'That's about it.'

I tell him about the last few weeks with as much economy as he permits, and while I am talking it strikes me that if anyone needed the sadness drawing out of him it is Mark.

'How about you?'

'Oh, you know.' He shrugs.

'What do I know?'

'I've been to church twice in the last fortnight. That sort of sums it up.'

He doesn't mean that this is the sum total of his activity; he means that he has reached the end of his tether. Mark takes drugs, goes to see bands, swears a lot, hates Conservatives, has periods of promiscuity. If, on meeting him for the first time, you were asked to name one thing that he didn't do, you would almost certainly choose churchgoing.

'How did it start?'

'I was driving to see you. I was feeling low, and I thought the kids would cheer me up, and it was Sunday morning, and . . . I dunno. I just saw the church, and it was the right time, and I went in. What about you?'

'I wanted to be forgiven.'

'For what?'

'For all the shitty things I do,' I say.

Mark only just made my guilt-list, and when I look at him now that seems almost laughably complacent. He's a very unhappy man, maybe even suicidal, and I didn't have a clue. All the lonely people . . . At least we know where they come from: Surrey. That's where Mark and I come from, anyway.

'You don't do anything shitty.'

'Thank you. But I'm human. That's how humans spend their time, doing shitty things.'

'Fucking hell. Glad I came here.'

I give him a cup of coffee, and he lights a cigarette – he gave up ten years ago – and I look for Monkey's saucer ashtray while he tells me about his hopeless job, and his hopeless love life, and all the stupid mistakes he's made, and how he has started to hate everyone and everything, including his nearest and dearest, which is how come he has ended up listening to a woman singing lines from *The King and I* at ten o'clock on a Sunday morning.

GoodNews has picked it all up already, of course. We sit down to a hastily assembled ploughman's lunch, and without invitation he wades into the stagnant, foul-smelling pond that is Mark's life.

'I'm sorry if you think I'm being a bit, you know,' he begins. 'But when we shook hands . . . Man, you nearly took my arm off.'

'I'm sorry,' says Mark, apologetic but understandably surprised: I saw the whole incident, and it seemed like a pretty straightforward handshake to me; at no stage did it look as though anyone would end up with a permanent disability. 'Did I hurt you?'

'In here you hurt me.' GoodNews taps his heart. 'Because it hurts when I know fellow human beings are in trouble. And if ever a hand was shouting for help it was yours.'

Mark cannot help it: he has a quick look, back and front, to see if there is any evidence of this manual distress.

'Nah, you won't see anything there. It's not a, like a visible thing. I mean, I feel it physically. Ow. You know?' And he winces and massages his hand, to demonstrate the pain that Mark so recently caused him. 'But sadness is a right sod for keeping itself hidden away. A right sod. Gotta come out sometime, though, and it's pouring out of you.'

'Oh,' says Mark.

The children munch on relentlessly. It depresses me that they are so accustomed to conversations of this kind that they cannot even be bothered to gape.

'I'm sure Mark would rather talk about something else,' I say hopefully.

'Perhaps he would,' says GoodNews. 'But I'm not sure it'd be a good idea. Do you know what you're sad about, Mark?'

'Well . . .'

'As far as I can tell, it's mostly in the area of relationships and work,' says GoodNews, apparently uninterested in anything Mark has to say. 'And it's starting to get serious.'

'How serious?' says David, concerned.

'You know,' says GoodNews, nodding meaningfully at the children.

'There's not much point in Mark being here, is there?' I say. 'Why don't you two sort it out between you?'

'Oh, we can't do that,' says GoodNews. 'In the end, Mark knows more about how unhappy he is than either of us.'

'Really?' I use a sarcastic tone of voice, and make a sarcastic face, and I even attempt a sarcastic posture, but it's no use.

'Oh, sure. I only get the vaguest sense of the causes.'

'I'd say work and relationships just about covered it,' Mark says.

'Do you want to do anything about it?' David asks him.

'Well, yeah, I wouldn't mind.'

'GoodNews rubs it out of you,' Molly says matter-of-factly. 'His hands go all hot and then you're not sad any more. I'm not sad about Grandma Parrot, or Poppy, or Mummy's baby that died.'

Mark nearly chokes. 'Jesus, Katie . . .'

'You should try it, Uncle Mark. It's great.'

'Can I have some more ham, Mum?' says Tom.

'We could really do a lot for you, Mark,' says David. 'You could leave a lot of things behind you here today if you wanted to.'

Mark pushes his chair back and stands up.

'I'm not listening to this shit,' he says, and walks out.

Getting married and having a family is like emigrating. I used to live in the same country as my brother, I used to share his values and his tastes and his attitudes, and then I moved away. And even though I didn't notice it happening, I started to speak with a different accent, and think differently, and even though I remembered my native land fondly, all traces of it had gone from me. Now, though, I want to go home. I can see that I made a big mistake, that the new world isn't all it was cracked up to be, and the people there are much saner and wiser than the people who live in my adopted nation. I want him to take me back with him. We could go home to Mum and Dad's. We'd both be happier there. He wasn't suicidal when he was there, and I wasn't careworn and guilty. It would be great. We'd fight about what television programmes to watch, probably, but apart from that . . . And we wouldn't make the same mistakes as before. We wouldn't decide that we wanted to get older and live lives of our own. We tried that, and it didn't work.

I follow him out, and we go and sit in the car for a while.

'You can't carry on like that,' he says.

I shrug.

'It's not impossible. What'll happen to me if I do?'

'You'll crack up. You won't be able to bring the kids up. You won't be able to work.'

'Maybe that's just because I'm pathetic. My husband's got a new hobby and he's invited a friend to stay. And OK, the hobby is redeeming souls, but . . . You know, I should be able to cope with that.'

'They're mad.'

'They've done some pretty amazing things. They got the whole street to take in homeless kids.'

'Yeah, but . . .' Mark goes quiet. He can't think of anything to say. It's always 'Yeah, but . . .' and then nothing when the homeless are brought into it.

'And, anyway, what kind of advertisement are you for the other side? Christ. You're thirty-eight years old, you don't have a full-time job, you're depressed and lonely, and you've started going to church because you've run out of ideas.'

'I'm not the other side. I'm just . . . normal.'

I laugh.

'Yeah. Normal. That's right. Suicidal and hopeless. The thing is, they're all mad in there. But I've never seen David so happy.'

Later that night, when I'm back cocooned in my bedsit, I read the arts pages of the newspaper, like the rounded adult I am desperately trying to become, and in a book review someone talks about how Virginia Woolf's sister Vanessa Bell led a 'rich, beautiful life'. I follow the phrase right the way up a blind alley. What can it possibly mean? How can one live a rich and beautiful life in Holloway? With David? And GoodNews? And Tom and Molly, and Mrs Cortenza? With twelve hundred patients, and a working day that lasts until seven o'clock in the evening some nights? If we don't live rich, beautiful lives, does it mean we've screwed up? Is it our fault? And when David dies, will someone say that he too lived a rich, beautiful life? Is that the life I want to stop him from leading?

Molly gets the birthday party she wants: the four of us and Hope go swimming, and then we go for hamburgers, and then we go to the cinema to see Chicken Run, which Hope doesn't really under-stand. After a little while Molly decides that Hope is to all intents and purposes blind, and begins a running commentary for her benefit, which eventually provokes an irritated complaint from the row behind us.

'Oi. Shut it.'

'She's not very clever,' Molly retorts, in aggrieved self-defence. 'And it's my birthday, and I invited her to my party because she hasn't got any friends and I felt sorry for her, and I want her to enjoy it, and she can't if she doesn't know what's happening.'

There is an appalled silence – or what I imagine, in my shame, to be an appalled silence – and then the sound of someone making an exaggerated vomiting noise.

'Why did that man pretend to be sick?' Molly asks when we have dropped Hope off at her house.

'Because you made him sick,' Tom says.

'Why?'

'Because you're disgusting.'

'That's enough, Tom,' says David.

'She is, though. So goody-goody.'

'And you don't like her being good?'

'No. She's just doing it to show off.'

'How do you know? And anyway, what difference does it make? The point is that Hope had a nice time for a change. And if that's because Molly was showing off, that's fine.'

And Tom is silenced, like everyone is silenced, by the unanswerable righteousness of David's logic.

'"Charity vaunteth not itself, is not puffed up",' I say.

'I'm sorry?'

'You heard me. You two are puffing and vaunting at every available opportunity.'

'Yeah,' says Tom darkly. He doesn't know what I'm talking about, but he can recognize an aggressive tone when he hears one.

'Where do you get all that stuff?' David asks. 'Where does it come from, the puffing and the vaunting?'

'The Bible. St Paul's Letter to the Corinthians, Chapter 13. They read it out in church on Sunday.'

'The one we had at our wedding?'

'What?'

'Corinthians, Chapter 13. Your brother read it.'

'Mark didn't read anything about charity. It was all about love. That corny one that everyone has.' Please forgive me, St Paul, because I don't think it's corny; I think, and have always thought, that it's beautiful, even if everyone else does, too, and the reading was my choice.

'I don't know. All I know is that Corinthians, Chapter 13 is what we had at our wedding.'

'OK, so I got the number wrong. But the one they read in church on Sunday was all about charity, and how true charity is not puffed up, and I thought of you and your puffed-up friend.'

'Thank you.'

'It's a pleasure.'

We drive on in silence, but then David suddenly thumps the steering-wheel.

'It's the same thing,' he says.

'What?'

'Love is not boastful, nor proud. It vaunteth not itself, is not puffed up. See? What Mark read was translated.'

'Not love. Charity.'

'They're the same word. I remember this now. *Caritas*. It's Latin or Greek or something, and sometimes it's translated as "charity" and sometimes it's translated as "love".'

That is why the reading seemed strangely familiar, then: because my own brother read it at my own wedding, and it is one of my own favourite pieces of writing. For some reason I feel dizzy and nauseous, as if I have done something terrible. Love and charity share the same root word . . . How is that possible, when everything in our recent history suggests that they cannot coexist, that they are antithetical, that if you put the two of them together in a sack they would bite and scratch and scream, until one of them is torn apart?

'"And though I have the faith to move mountains, without love I am nothing at all". That one.'

'We've got that song,' says Molly.

'It's not a song, idiot,' says Tom. 'It's the Bible.'

'Lauryn Hill sings it. On that CD Daddy bought ages ago. I've been playing it in my room. The last song, she sings that.' And Molly gives us a pretty, if occasionally off-key, rendition of St Paul's Letter to the Corinthians, Chapter 13.

When we get home, Molly plays us the Lauryn Hill song, and David disappears off upstairs and comes down with a box full of bits and pieces from our wedding day, a box that I don't think I knew we owned.

'Where did that come from?'

'The old suitcase under our bed.'

'Did my mother give it to us?'

'No.'

He starts to rummage through the box.

'Who did, then?'

'Nobody.'

'What, it just appeared on its own?'

'You can't think of any other explanation?'

'Don't be stupid, David. It's a very simple question. There's no need for all this mystery.'

'It's a very simple answer.'

And still I cannot think of it, so I make a frustrated, impatient growling noise and start to walk away.

'It's mine,' he says quietly.

'Why is it yours all of a sudden?' I say aggressively. 'Why isn't it ours? I was there, too, you know.'

'No, I mean, of course it's yours as well, if you want it. I just mean . . . I bought the box. I got the stuff together. That's how it came into the house.'

'When?' And still I can hear a snort in my voice, as if I don't believe him, as if he is somehow trying to put one over on me.

'I don't know. When we came back from our honeymoon. It was a fantastic day. I was so happy. I just didn't want to forget it.'

I burst into tears, and I cry and cry until it feels as though it is not salt and water being squeezed from my eyes, but blood.

13

'"Without love I am nothing at all,"' Lauryn Hill sings for the twelfth and seventeenth and twenty-fifth time on Janet's CD player, and each time I think, yes, that is me, that is what I have become, nothing at all, and I either cry again, or merely feel like crying. That's why David's box devastated me, I realize now – not just because I had no idea that my husband still felt anything at all about our wedding day, but because the part of me that should feel things is sick, or dying, or dead, and I never even noticed until tonight.

I'm not too sure when this happened, but I know that it was a long time ago – before Stephen (otherwise there wouldn't have been a Stephen), long before GoodNews (otherwise there wouldn't have been a GoodNews); but after Tom and Molly were born, because I was something and someone then, the most important person in the whole world. Maybe if I kept a diary I could date it precisely. I could read an entry and think, oh, right, it was on 23 November 1994, when David said this or did that. But what could David have possibly said or done to make me close down in this way? No, I suspect that I closed myself down, that something in me just got infarcted, or dried up, or sclerotic, and I let it happen because it suited me. And there is just enough for Molly and Tom, but it doesn't really count, because it's a reflex, and my occasional flashes of warmth are like my occasional desire to wee.

Maybe that's what's wrong with all of us. Maybe Mark thought he was going to find that warmth in church, and all those people in our street who took the street kids in thought they could find it in their spare bedrooms, and David found it in GoodNews's finger-tips – went looking for it because he wanted to feel it once more before he died. As do I.

Oh, I'm not talking about romantic love, the mad hunger for someone you don't know very well. And the feelings that constitute my working week – guilt, of course, and fear, and irritation, and a few other ignoble distractions that simply serve to make me unwell half the time – are not enough for me, nor for anybody. I'm talking about that love which used to feel something like optimism, benignity . . . Where did that go? I just seemed to run out of steam somewhere along the line. I ended up disappointed with my work, and my marriage, and myself, and I turned into someone who didn't know what to hope for.

The trick, it seems to me, is to stave off regret. That's what the whole thing is about. And we can't stave it off for ever, because it is impossible not to make the mistakes that let regret in, but the best of us manage to limp on into our sixties or seventies before we succumb. Me, I made it to about thirty-seven, and David made it to the same age, and my brother gave up the ghost even before that. And I'm not sure that there is a cure for regret. I suspect not.

The new patient seems vaguely familiar, but I'm not feeling very sharp: the little Turkish girl I have just seen probably has something seriously wrong with her, and I have been attempting to explain to her mother, through the Turkish-speaking health visitor, why I am sending her for a brain scan. So my nerves are jangling a little, and initially I don't have as much interest in the new patient's skin complaint as I would wish.

I ask her to take her top off, and she says something jovial about how she hates showing disgustingly slim doctors her fat stomach, and at the very moment the jumper covers her face, I recognize the voice. It belongs to the nice lady from the church.

She stands up so that I can see the rash on her back.

'Have you had this before?'

'Not for a long time. It's stress-related.'

'What makes you say that?'

'Because the last time I got it was when my mother died. And now I've got a lot of work problems.'

'What kind of work problems?'

This is an unprofessional question. I am always hearing that people have work problems, and I have never before shown the slightest interest, although if I am feeling especially sympathetic I might cluck a little. The nice lady, though . . . Of course I want to know about what is wrong with her job.

'It's utterly pointless, and I hate my . . . I hate the people I work for. Especially . . . Well, especially the boss.'

'You can put your top back on.'

I start to write a prescription.

'I was in your church last week.'

She flushes.

'Oh. I shouldn't have said anything.'

'It's fine. Patient–doctor confidentiality and all that.'

'Well, anyway, you know what my problems are, then.'

'Do I?'

'Isn't it obvious?'

I decide that it is best to say nothing, on the grounds that what was obvious to me – her rendition of 'Getting to Know You' was excruciating, all reference to the current rap hits is misguided to the point of lunacy – might not be obvious to her, and I will only succeed in making the angry red marks on her back positively furious. I write her a prescription and hand it to her.

'I enjoyed it,' I tell her.

'Thank you. But basically I no longer believe in what I'm doing, and I think it's all a waste of time, and my body knows it. So I feel ill every day.'

'Well, that's hopefully something I can help with.'

'Why did you come to my church? You haven't been before, have you?'

'No. I'm not a Christian. But I'm having a spiritual crisis, so . . .'

'Do doctors have spiritual crises?'

'Apparently they do, yes. My marriage is in big trouble and I'm very sad and I'm trying to decide what to do about it. What do you recommend?'

'I'm sorry?'

'What should I do?'

She smiles nervously; she's not sure whether I'm joking. I'm not.

I'm suddenly consumed with the desire to hear what she has to say.

'I've told you what to do about your rash. That's what I'm here for. You tell me what to do about my marriage. That's what you're there for.'

'I'm not sure you understand what the role of the church is.'

'What is it, then?'

'I'm not the one to ask, am I? Because I haven't got a clue.'

'Who has, then?'

'Have you tried counselling?'

'I'm not talking about counselling. I'm talking about what's right and wrong. You know about that, surely?'

'Do you want to know what the Bible says about marriage?'

'No!' I'm shouting now, I can hear myself, but I don't seem to be able to do anything about it. 'I want to know what YOU say. Just tell me. I'll do whatever it is you recommend. Stay or go. Come on.' And I mean it. I'm sick of not knowing. Someone else can sort it out.

The nice lady looks a little afraid, as she has every right to do, I suppose. I am seriously contemplating holding her hostage until she comes out with an answer, any answer, although I will not fill her in on this plan of action for the moment.

'Dr Carr, I can't tell you what to do.'

'I'm sorry, that's not good enough.'

'Do you want to come and see me in my office?'

'No. No need. Waste of time. It's a yes/no question. I don't want to spend hours talking about it with you. I've already spent months thinking about it. It's gone on long enough.'

'Do you have children?'

'Yes.'

'Is your husband cruel to you?'

'No. Not any more. He used to be, but he saw the light. Not your sort of light. Another one.'

'Well. . . ' She is on the verge of saying something, but then she stands up. 'This is ridiculous. I can't . . .'

I snatch the prescription out of her hand. 'In which case, I can't help you. You do your job and I'll do mine.'

'It's not my job. Please give me my prescription.'

'No. It's not much to ask. Stay or go, that's all I want. God, why are you people so timid? It's no wonder the churches are empty, when you can't answer even the simplest questions. Don't you get it? That's what we want. Answers. If we wanted woolly minded nonsense we'd stay at home. In our own heads.'

'I think you'll do what you want to do anyway, so it won't make any difference what I say.'

'Wrong. Wrong. Because I haven't got a clue any more. Do you remember *The Dice Man*, that book everyone read at college? Maybe not at theological college they didn't, but at normal college they did. Well, I am the Vicar Woman. Anything you say, I will do.'

She looks at me and holds up her hands, indicating defeat. 'Stay.'

I feel suddenly hopeless, the way one always does when two alternatives become one chosen course of action. I want to go back to the time just seconds ago when I didn't know what to do. Because here's the thing: when you get into a mess like mine, your marriage is like a knife in your stomach, and you know that you're in big trouble whatever you decide. You don't ask people with knives in their stomachs what would make them happy; happiness is no longer the point. It's all about survival; it's all about whether you pull the knife out and bleed to death or keep it in, in the hope that you might be lucky, and the knife has actually been staunching the blood. You want to know the conventional medical wisdom? The conventional medical wisdom is that you keep the knife in. Really.

'Really?'

'Yes. I'm a vicar. I can't go around telling people to break up families on a whim.'

'Ha! You think it's whimsical?'

'I'm sorry, but you can't start arguing with the decision. You wanted me to say something and I've said it. You're staying. Can I have my prescription now?'

I hand it to her. I'm starting to feel a little embarrassed, as perhaps is only appropriate.

'I won't say anything to anyone,' she says. 'I'm going to work on the assumption that you're having a bad day.'

'And I won't say anything about *The King and I*,' I say – somewhat gracelessly, given the circumstances. Our professional misconduct trials, should it come to that, are almost certain to have different outcomes, given the relative gravity of our crimes. She could argue that it is part of her brief to illuminate her sermons with highlights from the great musicals; I, on the other hand, would be hard pushed to make a case for the violent witholding of treatment until I had received inappropriate marital advice.

'Good luck.'

'Thank you.' I don't feel so graceless now, and I pat her on the back on her way out. I will miss her.

'Have you ever . . . Have you ever threatened a patient?' I ask Becca before I leave for the day. Becca has done many, many bad things, some of them during working hours.

'God, no,' she says, appalled. 'Is that what you think of me?'

So rehearsed is our good doc/bad doc routine that she never for a moment suspects that I am confessing, rather than accusing. That is why Becca is so good to talk to: she doesn't listen.

I want to speak to my husband when I get home, but his relationship is with GoodNews now. The two of them have become inseparable – joined, not at the hip, but at the temple, because whenever I see them they are hunched over their piece of paper, head joining head in a way that is presumably conducive to the mutual flow of psychic energy. In the old days, it would have been reasonable to ask David what was on the piece of paper; indeed, it would have been deemed both rude and unsupportive to show no interest. These days, however, everyone accepts that Molly and Tom and I are the footsoldiers and they are the generals, and any curiosity on our part would be regarded as impertinent, possibly even actionable.

I knock on the invisible office door.

'David, could I speak to you?'

He looks up, momentarily irritated.

'Now?'

'If possible.'

'Fire away.'

'Can we have dinner tonight?'

'We have dinner every night.'

'You and me. Out. GoodNews babysitting. If that's OK with him.'

'Tonight?' GoodNews consults his mental Psion Organiser and finds that, as it happens, he is indeed free tonight.

'OK, then. Do you think we need to talk?'

'Well, yes.'

'About . . . ?'

'There are a couple of things. Maybe we should talk about last night, for example. My reaction.'

'Oh, don't worry about that. We all get upset from time to time.'

'Yeah,' says GoodNews. 'Can't be helped. Like I said to your brother, sadness can be a right sod for keeping itself hidden away and then popping out.' He waves a magnanimous hand. 'Forget about it. It never happened.'

They smile beatifically and return to their piece of paper. I have been dismissed. I do not wish to be dismissed.

'I'm not looking for forgiveness. I want to talk about it. I want to explain. I want you and I to go out and attempt to communicate. As husband and wife.'

'Oh. Right. Sorry. That would be nice, yes. And you're sure you don't want GoodNews to come with us? He's very good at that kind of stuff.'

'I'm going through a really intuitive time at the moment, I have to say,' says GoodNews. 'And I know what you're saying about husband and wife and that whole intimacy thing, but you'd be amazed at the stuff I can pick up that's kind of zapping about between you.' And he makes a zigzaggy gesture, the exact meaning of which is lost on me, but which I presume is intended to indicate wonky marital communication.

'Thanks, but it's fine,' I tell him. 'We'll call you if we have trouble.'

He smiles patiently. 'That's not going to work, is it? I'm babysitting, remember? I can't just leave them here on their own.'

'We'll ask for a doggy-bag and come home immediately.'

He points a hey-you're-sharp finger at me. I have hit on the solution, and we are allowed out.

'So.'

'So.'

It's such a familiar routine. Two spicy poppadoms for him, one plain one for me, mango chutney and those onion pieces on a side plate placed between us for easy dunking . . . We've been doing this for fifteen years, ever since we could afford it, although before you get the impression that the variety and spontaneity have gone from our lives, I should point out that we've only been coming to this particular restaurant for a decade. Our previous favourite got taken over, and they changed the menu slightly, so we moved to find a closer approximation of what we were used to.

We need things like the Curry Queen, though. Not just David and I, but all of us. What does a marriage look like? Ours looks like this, a side plate smeared with mango chutney. That's how we can tell it apart from all the others. That mango chutney is the white smudge on the cheek of your black cat, or the registration number of a new car, or the name-tag in a child's school sweatshirt; without it we'd be lost. Without that side plate and its orange smear, I might one day come back from the toilet and sit down at a completely different marriage. (And who's to say that this completely different marriage would be any better or worse than the one I already have? I am suddenly struck by the absurdity of my decision – not the one handed to me by the vicar in the surgery, which still seems as good or as bad as any, but the one I made all those years ago.)

'You wanted to talk,' David says.

'Don't you?'

'Well, yes. I suppose so. If you do.'

'I do, yes.'

'Right.' Silence. 'Off you go, then.'

'I'm going to stop sleeping at Janet's.'

'Oh. OK, then.' He sips his lager, apparently unsure whether this news has any relevance to his life.

'Are you moving back home? Or have you found somewhere else?'

'No, no, I'm moving back home.' I suddenly feel a little sorry for him: it was not, after all, an unreasonable question. Most relationships in crisis probably provide some sort of clue to their eventual success or failure: the couples concerned start sleeping together again, for example, or attacking each other with kitchen knives, and from those symptoms one can make some kind of prognosis. We haven't had anything like that, however. I moved out without really explaining why, and then a nice lady vicar who doesn't know anything about me told me to move back in because I bullied her. No wonder David felt that his enquiry had several possible answers. He must have felt as though he were asking me who I thought would win the Grand National.

'Oh, right. Well, fine. Good. Good. I'm pleased.'

'Are you?'

'Yes, of course.'

I want to ask him why, and then argue with whatever he says, but I'm not going to. I've stopped all that. I have made my mind up – or rather, I have had it made up for me – and I have no wish to disassemble it.

'Is there anything I can do to make it easier for you?'

'Do you mean that?'

'Yes. I think so.'

'What am I allowed to ask for?'

'Anything you want. And if I don't think it's reasonable, we'll talk about it.'

'Is there any possibility that GoodNews could find somewhere else to live?'

'That really bothers you?'

'Yes. Of course.'

'Fine. I'll tell him he has to go.'

'Simple as that?'

'Simple as that. I'm not sure that it's going to make much difference, though. I mean, he'll still be round all the time. We work together. We're colleagues. Our office is in the house.'

'OK.' I think about this, and decide that David is right: it won't make much difference. I don't want GoodNews living in the house because I don't like GoodNews, but that problem will not be solved by him going to sleep somewhere else at nights. I have wasted one of my three wishes.

'What do you do exactly?'

'Sorry?'

'You say you and GoodNews work together. What do you do?'

A woman on the next table looks at me, and then looks away, and then looks at David. She is clearly trying to work out what my relationship with this man is. I have just told him I will move in with him, but now – somewhat late in the day, she must be thinking – I want to find out what he does.

'Ha! Good question!' When normal people give this answer to that question, they are usually making a joke. You know: 'Good question! Bugger all, really! Blowed if I know!', etc. But David means: 'Phew! How would I explain it, in all its knotty complexity!'

'Thank you.'

The woman on the next table catches my eye. 'Don't move in!' she's trying to say. 'He doesn't even recognize sarcasm!' I try to answer her back, using similar methods: 'It's OK! We've been married for donkey's years! But we've sort of lost touch recently! Spiritual conversion!' I'm not sure she picks it all up, though. It's a lot of information to convey without words.

'We're more at a strategic stage. We haven't got any actual projects on the go, but we're thinking.'

'Right. What are you thinking about?'

'We're thinking about how we can persuade people to give away everything they earn over and above the national average wage. We're just doing the sums at the moment.'

'How are they working out?'

'Well, you know. It's tough. It's not as straightforward as it sounds.'

I'm not making this up. This is actually what he says, in real life, in the Curry Queen.

'Oh, and we're sort of writing a book.'

'A book.'

'Yes. "How to be Good", we're going to call it. It's about how we should all live our lives. You know, suggestions. Like taking in the homeless, and giving away your money, and what to do about things like property ownership and, I don't know, the Third World and so on.'

'So this book's aimed at high-ranking employees of the IMF?'

'No, no, it's for people like you and me. Because we get confused, don't we?'

'We do.'

'So it's a good idea, don't you think?'

'It's a fantastic idea.'

'You're not being sarcastic?'

'No. A book telling us what to think about everything? I'd buy it.'

'I'll give you a copy.'

'Thank you.'

The woman on the next table doesn't want to catch my eye any more. We're no longer pals. She thinks I'm as daft as David is, but I don't care. I want this book badly, and I shall believe every word, and act on every suggestion, no matter how impractical. 'How to be Good' will become the prescription the nice lady denied me. All I need to do is quell the doubt and scepticism that makes me human.

When we get home, GoodNews is asleep in an armchair, a notebook open on his chest. While David is putting the kettle on, I pick the notebook up carefully and sneak a look. 'VEGETARIAN OR MEAT?????' it says in large red letters. 'ALLOWED ORGANIC???? Probly.' No doubt the book will tell us how to feed a family of four on organic meat when we have given away most of our income. I put the book back gently where I found it, but GoodNews wakes anyway.

'Did you have a cool time?'

'Very cool,' I say. 'But I've got a splitting headache.'

David comes into the living room with three mugs of tea on a tray.

'I'm sorry,' he says. 'You didn't tell me.'

'I've had it for a while. A few days. Anyone got any ideas?'

David laughs. 'You know GoodNews. He's full of ideas. But I didn't think you were interested.'

'I'm interested in having headaches taken away. Who wouldn't be? And I can't take any more paracetamol. I've been popping them all day.'

'You serious?' says GoodNews. 'You want the treatment?'

'Yeah. Why not?'

'And you're prepared for what might happen?' David asks.

'I'm prepared.'

'OK, then. Shall we go to the study?'

In a way, I wish I did have a headache, but I don't; I just have a soul-ache, and I want it taken away, whatever the cost. I have given up. I have not been able to beat them, so I will join them, and if that means that I never again utter a cogent sentence, or think a sardonic thought, or trade banter with colleagues or friends, then so be it. I will sacrifice everything that I have come to think of as me for the sake of my marriage and family unity. Maybe that's what marriage is anyhow, the death of the personality, and GoodNews is irrelevant: I should have killed myself, as it were, years ago. As I walk up the stairs I feel like I am experiencing my own personal Jonestown.

GoodNews ushers me in and I sit on David's writing chair.

'Do I have to take anything off?' I'm not afraid of GoodNews in that way. I doubt if he has a sexuality. I think it has been subsumed in some way, used as a stock for his spiritual stew.

'Oh, no. If I can't get through a couple of layers of cotton, I'm not gonna get through to the inner Katie, am I?'

'So what do you want me to do?'

'Just sit there. Where's the headache?'

I point to a place where a headache might feasibly be, and GoodNews touches it gently.

'Here?'

'Yeah.'

He massages it for a little while. It feels good.

'I'm not getting anything.'

'What does that mean?'

'I mean, are you sure the headache is there?'

'Maybe over a bit?'

He moves his fingers along a couple of inches and begins to knead my scalp gently.

'Nah. Nothing.'

'Really? Not even – ow! – just there?'

'Not even just there. Sorry.'

The tone in his voice suggests that he knows I'm faking it, but is too polite to say anything.

'Is that it, then?'

'Yeah. Nothing I can do. I can't find the pain.'

'Can't you just do the warm hands thing anyway?'

'That's not how it works. There's got to be something there.'

'What does that mean?' I ask this because I know he's not just talking about the headache. He is talking about something else, something that he thinks is missing, and I believe him to be right: there is something missing, which is why I came into this room in the first place.

'I dunno. That's just what my hands tell me. You're not . . . I'm sorry if this sounds rude, but you're not all there. In, like, the spiritual sense of the word.'

'And David was?'

'Must have been.'

'But that's not fair! David used to be a horrible, sarcastic, uncaring pig!'

'Yeah, well, I don't know about that. But there was something to work on. With you . . . It's like a flat battery in a car. You know,

I'm turning the ignition, and I'm turning the ignition, and it's just
. . . ker-chunk-ker-chunk-ker-chunk.'

The noise he makes is an uncanny articulation of how I feel.

'Maybe you need some jump leads,' says GoodNews cheerfully.
'Shall we go downstairs and drink our tea?'

14

Barmy Brian, Heartsink No. 1, is first on my Monday morning list, and he's not looking good. I know that a doctor's surgery is not the place to see people looking their best, but Brian has deteriorated rapidly since I last saw him, about three weeks ago. He seems to be wearing pyjamas under his raincoat, he is unshaven, his hair is wild, his face is grey, his breath you would have to file under alcoholic/agricultural.

'Hello, Brian,' I say cheerily. 'In a rush this morning?'

'Why do you say that?'

'Aren't those pyjamas you're wearing?'

'No.'

Even though Brian comes to see me regularly, he mistrusts me intensely and always thinks that I am trying to catch him out, as if I think that he is not who he says he is. Perhaps he isn't – perhaps he's Mental Mike, or Crazy Colin, or Loony Len – but my more or less constant position is that, whoever he is, he's not a well man, and therefore in need of my help. It's not the way he sees it, though. He seems to feel that if I succeed in unmasking him, I will banish him from the surgery.

'I see. You're just wearing matching pink-and-blue striped shirt and trousers.'

'No.'

I don't push it (although believe me, he is wearing pyjamas, and he is only denying it because to admit it would give me some sort of crucial information he'd rather I didn't have). There are unwritten rules for dealing with BB: you're allowed some fun – otherwise we would all be as barmy as he is – but not too much fun.

'What can I do for you?'

'I've got a bad stomach. I'm getting pains.'

'Whereabouts?'

'Here.'

He points to his abdomen. I know from previous experience that I am not allowed to touch any part of BB's body, but as most of BB's troubles are caused, not by physiological malfunction, but by the first B of his name, this is not usually much of a handicap.

'Have you been feeling nauseous? Sick?'

'No.'

'What about going to the toilet? Has that been OK?'

'How do you mean?' The tone of suspicion has returned.

'Now, come on, Brian. If you're having abdominal pain I need to ask you questions like this.' A couple of years ago Brian frantically denied that he ever passed stools, and would only admit to peeing; I was reduced to insisting that I, too, had bowel movements, but he wouldn't listen, and nor was he interested in hearing confessions from other members of staff.

'I've stopped going.'

'How long ago?'

'Couple of weeks.'

'That may well be your problem, then.'

'Really?'

'Yes. Two weeks without going to the loo is enough to give you a tummy ache. Has there been a change in your diet?'

'How do you mean?'

'Are you eating different things?'

'Yeah. Course.' And he snorts, to emphasize the stupidity of the question.

'Why?'

'Because my mum died, didn't she?'

If GoodNews were to touch my head now, he wouldn't say that I had a flat battery. He would say that there were all sorts of things going on: pity, sadness, panic, hopelessness. I hadn't realized that Brian had a mum – he is, according to my notes, fifty-one years old – but it makes complete sense. Of course there would have been a mum, and of course she would have kept the Brian show on the road, and now she has gone, and there are pyjamas and abdominal cramps.

'I'm sorry, Brian.'

'She was old old old. She said she'd die one day. But, see, how did she make the food hot? And how are you supposed to know what should be hot and what shouldn't? 'Cos sometimes we had ham. Cold. And sometimes we had bacon. Hot. And when you buy it they don't tell you which one is which. I thought they would. I've been buying it, but I don't know what to do with it. What about lettuce and cabbage? What about hot chicken and cold chicken? And I'm sure we had cold potatoes once, but they're not like the cold potatoes that you buy in the shop. They were horrible, the ones I bought. I think I bought hot ones by mistake, but they were cold hot ones. I get muddled. I got muddled when I ate them and now I get muddled when I buy them. I feel very muddled.'

This is, I think, one of the saddest speeches I have ever heard, and it is all I can do to stop myself embracing poor Brian and weeping on his shoulder. 'I feel very muddled, too,' I want to tell him. 'We all do. Not knowing what should be eaten raw and what you should cook isn't such a big deal, when you consider the things other people get muddled about.'

'I think maybe your tummy's gone funny because of eating things like raw potatoes,' I say eventually. 'But it's OK. There are all sorts of things we can do.'

And I do some of them. I prescribe him some liquid paraffin, and I recommend a bowel-loosening takeaway curry, and I promise that I will cook him dinner myself one evening. And when he has gone I call Social Services.

When I get home, David and GoodNews announce that after several weeks' deliberation, they have finally isolated their candidates for 'reversal' – their equivalents of Hope and Christopher, the people they feel most guilty about in their whole lives. I'm tired, and hungry, and not terribly interested, but they stand in front of me anyway and insist that they tell me.

'Go on, then,' I say, with as much weariness as I feel, plus a little extra for effect.

'Mine's called Nigel Richards,' David says proudly.

'Who's Nigel Richards?'

'He's a kid I used to beat up at school. Except he's not a kid now. He used to be. In the early seventies.'

'You've never mentioned him before.'

'Too ashamed,' says David, almost triumphantly.

I cannot help feeling that there must be someone else, someone more recent – a former colleague, a family member, me me me – but even on a day like today, when I am depressed and tired, I know better than to provide David with a long, thorny list with which he will flagellate himself for months to come. If he feels bad about Nigel Richards, then Nigel Richards it is.

GoodNews, meanwhile, has chosen his sister.

'What', I ask, 'did you do to your sister?'

'Nothing, really. I just . . . I can't stand her, that's all. So I never see her. And she's my sister. I feel bad about it, you know?'

'Do I still have to play with Hope, Mummy?'

'You've done your bit.'

'Well, we've never really done our bit, have we?' says David. 'It's a lifelong commitment.'

'So Nigel Richards is going to be your new best friend? We'll be spending all our time with Mr and Mrs Richards in the future?'

'I'm sure Nigel Richards won't need me as a best friend. I'm sure he's gone on to have millions of successful and fulfilling relationships. But if he hasn't, then I'll be there for him, yes.'

'You'll be there for someone you don't know because you thumped him twenty-five years ago?'

'Yes. Exactly. I shouldn't have done it.'

'And that's really the only thing you can think of that you shouldn't have done?'

'Not the only. The first.'

It looks like being a very long life.

It is, I confess, my idea to join forces – to combine Brian and Nigel and GoodNews's sister Cantata (for that is her name – self-chosen at the age of twenty-three, apparently, after a particularly intense experience under the influence of acid in the Royal Festival Hall) at the dinner table in the hope of expunging all our sins at one fell swoop – or at least, that is how I present it to David, who cannot see the prospect of anything but a very jolly evening, even if Nigel is now the chairman of a multinational bank and is seated next to Brian and his malfunctioning bowels for the entire evening.

The truth is that I have given up expecting anything approaching a pleasant or even tolerable social life, and so my motives for the suggestion are born from cynicism and a kind of despairing perversity: why not sit them all down together? The more the merrier! The worse the better! If nothing else, the evening will become an anecdote that may amaze and delight my friends for years to come; and maybe the desire for nice evenings with people I know and love is essentially bourgeois, reprehensible – depraved, almost.

GoodNews goes first. He phones the last number he had for Cantata, and then he is given another one, and then another one, and finally he tracks her down to a squat in Brighton.

'Cantata? It's GoodNews.'

But apparently not – she hangs up.

GoodNews phones the number again.

'Beforeyouputthephonedownagainlistento me . . . Thank you. I've been thinking a lot about you, and how badly I've treated you. And I wanted to . . .'

'–'

'I know.'

'–'

'I know.'

'–'

'Ah, now that wasn't my fault. I never called the police. That was Mum.'

'–'

'Well, I didn't run him over, did I? And I didn't leave the door open, either.'

'–'

'Oh, come on, Cantata. That cost seventy pence. And I'm pretty sure it was torn anyway.'

'–'

GoodNews jumps to his feet and then keeps jumping, up and down, like someone on a trampoline. Or rather, like someone who is trying to resolve a blood feud – the kind of problem that cannot be reached by healing hands, or answered on a piece of paper, or written about in a book, but only by jumping up and down, up and down, because that is the only response left to him. I wish I had thought of jumping up and down months ago. It would have been as useful as anything else.

'No!' GoodNews shouts. 'No, no, no! YOU fuck off! YOU fuck off!'

And then he slams the phone down and walks out.

'Aren't you going to talk to him?' I ask David.

'What am I going to say?'

'I don't know. Try to make him feel better.'

'He shouldn't have said that. I'm very disappointed in him. We're supposed to be above all that.'

'But we're not, are we?'

'I'm not talking about you. I'm talking about me and him.'

'That's the trouble, isn't it? You were human all the time. You just forgot.'

I go to talk to him. He's lying on his bed, chewing furiously, staring at the ceiling.

'I'm sorry I swore in front of the kids.'

'That's OK. They've heard that word a lot from their father.'

'In the old days?'

'Yeah, that's right. In the old days.' It had never occurred to me that David no longer swears in front of the children. That's a good thing, surely? OK, some would argue that this has been a Pyrrhic victory, achieved only by having a man with turtles for eyebrows coming to live with us for what seems like years, and at a cost to all semblance of a normal family life, but I choose to accentuate the positive.

'You shouldn't beat yourself up about it,' I tell him. 'I mean, I only heard your side of the argument, but she seems pretty unreasonable. What was all that stuff about seventy pence?'

'Her bloody Simon LeBon poster. She's never forgotten it.'

'I gathered that.'

'Katie, I can't stand her. She's awful. Always has been, always will be. Cantata! What a bloody idiot.'

With enormous self-control I pass up the opportunity for first-name-calling.

'It's OK.'

'No it's not. She's my sister.'

'But she's doing OK without you.'

'I don't know that.'

'If she needed you, you would have heard from her. Despite the unfortunate Simon LeBon poster incident.'

'Do you think?'

'Of course.'

'I still feel I'm a failure though. You know, it's love this, and love that, and I fucking hate her. Excuse my language.'

And in my opinion, he's right. He is a failure, and self-interest requires that I let him know. Who are these people, that they want to save the world and yet they are incapable of forming proper relationships with anybody? As GoodNews so eloquently puts it, it's love this and love that, but of course it's so easy to love someone you don't know, whether it's George Clooney or Monkey. Staying civil to someone with whom you've ever shared Christmas turkey – now there's a miracle. If GoodNews could pull that one off with his warm hands, he could live with us for ever.

'But think of all the people you help who do need you,' I tell him. 'Isn't that worth more?'

'D'you think?'

'Of course.'

And thus GoodNews is encouraged to wreak yet more havoc, by someone who should know better. But – irony upon irony – I know I'm doing the right thing.

It is easy to track Nigel down. David is a member of his Old Boys' Association, and within minutes he has a mobile phone number. We are all allowed to listen to the subsequent conversation, so confident is David of a warm and possibly even tearful welcome.

'Hello, is that Nigel?'

'–'

'This is David Grant.' He gives a small smile of anticipation.

'–'

'David Grant. From school.'

'–'

'Yes. That's right. Ha ha. How are you?'

'–'

'Good, good.'

'–'

'Fine, thank you. What are you up to these days?'

'–'

'Right, right. Excellent.'

'–'

'Gosh.'

'–'

'Wow.'

'–'

'Really? Well done. Listen –'

'–'

'That's a lot of megabytes.'

'–'

'That's a lot of turnover.'

'–'

'That's a lot of airmiles. Listen –'

'–'

'Really? Congratulations.'

'–'

'No, fifteen years is nothing nowadays. Look at Michael Douglas and . . .'

'–'

'Is she?'

'–'

'Does she?'

'–'

'That's a lot of magazine covers.'

'—'

'Did she? Well, I'm sure Rod must be heartbroken. He probably doesn't want to talk about it, ha ha . . . Anyway, I just wanted to catch up. And now I have. Bye, Nigel!'

And he hangs up. I look at him, and for a moment I see a flash of the man I used to know: angry, contemptuous, eaten up with envy and discontent.

'You didn't invite him to dinner.'

'No. I'm not sure it's much of a thing for him any more, the bullying.'

'Really?'

'Yeah. And I didn't know whether he'd get on with Barmy Brian.'

'Right.'

'And he's a pig. I'd have ended up thumping him again if he came round here.'

'Like I thumped Christopher?' says Tom cheerfully.

'Exactly,' David says.

'There are some people you just have to hit, aren't there?' says Tom. 'You just can't help it.'

David doesn't say anything, but the absence of an anguished correction is, I can't help feeling, significant. It seems a shame that some sort of epiphanic moment should come during a conversation between my husband and my son about perpetrating violence, but I'll take epiphanic moments where I can find them.

'Who are you going to try next?' I ask David as we are getting ready for bed.

'I dunno,' he says morosely. 'Because that didn't work, did it?'

'I'm not entirely sure what it was intended to achieve. But probably it didn't, no.'

David sits down heavily on the not-quite dirty clothes that cover our bedroom chair. There are so many clothes that he ends up all lop-sided, slanting towards the window like a house-plant starved of light.

'I know you think it's all stupid.'

'What? Phoning people up who don't remember you to apologize for something they've forgotten you ever did?'

'Not just Nigel Richards. All of it.'

I don't say anything. I just sigh, which is as good a way of answering the question as any.

'Well, so do I,' he says. 'I think it's incredibly stupid. Pointless. Pathetic.'

'You're just feeling discouraged. You've had a knockback. Apologize to someone else. That poor bastard whose life you used to make a misery on the local paper. That friend of your mum's you refused to invite to our wedding.'

'I'm not talking about apologies. I'm talking about everything. Feeding the poor. Telling everyone to give their money away. Writing that book. It's all mad, I know that. I've known it for a while. I just haven't let on.'

When GoodNews and David got on the phone earlier in the evening, it seemed like just another sweet, misguided and totally pointless scheme, and now it is clear that it was in fact a pivotal moment in familial history. It's like the Berlin Wall coming down: you couldn't see it happening, but then it seems clear that all the internal contradictions made the fall inevitable. It was always going to happen, just as David was eventually going to see that it was all mad. It feels strange, thinking that we are on the verge of returning to our old life. Sarcasm, bitterness, bad novels, a spare bedroom and one less mouth to feed . . . I have mixed feelings about it, if I am honest. For a while, things were interesting, special even.

'GoodNews told me about your flat battery,' says David. 'Well, I've got one, too. There's nothing there. That first flush I felt . . . It's all disappeared, and now I just feel nothing. That's why I can see how stupid it all looks. Like you can. And everybody else who's depressed and can't understand what they're supposed to be doing with their lives.'

I don't say anything. Tomorrow maybe I'll try to find a phone number for the organization that provides counselling for people who have been brainwashed by cults; I'm sure that depression of this kind is an entirely normal consequence of having your whole reason for living taken away from you.

'That's why I'm not going to give up,' David continues. 'I can't afford to. What am I going to do? Go back to writing nasty columns for the local newspaper about old people on buses? Ha! I don't think so. No, it's like a . . . well, it's like a marriage. You've got to work at it and hope the feeling comes back. And even if it doesn't, I know I'm doing something. Not just sitting around moaning and being mean.'

'So you're going to go round knocking on people's doors and telling them to give away all their savings even though you don't believe in it?'

'It's not exactly that I don't believe in it. More like, I dunno, I don't not believe in it.'

'And is that enough?'

'I don't know. I don't suppose so.' He looks at me. 'You tell me.'

'What do I know about it?'

'Aren't we both doing the same thing?'

'Are we?'

'How passionately do you believe in our marriage?'

'How passionately do *you* believe in our marriage?'

It's a fair question, I suppose, the one I have just angled back to David like a tennis player at the net, using the pace and the spin that he put on the ball to my advantage. Any marriage counsellor would support my right to ask it, but I know it's a cheat. That's the thing with failing relationships. You can always refuse to answer any question by repeating it. 'Do you love me?' 'Do you want a divorce?' 'Are you happy?' Your partner is invariably as ambivalent as you are, and if he or she is human – that is to say, cowardly but at the same time somehow full of moral self-righteousness – then he or she will not commit themselves through any expression of passion or commitment. After all, the absence of passion or commitment is the reason why the relationship is failing, surely? So in my experience it is both easy and advisable to reduce any serious discussion to a farcical stalemate almost immediately. Years can go by before you have to make a decision.

What is atypically pathetic in this case is that David isn't even really asking me to talk properly about us. He's using the marriage rhetorically, as an analogy, and yet still I won't be drawn. How feeble can you get?

'OK, OK,' I say, all of a rush. 'I don't feel passionately about the marriage at all. I'm just too frightened to pack it in. Too much depends on it. I don't want to be the bad guy.'

'Exactly,' says David soberly. 'Well that's just . . .'

'Hold on, hold on. Exactly? That's all? You don't mind me saying that? You knew all the time?'

'Katie, in the last couple of months you've had an affair and you moved out of our house. You're not exactly a blushing bride, are you? The point is, what are we going to do when we're both so, so . . . soul-dead? Me, I feel like I've come too far down one road to go back. And maybe you feel like that about our marriage. And that means that whatever we do is going to be really, really hard, much harder than it would be for anyone else who knew what they wanted and why. We've both got flat batteries, but we've still got to drive the car somehow. And I haven't got a clue how to do that. Have you?'

I shake my head. I don't like these sorts of talks. I prefer the 'Do you love me?/Do you love me?' kind, because they can go on for ever, and they never achieve anything, and nobody ever says anything worth thinking about ever again.

We make love that night, our first time for ages. We both agree afterwards that it's nice to feel some warmth, even if that warmth is located in the genitalia rather than the soul. But maybe something will catch.

'How passionately do you believe in our marriage?' I ask him just before I fall asleep. It's the right time for the question: my head is on his chest, and I'm asking because I want to know, not because I'm trying to get out of answering something he's asked me.

'Do you really want to talk about this now?'

'Is it a long answer?'

'No, not really. OK. I can't think of any good reason for giving up on it. Just like I can't think of any good reason for giving up the other stuff.'

'So I'm a charity case?'

'You're not, no. But the marriage is. The marriage is like one of those dogs you see in RSPCA posters. Thin. Pathetic.'

'Patches of skin showing through the fur. Pus-filled eyes. Cigarette burns.'

'Precisely.'

I was attempting to be frivolous, and for a moment I ache for David to share in the frivolity, to pick up the daft image and run with it, but he doesn't. Of course he doesn't.

'Anyway. That's what I think of the marriage.'

'What? It should be put down? Its owners should be prosecuted?'

'No, no. I mean, you know. I couldn't leave it in this state.'

'So you're going to nurse it back to health and then go.'

'Oh, no. I wouldn't do that. Because if it was healthy . . .'

'It's OK. I was joking.'

'Oh. I'm not very good at spotting that sort of thing any more, am I?'

'Not great, no.'

'I'm sorry.'

It's funny, but of all the apologies made over the last few months, this one seems the most pitiful, and the crime the least forgivable.

Brian has been moved to sheltered accommodation, which he hates.

'It's all full of old dears. They've got these emergency buzzers and they go off every five minutes. Every time they fall over. And they're always falling over. I shouldn't be in there. I don't fall over hardly ever. I mean, I have done. Everyone has, haven't they?'

I tell him that, yes, everybody has fallen over at some time.

'I mean, I'll bet you've fallen over, and you're a doctor. You've probably been to college and all that.'

I tell him that, yes, I've been to college, and even seven years of further education has not prevented me from losing my footing occasionally – thus confirming his suspicion, that it is age rather than intelligence which tends to govern the ability to stand upright, and even though he was never university material, he shouldn't be in sheltered accommodation with a lot of faller-overs.

'Well, there you are.'

'But you're eating better.'

'The food's all right. They send it round. Meals on Wheels. So they know what should be hot and so on and so forth.'

'Good.'

We lapse into silence. At the last count, I had fifteen patients waiting outside, but it is as if we are both waiting for a bus. Brian looks up at the ceiling and begins to whistle.

'Is there anything else?' The 'else' is a kindness on my part. It is my way of pretending that there was a good reason for Brian's visit in the first place, that he wasn't just wasting my time.

'Not really.' He goes back to whistling his tune.

'Well. It was nice to see you again. And I'm glad to hear that you're feeling better.'

I stand up, for added emphasis, and smile.

'I've come for my dinner,' says Brian matter-of-factly. 'You said.'

'Yes, but . . .' It's eleven o'clock in the morning. 'I meant an evening meal. Some time.'

'I'll wait. I won't get in the way.'

'Brian, you can't wait in here. People won't want you in here if I ask them to get undressed.'

'Oh. Yes. I never thought of that. I wouldn't want to see them undressed either. You've got fat people, haven't you? I don't like them very much. I'll wait outside.'

'Brian . . . I'm not going to finish work until six.'

'That's OK.'

So he waits for seven hours in the waiting area, and then comes home with me.

I have already called David to warn him, and when Brian and I get home there is a chicken in the oven, and several vegetables steaming away on the hotplates, and the table is laid, and there are even flowers. All my nearest and dearest know who Barmy Brian is, just as they know the names of every one of my heartsink patients, and

I have told David that if either of my children attach an adjective, any adjective, to his first name in his presence, then he or she will not be eating *en famille* for a statutory minimum two years, including Christmas Day and birthdays.

Brian takes off his coat, sits down and watches *Sabrina the Teenage Witch* with the children, while I make the gravy.

'What's going on here, then?'

'It's *Sabrina the Teenage Witch*,' Tom mumbles.

'How d'you mean?'

Tom looks at me nervously.

'That's the name of the programme,' I tell him.

'Oh, I see. Say it again.'

'*Sabrina the Teenage Witch*,' Tom enunciates.

Brian laughs, long and hard.

'Haven't you ever heard of it?' I ask him.

'Nooooo,' he says, as if even now he doubts whether such a programme really exists. 'But she's only a teenager?'

'Yes.'

'And she's already a witch? Blimey.'

We all smile politely.

'That's too young. Don't you think?'

'That's sort of the point of the programme,' says Tom. ''Cos most witches aren't teenagers.'

'How d'you mean?'

'Let them watch the programme, Brian.'

'I'm so sorry. Just wanted to get a couple of things straight in my head before I settle down to it.'

And settle down to it he does, with enormous if occasionally addled appreciation. Unfortunately the programme only lasts another thirty minutes, and then it is time to eat.

GoodNews joins us just as we are serving up.

'Hi,' he says to Brian. 'I'm GoodNews.'

'How d'you mean?' Brian asks nervously.

'How do you mean?' says GoodNews with great formality, and he shakes Brian's hand. GoodNews, who has also been informed that he will be spending the evening with an eccentric, is clearly under the misapprehension that 'How d'you mean?' is Brian's eccentric salutation, a weirdo's version of 'How do you do?'

'No!' Tom shouts. 'He doesn't understand your name!'

'He doesn't understand it?'

'You've got to have a name like Tom or Brian or David or Dr Carr,' says Brian. 'What's your name like that?'

'Yes,' I say. 'What is your name like that?'

'It doesn't really matter,' GoodNews tells Brian. 'GoodNews is my name now. Because that's what I want to bring, see.'

'Well, I want to bring Brian,' says Brian firmly. 'So Brian can have his dinner.'

'Good for you,' says David.

We eat in silence, and, in Brian's case, with enormous speed. I have just finished pouring my gravy when he puts his knife and fork together on an empty plate.

'That', he says, 'was the best meal I've ever had in my whole life.'

'Really?' says Molly.

'Yeah. Course. How could I have ever had a better meal than that? My mum couldn't have cooked that.'

'What about you?'

'No. See, I don't know what should be cooked and what shouldn't. I get muddled.'

'Really?'

'Oh, yeah. Muddled as anything.'

'Can I test you?' Molly asks.

'If you want, but I won't know the answer.'

'Just eat your dinner, Mol,' I tell her. 'Do you want some more, Brian?'

'There isn't usually any more.'

'There is here, so you can have some if you like.'

'And it doesn't cost any extra?'

I look at him, forgetting for a moment that Brian is incapable of pulling legs.

'You know you won't have to pay for this, don't you, Brian?'

'How d'you mean?'

'We're not like a restaurant. You're our guest.'

'Well, I . . . I don't know what to say. You told me that I had to drink that stuff, and I had to pay for that, and then you said to eat a curry, and I had to pay for that. And then you said I had to come round for dinner with you, and I thought I had to pay for that, too. I brought five pounds with me. The curry was five pounds. £4.95.'

'We don't want your money, Brian.'

'That's amazing. So it's on the NHS?'

'It's on the NHS.'

Molly is fascinated by Brian, and begins to ask him question after question – where does he live? What does he do all day? Who are his friends? Has he got any family?

And each answer is like a hammer driving the heads of the adults further and further down towards the table, until at the end of Molly's inquisition our noses are almost touching our roast potatoes. Brian doesn't really do anything all day, apart from the days he has to see me; he has no friends (he thinks that he used to have a couple when he went to school, but he doesn't know where they are now); he has a sister, but his sister calls him Barmy Brian and won't have anything to do with him. (This reply is followed by a particularly tense silence, and I am pleased and amazed to say that both of my children ignore the enormous juicy worm dangled in front of them.)

'Wouldn't you like to live with somebody?' Molly asks.

'I'd love to,' says Brian. 'I thought I was going to live with my wife. But then I couldn't find one.'

'Mum,' says Molly. I start to cough frantically, and get up to pour myself a glass of water.

'Mum,' says Molly, after I have finished with the water, and also a long explanation as to what I think it might have been that caused me to cough in that way.

'Do you want some more?' I ask her. She ignores me.

'Mu-um.'

'How about you, Tom? David? GoodNews?' Sooner or later, I know, I will have to let my daughter speak. One day there will be no more delaying tactics left, but hopefully that day will not arrive for several years yet. 'Do you want to get down, kids?'

'Mu-u-um.'

'Molly. It's rude to speak when . . . when . . . no one wants to listen to you.'

'Mum, can Brian come to live with us?'

'Thank you,' says Brian. 'I'd love that. It's very lonely, where I am, because I don't know anybody, and I don't have anything to do. You could be my family. You could look after me like my mum used to do.'

'What happened to your mum?' Molly asks.

'Nothing,' I snap, although even as I am snapping I realize that this is an inadequate answer, almost certainly provoked by panic.

'She died,' says Brian. 'She said she wouldn't, but she did.'

'That's really sad,' says Molly. 'Isn't it, Mum?'

'It is,' I admit. 'It's very sad.'

'That's why Brian should live here.'

'Thank you,' says Brian. 'I shall enjoy that.'

'Molly, Brian can't live here.'

'He can, can't he, Dad?' says Molly. 'We had Monkey living here for a while, Brian. So if we can have Monkey, we can have you.'

'I couldn't live here just for a while,' says Brian helpfully. 'It would have to be for ever.'

'That's OK,' says Molly. 'Isn't it, Dad? For ever? That's what we do here,' says Molly. 'It's great. We look after poor people. We're very good. Everyone thinks so.'

'I'm not poor,' says Brian. 'I've got some money.'

'You're a different sort of poor,' says Molly.

Tom, who has been ominously quiet, stands up violently. The movement of his lower lip presages an explosion.

'If he comes to live here . . .'

'Sit down, Tom,' I tell him. 'I'll deal with it.'

'You won't. Because Dad'll tell you what to do and then you'll do it. And Dad'll say . . .'

'Go and watch TV. Go on. Scram.'

I am dimly aware that this is a defining moment in our family's history. Not just because Barmy Brian might live with us until the day I die and possibly well beyond – and that would define us all right, rather like a chalk outline defines a murder victim – but because if we go the other way, if I tell Brian that he cannot live with us, then things might be different for us afterwards.

'Molly, Brian . . . You can't come to live here.'

'Why not?' Molly asks.

'Yes, why not?' Brian asks. 'How come you're allowed a family and I'm not?'

'Yeah,' says Molly. 'That's not fair.'

She's right, of course. It's not fair. Love, it turns out, is as undemocratic as money, so it accumulates around people who have plenty of it already: the sane, the healthy, the lovable. I am loved by my children, my parents, my brother, my spouse, I suppose, my friends; Brian has none of these people, and never will, and much as we would like to spread it all around a little, we can't. If ever anyone needed looking after in a household, it's Brian, and if Brian only knows one household and it happens to be ours, then we, surely, are the people who should offer him hospitality. I catch David's eye: he knows that the path I am on is slippery, glacial, and that no one can step on it without sliding all the way to the bottom.

'Molly, that's enough. We're not going to have this conversation in front of Brian. It's rude. And it's not something we can decide in two minutes.'

'I'll wait,' says Brian. 'I've got nothing to do this evening.'

But he goes, in the end, after a cup of tea and a fun-sized Mars Bar; I drive him back to his new home (or, rather, to the corner of the street – now that we are alone again, he has regained much of his old suspicion, and refuses to let me see where he lives).

'Thank you,' he says, as he is getting out of the car. 'And you'll tell me about the other thing tomorrow? Because if I'm going to move I'll have to tell them here. And I've got to pack.'

'Brian . . . You can't come to live with us.'

'I thought you were going to talk about it?'

'We will, but I know what we're going to decide.'

'Oh.'

'Are you disappointed?'

'Yes. Very. I was really looking forward to it. I liked that pro-gramme, that teenager programme.'

'You can get that on your TV.'

'Can I?'

'Yes.'

'Are you sure? I've never seen it before.'

'It's on ITV, I think.'

'Oh. Well. I don't watch that one so much. What number's that? On my remote thing?'

'Three, I expect. It is on ours.'

'That's not so bad, then.'

'Isn't it?'

'No. What about the chicken? Can I have some of that again?'

'Of course you can. Every time we have roast chicken you can come round for supper.'

'And you're not saying that because you know you'll never have it again? Because that's what I'd say. To trick you.'

'I'm not tricking you.'

'OK then. Bye.'

And he wanders off down the street.

I have just invited one of my heartsink patients round to eat with us once every couple of weeks for ever. A few months ago this would have been a surefire indication of my own barminess, and yet now it signifies only a cold-hearted and pragmatic sanity. I feel like getting out of the car and dancing on the roof. Molly will take the news much harder than Brian, but then, that's the thing with this brand of charity. It's all about what it does for us, not for people like Brian.

Some of us – Tom has not yet moved from in front of the TV – are waiting for me when I get back.

'We're going to talk,' says Molly seriously. 'We're going to talk about whether Brian is coming to live with us.'

'OK.' I sit down at the table. 'Can I talk first?'

'If you want.'

'He's not. And I've told him.'

'That's not fair!'

I am not going to say that life is unfair. I refuse.

'I know. I'm sorry. I've promised him that he can have roast chicken with us the next time we have it.'

'I bet you didn't even mean that.'

'I did mean it. I meant it with all my heart. But that's as far as it goes. The outer limits of our hospitality.'

'But you said . . .'

'Molly. There was nothing to talk about. Brian couldn't come to live here. He's not our family.'

'But he could be.'

'No. He couldn't.' I look at David, who looks right back at me. He's not about to help me out.

'Molly, this is our family. You, me, Daddy, Tom. That's it. Not GoodNews, not Brian, not Monkey, nobody else. Tough. There's nothing you can do about it. These are the people we have to worry about first.'

'Why?' Finally, a contribution from my husband. Not a helpful contribution, but a contribution nevertheless.

'Why? Why? David, we're barely able to look after ourselves. We're almost broke, partly because you refuse to work. Tom's been stealing things from people at school . . .' I can feel a hot torrent of words building up inside me, and could no more prevent this torrent from coming out of my mouth than I could stop myself from vomiting if I were ill. 'Molly's turning into a prig, I've had an affair . . .'

'What's a prig? What's an affair?'

'It means Mummy's had a boyfriend,' says Tom, without missing a second of the television programme he is watching.

'You and I have been on the verge of divorce for months, although now we've made the decision to lock ourselves in and throw away the key, thus condemning each other to what might be a lifetime of frustration and mutual loathing. And you ask why we have to look after each other first? Because life's fucking hard enough as it is, that's why, and . . .'

'Katie, stop. You're upsetting the kids.'

'Good. Maybe they should be upset. Maybe they shouldn't go through life thinking that everything's OK, everything's great, everything's so great, in fact, that it doesn't matter who we give money to or who we take in, because it does matter. I wish it didn't. I wish we were competent enough to handle lives other than our own, but we're not. And I'll tell you something for nothing. All my life I have wanted to help people. That's why I wanted to be a doctor. And because of that I work ten-hour days and I get threatened by junkies and I constantly let people down because I promise them hospital appointments that never come and I give them drugs that never work. And having failed at that, I come home and fail at being a wife and a mother. Well, I haven't got the energy to fail at anything else. And if that means that Brian goes on living in sheltered accommodation, or Monkey has to sleep rough, well, so be it. Too bad. If in twenty years' time, we're all still speaking, and Molly's not an anorexic, and Tom's not inside, and I'm not hooked on tranquillizers, and you're not an alcoholic, and you and I are still together, well, that'll be a bloody miracle in itself. I'm not asking for any more than that. And if on top of all that we manage to buy a few copies of the *Big Issue*, and take them to the recycling centre, then hurrah for us. Haven't we done well? Hurrah for us. Hur-rah-for-us! Hur-rah-for-us. Come on! Join in!'

Nobody does.

It's over, now. I've emptied the contents of my throat all over the family, and there's nothing left.

'You're not really going to get divorced, are you?' Molly asks. She's crying, but then, that was the idea.

'Not if you're good,' I tell her. It's a terrible thing to say, I know that. But it's weirdly appropriate too.

15

For the first time in months and months I have to go to a bookshop, to buy a birthday present for my father. I don't know what to get him, and he doesn't know what he wants, so I wander around aimlessly. I used to spend a lot of time in bookshops; I used to know what most of the books were, what they meant, but now I'm simply perplexed and vaguely panicky. I pick up a novel by a young woman writer and read the blurb: perhaps I would like this, I think. I was halfway through *Captain Corelli's Mandolin* when I moved out of Janet's, and even though no further progress has been made, there is a possibility that I may well wish to have another go at reading a novel some time in the new Millennium. But when I try to decide whether this might be the book for me, I realize that I no longer have the capability to do so. How am I supposed to know whether I would enjoy it or not? How does one tell? I would enjoy a shoulder massage. I would enjoy a week lying by a swimming pool in the sun, sleeping. I would enjoy a large gin and tonic, as long as I didn't have to do anything after I had drunk it. I would enjoy some chocolate. But a book . . . This one is about a girl who, after being forced by political persecution to leave her African homeland, comes to live in Bromley, where she meets and falls in love with a young white racist skinhead ballet dancer. 'It is as if *Billy Elliott* had mated with *Wild Swans* to produce *Romeo and Juliet*,' says a review on the back. I put the book down again – not because it sounds like tosh, but because I have not been forced to leave my African homeland, and I do not live in Bromley. Really! Really and truly! That is the logic I use to help me make up my mind! This means, of course, that there is very little to separate me from Poppy, the family cat that was found in the road – although I have managed to remain three- rather than two-dimensional, and I still have my own viscera. Poppy liked being stroked, just as I enjoy shoulder massages; Poppy enjoyed fish, just as I enjoy chocolate. Poppy also loved sleeping in the sun, and she would have put this novel down if she had picked it up in a bookshop, for exactly the same reasons. I become so alarmed by the comparison that I buy the book immediately, even before I have found anything for Dad. I will not turn into a pet. I will not.

Biographies. Would he like a biography? Hitler? Montgomery? Dickens? Jack Nicklaus? The woman out of *Eastenders* who ran the pub? But Dad's not much of a pub man, I think, so he's not likely to . . . Jesus, Katie. It wasn't a real pub. The point of this book is that the woman used to be in *Eastenders*. Dad doesn't watch *Eastenders*. That's why you're not going to buy him this book. I find a reassuringly present-sized biography of God on the 'Staff Picks' table, and just as I am about to take it to the till, I see the book about Vanessa Bell, Virginia Woolf's artist sister, the woman who, according to the book review I read, lived a rich and beautiful life. So I buy that, too, to see how it's done. And when David and GoodNews have finished 'How to be Good', we can sit down and compare notes.

David has gone back to writing company brochures. He is no longer interested in his novel, and even if he were angry any more – which he isn't – he would not be able to vent his spleen in the local paper, because he has been displaced, dethroned, out-raged: there is a new, and even angrier, Angriest Man in Holloway now – which is as it should be, I suppose. If the new columnist were not angrier than David at his angriest, then he would be the Second Angriest Man in Holloway, and that would look a bit feeble on the page. And anyway, people get angrier all the time. It was inevitable that David's anger levels would end up looking a bit late 90s. He was never going to hang on to the title for ever, just like Martina was never going to remain Wimbledon champion for ever. Younger, meaner people come along. The new chap has just called for the closure of all public parks, on the grounds that they are magnets for gays, dogs, alcoholics and children; we have to hold up our hands in defeat. The better man has won.

In the old days, David's failure to have remained angry enough to keep his job would have made him furious – furious enough to become angry enough to keep his job. This David, though, just shrinks back into himself a little more. He has offered the paper a different sort of column, one based on the book he is writing with GoodNews, but no one was interested. He is properly depressed now, I think, and if he were to come to see me in the surgery I would prescribe something. But he won't. He still spends all his spare time with GoodNews, scribbling notes for 'How to be Good', although spare time is much harder to find now – there are a lot of brochures to be written.

After much heart-searching, GoodNews has been given three months to find somewhere to live. He says he appreciates that he has been a burden on us; we are, after all, a middle-class nuclear family, he knows that, and he should respect our, y'know, our nuclearness. We know we are being insulted, but we don't care very much – or at least, I don't. David agonizes about it every night just before we go to sleep, wonders aloud whether we want to be nuclear, whether we should become a denuclearized zone, but much of his conviction has gone.

The children seem pretty depressed, too. They were shaken by my outburst, and I have had to talk to them about my boyfriend, and they watch their parents with panic-filled eyes each time we eat, or go out together anywhere. We have only had one argument in the last few days, David and I – about a grillpan – and the kids needed counselling afterwards. I suspect that after a few months of dullness they will forget our woes, but right now I feel sorry for them, and I wish that we had not contrived to make them feel so insecure.

Me, I don't think I'm depressed. That's not the right word. I'm daunted. I no longer think about whether I want a divorce or not – the nice vicar took that option away from me. It is just beginning to register that those post-divorce fantasies I had before I was married were untenable, and that I am likely to remain married at least until the children are adults. So that's . . . Fifteen years? By which time I will be in my mid-fifties, and one part of life – the Kris

Kristofferson part – will be a long way behind me. But there is a sort of virtue in having no choices remaining, I think. It certainly clarifies the mind. And there is always the possibility that David and I will be able to say to each other one day 'Do you remember when we nearly packed it in?', and we will laugh at the sheer idiocy of these last few months. It is, I cannot help feeling, a remote possibility, but it is there nonetheless. I'm sure it's right, that thing about leaving the knife in when you've been stabbed. Maybe I should check it out again. Just to be sure.

We are cooking my father's birthday dinner, and my mother has called to say that he has given up red meat. David buys a free-range chicken, and it is nearly ready when Molly asks us what we are eating.

'Hooray!' she says, with more excitement than the menu really warrants.

'I didn't know you liked chicken that much.'

'I don't. But it means that Brian can come for dinner.'

'It's Grandpa's birthday.'

'Yes. But chicken. You promised.'

I had forgotten my promise. When I made it, it seemed like the best and easiest deal I could possibly strike; now it is preposterous, unreasonable, a deal with God made by an atheist at a time of crisis, forgotten when the crisis has passed.

'Brian can't come tonight.'

'He has to. That's why he's not living with us, because he was allowed to come whenever we're having chicken.'

'Grandpa won't like Brian.'

'Why did you promise, if you were going to break it straightaway?'

Because I didn't mean it. Because I did it to get myself out of a hole. Because we have done enough for Brian, even though we have done almost nothing, and even though he is a sad and pathetic man who will devour any crumb of comfort that is thrown at him, like a duck in winter.

'I didn't mean birthdays.'

'Did you tell him that birthdays didn't count?'

'Molly's right,' says David. 'We can't just go around making promises to people like Brian and then breaking them when it is inconvenient.'

'Brian is not coming to my father's birthday dinner,' I say. Of course he isn't. It's obvious, surely? It's common sense.

'You're a liar, then,' Molly says.

'Fine.'

'You don't even care you're a liar.'

'No.'

'OK. Well, I'll be a liar, too, whenever I feel like it.'

I suddenly realize that David's part in the chicken debacle might not be entirely innocent.

'You bought that chicken deliberately,' I say to him.

'Deliberately? Well, it wasn't an unconscious purchase, if that's what you mean.'

'You know that's not what I mean.'

'OK. I wasn't entirely unaware of your promise to Brian and Molly when I put it in the trolley.'

'So you were trying to catch me out?'

'It didn't occur to me that you would need catching out. It didn't occur to me that your offer was anything but genuine.'

'Liar.'

'So what you're saying is I should have realized that you didn't really mean it? Even though you said you meant it with all your heart?'

'Is this really what it's all come down to, David? Playing games with chicken dinners?'

'It rather looks like it. I don't know what else is left. I couldn't get you to do anything else. I'd rather hoped we'd drawn the last line in the sand.'

'I just want my dad to have a nice birthday. Is that too much to ask?'

'That's been the question all the time. Or a version of it.'

We end up compromising. The night after my father's birthday dinner, we cook another roast chicken, and we invite Brian round, and thus the spirit of the Brian treaty is upheld. Stuffing our faces with meat and three vegetables on consecutive nights may seem like a peculiar way to make the world a better place, but it seems to work for us.

OK, Vanessa Bell. She was a painter, so, you know, easier for her to live a beautiful life than it is for someone who has to deal with Mrs Cortenza and Barmy Brian and all the Holloway junkies. And she had children by more than one man, which might have made things a bit richer than they might otherwise have been. And the men she knocked around with were, it is only fair to say, more interesting and more talented than David and Stephen. They tended to be writers and painters and what have you, rather than people who wrote company brochures. And even though they didn't have money, they were posh, whereas we're not. It must be easier to live beautiful lives when you're posh.

So, what I'm beginning to think – and I'm only halfway through the book, but I'm sure the second half will be more of the same – is that Vanessa Bell isn't going to be too much help. OK, my brother may well end up filling his pockets with stones and jumping into the river, just as her sister did, but beyond that . . . Anyway, who lives a rich and beautiful life that I know? It's no longer possible, surely, for anyone who works for a living, or lives in a city, or shops in a supermarket, or watches TV, or reads a newspaper, or drives a car, or eats frozen pizzas. A nice life, possibly, with a huge slice of luck and a little spare cash. And maybe even a good life, if . . . Well, let's not go into all that. But rich and beautiful lives seem to be a discontinued line.

What helps is not Vanessa Bell, but reading about Vanessa Bell. I don't want to be like Poppy the squashed cat any more. Ever since I moved back into the house after my stay at Janet's, I have had the nagging feeling that I miss something, without quite being able to describe precisely what that something was. It's not my former flatmates, or the chance of sleeping on my own in a bed (because, like I said, David and I fit, or have learned to fit, and sharing a duvet with him is frequently a comfort rather than a hardship), but something else, something that is clearly not important enough to me, in both senses: it should be more important to me than it is, because I miss it, and yet life is clearly not impossible without it, because I have been managing to survive despite its absence – in other words, it's some spiritual equivalent of fruit, which I am bad about eating. And it is only when I have shut the bedroom door for the third or fourth time on my husband and children in order to find out precisely how Vanessa Bell's life was better than my own that I work it out. It is the act of reading itself I miss, the opportunity to retreat further and further from the world until I have found some space, some air that isn't stale, that hasn't been breathed by my family a thousand times already. Janet's bedsit seemed enormous when I moved into it, enormous and quiet, but this book is so much bigger than that. And when I've finished it I will start another one, and that might be even bigger, and then another, and I will be able to keep extending my house until it becomes a mansion, full of rooms where they can't find me. And it's not just reading, either, but listening, hearing something other than my children's TV programmes and my husband's pious drone and the chatter chatter chatter in my head.

What happened to me? However did I get it into my head that I was too busy for all this stuff? Maybe I can't live a rich and beautiful life, but there are rich and beautiful things for sale all around me, even on the Holloway Road, and they are not an extravagance because if I buy some of them then I think I might be able to get by, and if I don't then I think I might go under. I need a Discman and some CDs and half-a-dozen novels urgently, total cost maybe three hundred pounds. Three hundred pounds for a mansion! Imagine asking a building society manager for three hundred pounds! He'd give you cash out of his own pocket. And I could shave even that pitiful amount down. I could go to the library, and I could borrow the CDs . . . but I need the Discman. I don't want anyone else to hear what I am hearing, and I want to be able to block out every last trace of the world I inhabit, even if it is just for half-an-hour a day. And yes, yes: just think how many cataract operations or bags of rice could be bought for three hundred pounds. And just think how long it would take a twelve-year-old Asian girl to earn that in her sweatshop. Can I be a good person and spend that much money on overpriced consumer goods? I don't know. But I do know this: I'd be no good without them.

For the last three days, it has been raining and raining and raining – it has been raining harder than anyone can remember. It's the kind of rain you're supposed to get after a nuclear attack: rivers have broken their banks all over the country, and people are wading down High Streets, sandbagging their houses, abandoning their cars, rowing across fields. The traffic all over London has slowed and slowed and then, finally, stopped, and the trains aren't running, and the buses are overstuffed like a human sandwich, with bits of arms and legs hanging out of them. It's dark all day, and there's this relentless, terrible howling noise. If you believe in ghosts, the kinds of ghosts who have been condemned to haunt us because they died terrible, painful deaths or did terrible, painful things to their loved ones, then this is your time, because we would listen to you now. We would have no option but to listen to you, because the evidence is all around us.

The last time it rained like this was in 1947, according to the news, but back then it was just a fluke, a freak of nature; this time around, they say, we are drowning because we have abused our planet, kicked and starved it until it has changed its nature and turned nasty. It feels like the end of the world. And our homes, homes which cost some of us a quarter of a million pounds or more, do not offer the kind of sanctuary that enables us to ignore what is going on out there: they are all too old, and at night the lights flicker and the windows rattle. I'm sure that I am not the only one in this house who wonders where Monkey and his friends are tonight.

Just as we were eating, water started to pour into the kitchen under the French windows; the drain outside, placed incompetently in the dip between the garden and the house, cannot cope. David digs out an old pair of wellingtons and a cycling cape and goes outside to see if anything can be done.

'It's full of rubbish,' he shouts. 'And there's water pouring down from the gutter outside Tom's room.'

He clears as much muck from the drain as he can with his hands, and then we all go upstairs to see what can be done with the guttering.

'Leaves,' David says. He's half out of the sash window, holding on to the frame – which, I can see now, is rotten, and should have been repaired years ago. 'I could reach them with a stick or something.'

Molly runs off and comes back with a broom, and David kneels on the windowsill, and starts to take wild pokes at the gutter with the handle.

'Stop, David,' I tell him. 'It's not safe.'

'It's fine.'

He's wearing jeans, and Tom and I grab hold of one back pocket each in an attempt to anchor him, while Molly in turn hangs on to us, purposelessly but sweetly. My family, I think, just that. And then, I can do this. I can live this life. I can, I can. It's a spark I want to cherish, a splutter of life in the flat battery; but just at the wrong moment I catch a glimpse of the night sky behind David, and I can see that there's nothing out there at all.

NICK HORNBY

ABOUT A BOY

'A delightful, observant, funny and good-hearted novel' Terence Blacker, *Mail on Sunday*

'How cool was will Freeman?'

Too cool! At thirty-six, he's hip as a teenager. He's single, child-free, goes to the right clubs and knows which trainers to wear.

But then Will meets Marcus, the oldest twelve-year-old on the planet. Marcus is a bit strange: he listens to Joni Mitchell and Mozart, looks after his mum and has never owned a pair of trainers. But Marcus latches on to Will - and won't let go. Can Will teach Marcus how to grow up cool? And can Marcus help Will just to grow up?

'About the awful, hilarious, embarrassing places where children and adults meet, and Hornby has captured it with delightful precision' *Irish Times*

'It takes a writer with real talent to make this work, and Hornby has it – in buckets' *Literary Review*

'A very entertaining and endearing read' *The Times*

NICK HORNBY

JULIET, NAKED

Annie and Duncan are a mid-thirties couple who have reached a fork in the road, realizing their shared interest in the reclusive musician Tucker Crowe (in Duncan's case, an obsession rather than an interest) is not enough to hold them together any more. When Annie hates Tucker's 'new release', a terrible demo of his most famous album, it's the last straw – Duncan cheats on her and she promptly throws him out. Via an internet discussion forum, Annie's harsh opinion reaches Tucker himself, who couldn't agree more. He and Annie start an unlikely correspondence which teaches them both something about moving on from years of wasted time.

Juliet, Naked is about the nature of creativity and obsession, and how two lonely people can gradually find each other.

'*Juliet, Naked* is Hornby's best novel to date' *Spectator*

'Ingenious, funny and moving' *Daily Mail*

'Hornby writes so well that you can almost smell the birdseed odour of badly dried clothes combined with failure that pervades Annie's house; his triumph though is to find infinite amounts of warmth and humour in this seeming world of desolation' *Sunday Telegraph*

He just wanted a decent book to read ...

Not too much to ask, is it? It was in 1935 when Allen Lane, Managing Director of Bodley Head Publishers, stood on a platform at Exeter railway station looking for something good to read on his journey back to London. His choice was limited to popular magazines and poor-quality paperbacks – the same choice faced every day by the vast majority of readers, few of whom could afford hardbacks. Lane's disappointment and subsequent anger at the range of books generally available led him to found a company – and change the world.

'We believed in the existence in this country of a vast reading public for intelligent books at a low price, and staked everything on it'
Sir Allen Lane, 1902–1970, founder of Penguin Books

The quality paperback had arrived – and not just in bookshops. Lane was adamant that his Penguins should appear in chain stores and tobacconists, and should cost no more than a packet of cigarettes.

Reading habits (and cigarette prices) have changed since 1935, but Penguin still believes in publishing the best books for everybody to enjoy. We still believe that good design costs no more than bad design, and we still believe that quality books published passionately and responsibly make the world a better place.

So wherever you see the little bird – whether it's on a piece of prize-winning literary fiction or a celebrity autobiography, political tour de force or historical masterpiece, a serial-killer thriller, reference book, world classic or a piece of pure escapism – you can bet that it represents the very best that the genre has to offer.

Whatever you like to read – trust Penguin.